MW01093921

Funny
Fantasy

Edited by
ALEX SHVARTSMAN

UFO Publishing
Brooklyn, NY

PUBLISHED BY:

UFO Publishing
1685 E 15th St.
Brooklyn, NY 11229
www.ufopub.com

ISBN: 978-0-9884328-8-8

Visit us on the web:

www.ufopub.com

Table of Contents

FOREWORD
ALEX SHVARTSMAN

IN THE AGE of gritty, grimdark fantasy epics like *Game of Thrones*, it is sometimes nice to take a break and enjoy a lighter, humorous approach to the genre. This book collects fourteen such stories, all originally published in the past decade. There is traditional fantasy, urban fantasy, fairy tale retellings and even a mash-up of fantasy and space opera.

This book follows in the footsteps of *Funny Science Fiction*, an anthology that similarly collected stories from that other side of the speculative spectrum. It was very successful and warranted some sequels. (*Funny Horror* is forthcoming later this year.)

As I worked on this volume, it struck me how different fantasy humor tends to be from science fiction humor. While humorous science fiction stories are more likely to explore new ground and provide social commentary by thrusting their characters into unexpected settings, fantasy stories often play off the tropes we recognize from pop culture, be it zombies, vampires, or the Judeo-Christian concept of the afterlife.

A very common tactic for humorous fantasy stories is to retell or subvert fairy tales, often remixing and infusing them with modern tropes—you will undoubtedly recognize several such tales in this book.

When parsing through hundreds of excellent short stories, I tried to select a mix that would represent the sub-genre well and still manage to surprise and delight the reader. I also wanted to recognize magazines and anthologies that are currently publishing funny fiction (there's never enough of it!) as well as involve some of the iconic authors especially known in the SF/F fandom for penning such fare.

Those of you who are fans of *Unidentified Funny Objects*—an annual anthology of humorous SF/F I curate—can expect this book to serve up a somewhat similar mix of zany and lighthearted. And if you aren't already a reader of the UFO series, and you find yourself enjoying *Funny Fantasy*, I'd encourage you to give them a try.

I daren't delay you from enjoying the stories any longer. After all, there's a wise opossum waiting to take you on a quest, on the very next page.

Happy reading!

DAVE THE MIGHTY STEEL-THEWED AVENGER
LAURA RESNICK

IT WAS WHEN a rat rose up on its hind legs and spoke to me in the middle of the street at one o'clock in the morning that I realized that this night was going to be different from all other nights.

"Hello, Dave," it said.

"Whoa," I said in reply. "Is that a *rat* talking to me?"

Okay, I should definitely not have had that second beer. I can't hold my liquor at all, so I knew even while I was doing it that having two beers in a row was a bad idea.

And here, now, right in front of me on the dark street, was proof positive.

"*Excuse* me?" asked the creature.

"A talking rat?" I asked incredulously.

There was a moment of silence as I stared slack-jawed at the rat, which stared back at me.

Was I hallucinating, I wondered? If so, did this mean that two beers were enough to give me alcohol poisoning? Should I proceed immediately to the campus medical center and check myself into the detox unit?

Or was this a practical joke? Maybe it was a set-up to covertly film me—and then immortalize me on YouTube—making a fool of myself. In which case, I was impressed with the technical skill of the perpetrators, because the rat looked completely real.

"Rat?" the creature repeated. *"Rat?"*

I looked around in the dark, expecting to see someone recording this scene.

"First of all," the rat said coldly, still on its hind legs, "the word 'rat' is considered pejorative. The appropriate term is 'urban rodent.'"

"A politically correct rat?"

"I am not a rat!"

"Hey!" I fell back a step when the thing bared its little fangs at me. Maybe it had rabies.

Or maybe *I* had rabies. I was talking to a rat, after all.

"I am an opossum!" it cried. "I do not in any way resemble an urban rodent."

"Sorry," I said inanely. "I don't really know that much about—"

"I am, in fact, *the* opossum! The marsupial who has been foretold in song and story," it raged, advancing on me. "How *dare* you mistake me for a rat!"

"Joke or no joke," I warned as I backed away from it, "if I get bitten, I'm filing a formal complaint."

The animal paused, made a squeaky sound, then raised a little paw. It had weird-looking pink digits. "I apologize, Vworntokthalis. I did not mean to appear aggressive. It's just that I have looked forward to this meeting for so long and have imagined our first exchange of greetings so many times."

"Huh?"

It brushed its whiskers with the other weird-looking pink paw. "I must admit, I feel some disappointment at how it's going so far."

"Yeah, well... whatever." I turned and walked away. "I'm out of here."

"Wait!" cried the creature, following me. "I have sought you now because, exactly as the Wizened Ones of Loremead have long feared, Grok the Valkslayer has roused the Dread Grzilbeast from its prison of enchanted sleep in the Caverns of Mimnoth."

"Oh, well," I said, picking up my pace. "I'm sure things will work out."

"Can you slow down?" my furry friend asked. "This is a demanding speed for me when I'm talking."

I reached the end of the street, turned the corner, and walked faster.

"Stop!" cried the opossum, panting a little. "You must listen to me! *This* is the dark night described in the Prophecies of Joralion! The doom that was foretold in the Codex of the Ninth-Born has come to pass! Now is the time prognosticated in the Calendar of C'ghu'nim and secretly coded into the Long Island Railroad timetable for Oyster Bay!"

I stopped in my tracks and stared at the opossum. "So it *is* a joke," I said with certainty.

"It is no jest, Vworntokthalis!" cried the animal, his little sides heaving as he came to a stop, too. "Now is the time for the Avenger of the Valk to lay rightful claim to Jasmine Truethunder, confront Grok—"

"How did you know I'm from Oyster Bay?" I challenged.

I looked around again. Yes, it was dark, but I had covered more than a block since being accosted by a talking marsupial, so by now I should have seen or heard whoever was following me with a camera.

It replied, "I know because I am Briddlecroonak the Seer, the marsupial foretold—"

"—in song and story. Yeah, I know."

"My visions told me that Vworntokthalis the Avenger hailed from a town called Oyster Bay. So I went there." Briddlecroonak the Seer continued, "But it turned out that you had left that hamlet as a callow youth."

"Who told you I was *callow?*"

"Fortunately, though, as time passed, you became aware of your destiny to avenge the Valk by slaying Grok and mastering the Dread Grzilbeast."

I sighed. "Can we just stop now?"

The opossum raised one paw to pat his whiskers fretfully. "Er, you did realize your true identity, didn't you, Vworntokthalis?"

"Why do you keep calling me that?"

"That is... I mean, I had naturally assumed that you moved to this dreary little town of cheap taverns and no symphony because you recognized that your destiny lay here."

"I moved here to attend law school," I said morosely.

"Yes! Becoming an under-achieving student at a second-rate law school was an excellent way of eluding your enemies while you prepared for your inevitable confrontation with Grok the Valkslayer," said the marsupial. "The last mighty steel-thewed avenger I knew couldn't resist showing off to random maidens and passing strangers, while awaiting the challenges foretold in the prophecies about *him*. And thus it was that he met an early grave and never fulfilled his destiny. But not you! No, *you* have been prudent, cunning, and wise. To immerse yourself so completely in an identity of such consistent mediocrity was brilliant!"

"Gee, thanks."

"But I, Briddlecroonak the Seer, can sense that you have been unhappy and restless while waiting for your glorious fate to unfold."

I wondered which one of my classmates had decided to use my anxieties as fodder for this weird joke. Maybe it was someone from my Antitrust Law class, which was the course I hated the most—and the one I was the closest to flunking.

The possum continued, "If you continue on this path, Vworntokthalis—"

"Stop calling me that."

"—you will graduate in the bottom third of your class at this poorly-ranked law school, after which your *best* possible fate will be a career as an ambulance-chaser. Most likely, though, you'll struggle to find even a moderately remunerative white-collar job and spend many years paying off massive student loans without ever even entering the legal profession for which you trained with a mixture of ambivalence, apathy, and reluctance."

I glared at the marsupial. Everything it was saying was true. I had spent the past few weeks thinking over my situation and trying to escape exactly the conclusions this furry little fellow was now voicing. It was why I'd gone to a bar and had two beers tonight—which is about one-and-a-half beers more than I ever drink.

I'd had no idea what to do with my life after graduating from college, or how to find a job with my B.A. in philosophy. So I had applied to law school simply because I didn't know what else to do. Now in my second year of the program at (Briddlecroonak was right) a second-rate law school, I *still* didn't know.

And I was getting angry about my problems being made the butt of this elaborately weird prank. So, acting on impulse, I bent over, picked up the opossum, hoisted it into the air, and started shaking it, trying to detect or dislodge whatever audio device someone must have attached to it.

"Who *are* you?" I demanded.

"I told you! I am Briddlecroonak the Seer." The opossum struggled against my grip as it added, "And I hate heights! Put me down, Vworntokthalis!"

Its warm breath brushed my face as it spoke in a shrill voice while struggling against my hold. It was definitely a real animal, and—I realized with a mixture of shock and recognition—it was really speaking. There was no audio device attached to it, and with its face so close to mine, I could tell that its voice was coming from its own mouth.

"Yikes!" I dropped Briddlecroonak and stumbled backward, staring at him in amazement.

"Oof!" He hit the pavement like a bag of wet cement and lay there motionless.

"Briddlecroonak?" I took a tentative step closer. There was no response. "Uh, are you okay?"

"I just need a moment," was the faint reply.

I looked around. We were still alone. I had chosen a Wednesday for my drinking binge, so hardly anyone was around now, though the streets would be crowded at this late hour if it were a weekend night.

I decided to accept that there were no pranksters or video cameras involved in this strange event. Sure, I might be hallucinating under the influence of two beers. Or maybe I was cracking under the stress of realizing how much time and money I had already thrown away on studying for a profession that I didn't really want to pursue. But if there was even a faint chance that I was *not* delusional... then this was certainly the most interesting thing that had ever happened to me, and I wanted to see where it would lead. Especially since Briddlecroonak's stark description of my life was depressingly accurate.

So I said, "I'm sorry about manhandling you just now."

"Oh... that's all right, I guess." The opossum started scraping himself off the street.

"I suppose I... lost my composure."

The marsupial grunted, pulled himself together, and then sniffed his fur. He made a little noise, then looked at the pavement where he had been lying. "I think someone vomited here recently."

"I wouldn't be at all surprised." This street ran directly between the bar district and the main campus. "Are you feeling okay? Didn't crack your skull or anything?"

He touched his snout gingerly with one pink paw, rubbed his rump, then shook his head. "Oh, don't worry, Vworntokthalis. I survived much worse treatment at the hands of the fanatical Plikazar sect during the Schism of the Sirikirai. Not to mention what Yurg the Destroyer did to me when I helped rescue the Scrolls of Calarnius from the Fires of—"

"Okey-dokey," I said quickly. "If you're feeling all right, then maybe you can walk me slowly through this whole Grok-Grizzle-Valkyrie thing."

"Valk," he corrected. "Just Valk. The Valkyrie are... well, they're a whole other thing, and we don't need to worry about them right now."

"Who or what is a Valk?"

"By thunder, Vworntokthalis, we have no time for a history lesson! Nor can we 'walk slowly' through explanations!" Briddlecroonak cried. "Have I not impressed upon you the urgency of the situation? The Dread Grzilbeast is free! Grok the Valkslayer intends to bring about the doom foretold by the chroniclers and prophesied by the . . . the . . . the prophets!"

"It sounds like you're saying this is a *bad* thing."

"Only *you* can defeat Grok, return the Grzilbeast to its prison of enchanted slumber, and save the last of the Valk from being slain!"

"So I gather we *don't* want the Valk to be slain?"

"Of *course* not," said Briddlecroonak (with noticeable exasperation). "If the last of the Valk is slain, then the Incarnation of Konax can never come to pass! In which case, the Age of Ilak cannot be averted, and darkness shall smother the Five Kingdoms."

"This is getting so complicated," I said. "Maybe I should take notes."

"You don't need notes, you have a seer. *The* seer. Me!"

"In that case, can you 'see' what we're supposed to do now?"

"Why are you making that gesture with your hands?" he demanded. "Are those supposed to be quotation marks?"

I folded my arms. "Sorry, I wasn't trying to be rude."

"I am *literally* a seer," Briddlecroonak said with wounded dignity. "So, yes, of *course* I can see what we're supposed to do now."

"Then, by all means, share it with the class."

"Huh?"

"Tell me what to do," I said. "Because, uh, by thunder, I have no idea what's going on."

"Fortunately, what you must do is very simple," said the possum. "Impossibly dangerous and probably fatal—"

"What?"

"—but quite simple. Follow me, Vworntokthalis!"

Briddlecroonak started waddling down the street at a brisk pace.

I followed. "Hold on. *How* dangerous?"

"Well, not necessarily as dangerous as the time I had to help retrieve the Three Golden Arrows from the Mountain of Ghouls." He was panting a little as he kept talking at this (for him) brisk pace. "But probably more dangerous than the time I—"

"Never mind," I said. "Did you say *fatal?*"

"Well, probably fatal for Dave, the ordinary fellow you have pretended to be while awaiting this night foretold in song and story," he said cheerfully.

"I *am* Dave."

"But surely not for Vworntokthalis, the mighty steel-thewed Avenger of the Valk!"

"I should probably mention that my thews really aren't all that steely," I said, plodding behind the opossum. "I never go to the gym. Jogging makes me vomit, and I fainted the only time I ever tried to do a bench press, so..."

"Do not trouble yourself with such reflections, Vworntokthalis. Gymnasiums are for people who are going to be lawyers," Briddlecroonak said dismissively. "Or for those in search of easy sexual conquests."

"Seriously?" I'd always thought that was an urban myth.

"Your strength arises from your birthright and has lain slumbering inside you, ready to awaken when the time is ripe."

"Well, I guess that's some comfort... But if you were going to calculate odds on me surviving my confrontation with the Valkyrie-slayer, what would you say my chances—"

"*Valk*slayer. Valk," said my companion. "And his name is Grok."

"I'm just wondering exactly how dangerous Grok is," I said as we arrived at the main entrance to the oldest part of campus, which conveniently abutted the bar district.

There was a big, pretentious gate, an old building with a clocktower, and a notoriously dirty fountain that surrounded a marble statue of the minor statesman who'd founded this university with the fortune he'd made by exploiting child labor.

"Here we are," said Briddlecroonak, coming to a halt in front of the fountain.

I looked around and didn't see anyone. Certainly no Valks, Groks, or Grzils. (I had no idea what any of those things were, but I had a feeling they'd stand out around here as much as—oh, for example—a talking marsupial.)

I looked again at the opossum. "I mean, on a scale of one to ten, would you describe Grok as a nine? A two?"

"Before you can defeat Grok in glorious combat—"

"Are we sure it has to be combat? Maybe Grok and I could just talk. You know—work things out like adults."

"—you must first claim Jasmine Truethunder."

Momentarily distracted, I asked, "What if she doesn't want to be claimed? Has anyone asked *her* how she feels about this?"

Briddlecroonak started wheezing. I only realized it was laughter after he said, "Ah, thank you, my brave friend. That witticism helped break the tension."

"*I'm* still tense."

"Now is the time! This is the place!" Briddlecroonak rose up on his hind legs and waved his little pink claws majestically. "Jasmine Truethunder has lain in wait for years beyond counting, sleeping until this moment! Claim her, Avenger of the Valk! Claim her and know your destiny!"

I looked around again and still didn't see anyone.

"Claim her!" the opossum repeated.

"Is there a sleeping princess somewhere that I'm supposed to kiss?" I asked in confusion.

The seer's nose twitched and his lips curled up over his fangs for a moment. Then he said, with forced patience, "Reach into the fountain."

"What? No *way*. Do you have any idea how many drunken students have pissed in this fountain since the last time it was cleaned—which was probably when Ronald Reagan was president?"

Briddlecroonak got back down on all fours. "Look, if you won't even touch a little dirty water, then this night is going to be a disaster. And the Five Kingdoms are doomed."

I looked into the murky water. "Oh... *crap.*" And considering the way it smelled, that was another substance that was probably floating in it. "All right." I rolled up my sleeve, thinking that as soon as we were done here, I was going to the med center to have my whole arm sterilized.

As I plunged my hand and forearm into the slimy water, I acknowledged that all my behavior tonight—and particularly this moment—confirmed that it was past time for me to drop out of law school and come up with a better plan for my life. Except that I was still in law school because I didn't *have* any other plan. I was every bit as aimless and unfocused as I had always—

"Whoa!"

I was so surprised I nearly fell into the fountain when a bright, iridescent light suddenly spread across the water, turning it a dozen shades of glimmering blue, violet, and turquoise. Even more surprisingly, the water was suddenly crystal clear, as if no one in the whole history of the college had ever pissed, spat, or vomited into it.

And from the depths of the crystal-clear water that shimmered and glowed with strange enchantment, there arose a gleaming steel blade. As I reached for it, it whirled away and spun around in a dizzying circle, then floated up to the surface—up, up, up until it broke through the water and soared into the air. Still trying to grab it, I stumbled forward, and now it came into my outstretched hand as if escorted there by destiny itself.

"Wow," I said.

"Your weapon, Jasmine Truethunder," Briddlecroonak said triumphantly.

"Weapon? It's, um, a penknife." I folded the blade closed, then opened it again. "See?"

"As legend foretold, she gave herself into the hand of the true Avenger of the Valk," the opossum said somberly. "You and no other are destined to slay Grok and master the Grzilbeast—or die trying!"

"Die?" I repeated. "Did you say—?"

"Embrace your true identity, Vworntokthalis! Bond with Jasmine Truethunder, for she will not fail you." Briddlecroonak added, "Well, probably not."

I was very impressed by the whole event, of course, but even so... "This is a penknife."

The seer placed a little pink claw on my ankle. "Now you are ready for deadly combat, Vworntokthalis. Now you must face Grok the Valkslayer."

"If I'm honest, that suffix, *slayer*, has me a little worried," I said. "How many Valk has he slain, for example? And in addition to having a secret identity as their avenger, do I also have a secret identity as a Valk? If so, then isn't it likely Grok might slay me, given that—"

"You really have been in law school too long, haven't you?" asked the seer.

"But not for much longer!" said a menacing, gravelly voice behind us. "Mwa-ha-ha-ha-ha!"

Moving as one man (so to speak), Briddlecroonak and I whirled around to confront the owner of that voice, and we found ourselves facing...

"Professor James?" I said in surprise, seeing my notoriously unpleasant Antitrust Law lecturer standing there in the dark, laughing maniacally. I recognized him even though his eyes, normally a dull brown, were now bright red and *glowing*—which, I don't mind admitting, I found pretty unnerving. A split second later I saw the *thing* crouching next to him on all fours, and I nearly wet myself. "What the hell is *that?*"

"Grok!" exclaimed Briddlecroonak.

"That's Grok?" I said in horror, staring at the thing beside Professor James. "How am I supposed to fight *that?*"

It was some sort of animal, roughly the size of a Saint Bernard, but clearly feline in nature. It looked as if someone had crossed a domestic tabby cat with a prehistoric saber-toothed tiger—and then did something to make the offspring very, very angry. The thing was growling and crouching as if preparing for attack, its hackles raised, its long fangs bared and dripping with saliva.

"Seer! So we meet again after all these years," Professor James said in a menacing voice. Then to me, he said, "Hello, Dave."

"That's Grok?" I repeated. "What am I supposed to do with a *penknife?*"

Too scared to look away from the giant crouching cat, I waved my implement around in Briddlecroonak's general direction, though probably five feet above his little head.

Professor James gasped and fell back a step. "Jasmine

Truethunder!"

"Hah! That's right, Grok!" said the opossum. "I found Vworntokthalis first. You are too late to prevent the Avenger of the Valk from bonding with his fateful weapon and... and... and avenging the Valk you have slain!"

"Jesus, kill a few lousy Valk and the Wizened Ones of Loremead send half the heroes in the Five Kingdoms after you," grumbled Professor James. "This is getting so tedious. But, oh, well, I guess I'll have to kill another warrior."

"*You're* Grok the Valkslayer?" I said in astonishment, gazing into his glowing red eyes. James was the most burned out, snide, and unpleasant professor in the whole law school (which was saying something). He had been here for decades and seemed embittered and overdue for retirement. "I don't believe it."

"Frankly, I'm having a hard time believing that *you're* the Avenger," he shot back. "You have maintained an impressively convincing disguise of utterly forgettable mediocrity during your sojourn at this institution. I congratulate you, Dave."

"Um, thanks."

Except for the glowing eyes and the menacing creature beside him, his behavior seemed completely normal (yes, he was like this all of the time).

"You're really Grok the Valkslayer?"

"Long have I awaited this moment, Avenger," he intoned. "It was foretold by the ancients that you and I should meet in mortal combat, and the fate of the Valk would be decided between us."

"I don't suppose we could just *talk* about the Valk?" I said without much hope. As far as anyone knew, James had never once agreed to a student's reasonable request.

"Heresy!" he thundered. "Even the Codex of the Ninth-Born and the secretly-coded Long Island Railroad timetable proclaim that one or the other of us must die this dark night, Avenger! Face up to your destiny!"

"You've had a little more time to prepare for this than I have," I pointed out.

"Always with the excuses, Dave," he said with disgust. "If you failed to prepare for this test, it's your own fault."

"Oh, now wait just a damn minute. I was walking along tonight, minding my own..." I came to my senses and shook my head. "No, never mind. Forget it. Let's just get on with this."

It was my Antitrust mid-term all over again.

"Mwa-ha-ha-ha-ha!" he laughed.

Seriously, except for the glowing red eyes and the giant snarling feline at his side, this was *just* like being in his classroom.

I glanced anxiously at the creature beside him. "So I guess that's the Dread Grzilbeast that you freed from its enchanted sleep in the Caves of... of..."

"The Caverns of Mimnoth!" he snapped. "Didn't you prepare at *all*, Dave?"

God, I hated this guy. I'm generally opposed to physical violence, let alone mortal combat. But I realized, standing there in the dark as Professor James, a.k.a. Grok the Valkslayer, sneered and jeered at me, that if I was ever going to kill anyone, then I really wanted it to be him. In fact, as memories of the frustrating injustices and undeserved humiliations I had suffered in his class flashed through my memory, I realized that something inside me understood, believed, and knew that I was indeed *destined* to kill him—or die trying.

So I said grimly, "Oh, believe me, Grok, I am prepared for this, all right. *You* prepared me."

"What's that supposed to mean, Avenger?" he said with a sneer.

"That's *Mister* Avenger, to you," I said with a half-decent sneer of my own.

"Oh, this is going just like the Prophecies of Joralion said it would!" Briddlecroonak clapped his paws and gave an excited little hop. "Prepare to meet thy doom, Valkslayer!"

"Hah!"

Moving with the speed and agility of a young athlete, which took me by complete surprise, Grok leaped straight at me. He was brandishing a dagger (where had *that* come from all of a sudden?) with three long, shiny blades—all of them aimed at my throat.

I shrieked, staggered backward, and reflexively threw my penknife at him. Hey, I was new to this whole mortal combat thing and hadn't expected the old man to jump me so fast or fiercely. So I panicked.

Jasmine Truethunder flew straight into Grok's forehead and hit him right between the eyes with a solid *thud!* Grok froze in mid-leap, hovered motionless for a moment, then keeled over and lay there on the ground, his eyes remaining wide open as the strange red glow slowly faded from them. My penknife was sticking out of his head, its blade having sunk into his skull.

Briddlecroonak squeaked and squealed with excitement, running around in little circles. "You have done it, Vworntokthalis! Hip-hip-hurrah! You have triumphed over the

Valkslayer!"

"I have?" I tiptoed closer to Professor James's prone body. "Is he... *dead?*"

I had barely finished asking the question when a putrid yellow mist arose from the corpse. The body began liquefying, bubbling and gurgling noisily, churning itself into the thickening yellow mist that stank of sulfur as it soared upward and away.

"Whoa!"

"Hurrah! Hurrah! The Valkslayer is slain! He has fallen to the Avenger's mighty blow!"

I stood back and held my nose, gagging at the stench, as the body disintegrated and evaporated, roiling skyward and then dissipating on the wind.

When there was nothing left of Grok's body except a little sticky slime and the penknife which had slain him, I bent over, picked up Jasmine Truethunder, and used my sleeve to wipe clean the blade of my bonded weapon.

Then I held Jasmine Truethunder aloft and proclaimed, "This is the true hero of this dark night."

Briddlecroonak patted my ankle. "But you certainly helped."

I shrugged. "And, happily, I don't have to try to explain the corpse of my most hated professor to the law school dean."

I heard a loud snarl, looked over my shoulder, and realized that *I* was about to become a corpse. The Dread Grzilbeast gave a mighty roar and then launched itself at me.

In my terror, I dropped my penknife rather than throwing it.

Fleeing for my life, I turned, ran—and immediately fell into the fountain. Now that it had surrendered Jasmine Truethunder to me, it was no longer glowing and clear, but had returned to its usual putrid condition. But since this was no time to be fastidious, I simultaneously staggered, flailed, and swam as fast I could, moving further into the murky water as I felt the Grzilbeast enter the fountain behind me, its immense claws reaching for me.

"Agh!" I made a desperate lunge to escape the big, bloodthirsty monster.

"Meow!" a pathetic little voice wailed directly behind me. "Meow!"

I glanced over my shoulder and saw... a small tabby cat dog-paddling in the filthy water, trying not to drown as it cried for help.

There was no sign of the Grzilbeast.

"What the...?"

I reached instinctively for the drowning tabby cat, which clung to me and cried pathetically. I clutched it to my chest as I looked around, dreading the renewed sight of the long-fanged beast that had been chasing me only a moment ago.

"You have returned the Dread Grzilbeast to its enchanted sleep!" cried Briddlecroonak, punching the air with a little, pink fist. "Yes!"

"I've done what?" I said, standing in the middle of the stinking fountain.

The seer gestured to the frightened cat that clung to my chest as I started wading to the edge of the fountain. "*This* is the Grzilbeast in its enchanted form."

"Seriously?" I looked down at the sputtering cat. "It looks just like the mouser that lives in the basement of the law library."

"Yes, that is where Grok woke it, intent on using its unleashed ferocity for his own evil purposes."

"The library basement?"

The opossum nodded. "Also known as—"

"Let me guess," I said. "The Caverns of Mimnoth?"

"Precisely. And we must return the sleeping Grzilbeast to the Caverns of Mimnoth—"

"Or, in local dialect, we must return Stripes to her kitty bed in the basement of the library—"

"—and flee this realm before the Minions of Grok find, torture, and dismember us."

"Well, *I* was going to say, 'Before anyone notices Stripes is missing,' but, hey, you say tomato, I say to-mah... Wait... *What* did you just say?"

"That sulfuric mist rose from the body to be carried on the winds to the Cliffs of Nomhara, where the Minions of Grok will be alerted to the slaying of their revered idol."

"That guy had minions?"

"They will want to punish the hero who slew him," said my companion. "And believe me, you do *not* want to mess with minions."

"But why did—"

"Garrgh!"

Briddlecroonak the Seer had a vision. Peering sightlessly into this dark night, he drew in a long, deep, noisy breath through his little pink nostrils and made a humming sound. Then he said, "The mist has already reached some of the minions."

"That was fast." Still clutching the cat, I hauled myself out of the fountain, soaking wet and smelling incredibly rank. "What should we do now?"

"We must flee to the Valley of Sohn where we can rally with the Exiled Ones and mount a defense."

"Okay, that's pretty specific," I said with a nod. "I guess you know where this valley is?"

He waggled his paw. "More or less. We might need to ask directions along the way."

"But why are we going to rally with the Exiled Ones?" I asked as we headed rapidly in the direction of the law library, so we could return Stripes to her proper place before departing. "Shouldn't we go find the Valk? I mean, I'm their Avenger, right? I just slew Grok the Valkslayer, and all that."

"Oh, the Valk will shower you with gratitude and glory when next we meet them," said Briddlecroonak, "but they're basically a species of decorative butterfly and, as such, not very useful in a situation like this. So we'll rally with them some other time, Vworntokthalis."

"All right. That makes sense," I said. "But there's just one thing I have to say before we go off on another adventure."

"Yes, of course." The opossum nodded. "I know what it is."

"Oh, right. You're a seer."

"You're not sure this is the right path for you, leaving behind all that you know in order to travel to strange lands, face more deadly foes, meet with danger and constant—"

"Oh, no, that's all fine. No problem there."

He stopped waddling and stared at me. "No?"

"No. I've finally figured out what to do with my life. I'm on board. Avenging the Valk, heroic deeds, deadly enemies, mortal combat—count me in all the way. But..."

"Yes?"

"I'd really rather you just call me Dave, if you don't mind. I can't even pronounce Vw... Vw... the name you've been calling me."

"Oh! All right. If you wish it, of course I can call you Dave."

"Great." I gave my furry partner a friendly little pat on the back. "Now let's get Stripes to safety and then go rendezvous with the Exiled Ones in the Valley of whatever."

And thus it was that I dropped out of law school and embarked on my true path in life.

the king, no way of obtaining a plump enough gift for the king without a choice assignment. Sir Hanson the Hawk-eyed could have changed his name to Sir Hanson the Knightly-scutwork-until-you-die without violating any truth-in-advertising laws.

The quest to which he was presently assigned was a case in point. It was a simple Missing Persons affair, and while the Persons thus Missing were important enough, none involved were princess-level important.

"Maybe it's a dragon that's responsible," Sir Hanson muttered to himself as he leaned slightly forward upon the pommel of his saddle. "There aren't supposed to be any dragons in the Dark Woods, just trolls and goblins and giants and flesh-eating witches, but you never can tell with dragons: They pretty much turn up wherever they like. Who's going to tell them *not* to? And where there's dragons, there's hoards of gold. It can't be helped." He ended on an optimistic note that rang somewhat tinny, even to his own ears.

He consulted the scrap of parchment in his hand one more time. Sir Hanson had requested that the palace scribe write down the particulars of the case, being a firm believer in the Rule of the Six P's, viz.: *Prior Planning Prevents Poorly Prepared Paladins.*

"Vanishments," Sir Hanson read. "Mysterious vanishments within the Dark Woods, cause unknown, sorcery suspected." He shook his head. "But that's impossible. Who'd go *into* the Dark Woods, these days? Everyone *knows* that they're rife with witches who'd turn a child into gingerbread and gobble him up before you can blink. And since the construction of the Dark Woods Bypass, there's no need to risk traveling through this unholy place. Only a fool would do so."

Once more, Sir Hanson's head filled with the king's indignant voice giving him his assignment: *We're not talking about a bunch of children or village idiots here, Hanson; we're talking about some of the most cunning, ruthless, successful merchants in my realm! These were not stupid men, and yet, they were all last observed going into the Dark Woods and not coming out again.*

Men? Sir Hanson had echoed. *But in the old tales, isn't it always children who—*

His Majesty cared not a festering fig for the old tales. *Do you think I'd be wasting any of my manpower if this was about* children? *Children do not pay taxes, or see fit to remember their beloved king with appropriately lavish gifts at Yuletide. To the fuming pits with the children: These are* real *people who've vanished, and I want to know the reason why.*

It was interviews like that which sometimes made Sir Hanson the Hawk-eyed pause to wonder just what, exactly, Good King Donald was good *for*.

Sir Hanson took up the reins, and urged his steed forward. "On, Barbelindo!" he cried, lifting his chin and striking a heroic pose.

The horse just stood there and, very slowly and with supreme contempt, turned to look at him. In spite of the grandiloquent name Sir Hanson had bestowed upon his mount, they both knew the truth: Barbelindo the Bold was really Bessie, a stolid, serviceable stopgap steed from his father's modest stable. Instead of a proper knight's horse—a fiery stallion with coat of midnight and eyes of flame—all Sir Hanson could afford was Bessie, a mare with coat of oatmeal, eyes of hazelnut, and an expression that made him swear she was always laughing at him.

Covert equine insubordination aside, she was obedient enough. Her one non-negotiable point, however, was her name. And so, muttering angrily under his breath, Sir Hanson managed to grit out a terse, "Giddup, Bessie," before the beast would consent to carry him on to adventure 'neath the Dark Woods' drear and dreadful boughs.

They rode down a forest path that was not entirely unfamiliar to him, even though he had never traveled its tree-shadowed twists and turns himself before now. The Dark Woods and its reputed perils were old hat to Sir Hanson, who had grown up bored halfway out of his skull by tales of this selfsame place of dangers dire and dolorous, whenever Auntie Gretel came to visit. It never failed: The conversation with her brother Hansel always slewed back to their childhood adventures with the Dark Woods, the breadcrumb trail, and the witch they'd so cleverly slaughtered.

"Ah, there was gold aplenty in that gingerbread house!" Auntie Gretel cackled. "God knows how the crone came to have it."

"Who cares how she got it?" her brother Hansel responded. "What matters is *we* did. Gold's a good dog: It knows its proper master!"

"True, dear brother, true." This was invariably the point where Auntie Gretel sighed happily and twirled the fat strand of pearls around her neck.

Unfortunately this was invariably also the point where young Hanson let loose a cavernous yawn. (Family histories are wasted on the young.) That yawn made young Hanson's father cuff his ear and deliver a lecture about how the witch's purloined riches became the foundation of the family's modest fortune.

"Aye, and the reason why a poor woodchopper's son like me will become the father of a belted knight some day!" he concluded, clouting young Hanson in the other ear for good measure.

Sir Hanson's mother was just as weary as her son of hearing the old, old story. She took pains to confide a few salient details that Dad and Auntie Gretel left out, details she'd learned once upon a time *in vino veritas*, when her husband had turned truthful in his cups.

"Abandoned by their parents in the Dark Woods?" she said with a sarcastic lift of one eyebrow. "Did you never *meet* your grandparents? Your Grandpa Hansel-the-Elder would sooner chop off his own arm for the stewpot! Your pa and auntie ran off into the Dark Woods on purpose, by themselves, because they'd heard about the witch's gold and decided it'd be great sport to rob her. That whole bit about the witch caging your pa to fatten him up while making your auntie keep house for her, that's trash and moonshine. Gretel's such a slob, she wouldn't know which end of a broom to hold if you shoved it up her— er, never mind.

"You see, the witch was a keen cardsharp—loved gambling to the point where she couldn't think straight when the gaming fever was on her. Gretel challenged her to a long sit-down over the devil's pasteboards—hand after hand of Trim the Brisket, Five Yellow Dogs, Seeking Aubrey's Ankle and Camelot Hold

'Em—and by the time the sun went down, she'd won most of the old woman's gold."

"And the witch let her go home with her winnings?" young Hanson inquired of his mother.

Her laughter shook cobwebs from the ceiling corners. "After she caught on that Gretel'd marked the cards? Fat chance! But while Gretel was separating the witch from her treasure, your pa'd been rummaging through the old besom's books until he found one full of simple spells.

"The witch was just about to mount her broomstick and fly after those treacherous brats when your pa launched an incantation that brought the gingerbread cottage tumbling down on the crone's skull. She was crushed beneath an avalanche of stale cake and candy pieces, your pa and auntie took to their heels with her gold in a little casket between 'em, and that, dear heart o' mine, is what *really* happened."

"Oh," said young Hanson, who rather liked the family history account better.

Now he rode along the way his pa and aunt had trodden so long ago. It did not take him long to notice that something was not quite right about the path through the Dark Woods.

"A troll-haunted woodland road with *fresh* wagon ruts? And so many?" He blinked at the evidence of his eyes. True, merchants had vanished 'neath the not-so-jolly greenwood shade, but Sir Hanson was expecting to find the hoofprints of horse or donkey, something proper to a lone wayfarer who'd taken a wrong turn into the forest and was waylaid by crone or creature. When a merchant went into the Dark Woods with a wagon heavily laden enough to leave ruts this deep, it meant he'd gone in with property and purpose.

Sir Hanson had just reached this conclusion when his musings were shattered by a loud, ungodly bawling. It came from under an abandoned wagon dead center on the forest path. He dismounted and peered into the shadows beneath the cart, expecting to encounter a banshee, at the very least. Instead, he found a weeping child.

It didn't take much parley to persuade the tyke—a dirty-faced, towheaded boy who looked barely nine years old—to come out and accept an apple. As the lad crunched into the rosy fruit with the grace of a starving dog, Sir Hanson tried to question him, thus:

"Boy, how did you come to be here?"

"Mumf vavver tol' mezoo wait here furrim 'til heecumback f'me," the boy replied, cheeks bulging like a chipmunk's. Then he swallowed and repeated: "My father told me to wait here for him until he comes back for me."

"Your father left you here?" Sir Hanson had a bad feeling about this. The whole thing smacked of mid-woodland child abandonment, something with which he was more than a little familiar.

On the other hand, there was still the matter of the wagon. People abandoned children far more readily than they gave up all claim to a fine vehicle like this one. Come to think of it, though the cart was here, where were the beasts to pull it? The roadway bore ample, pungent evidence that the cart had been brought this far by the labor of oxen, yet oxen here were none. It was all most puzzling.

"Lad, did your father happen to mention where he was going and why he took the oxen with him but left you behind?" Sir

Hanson handed the boy a piece of bread and a small chunk of cheese to grease the wheels of conversation.

The boy was not quite so desperate for food after the apple, so he munched the bread and cheese in smaller bites while replying: "Oh, he had to take the oxen. They're all he had to offer up after the last time. But kids ain't allowed to go into the candy house. My father said that *she* turns away anyone who tries to bring one in, 'cause it's no fit place for children."

"Whereas the Dark Woods is quite the *ideal* place to leave a child alone." Sir Hanson's mouth tightened. "The candy house, you say? Odd. That sounds very much like the place where my father and auntie once met a woodland witch."

"A witch, that's right!" The boy bobbed his head happily, licking crumbs from his lips. "That's her, the one my father's gone to see; a witch top to toe, he says."

Sir Hanson liked what he was hearing less and less. His hands began to twitch, as though they dreamed their own dexterous dreams of what they would do to this child's father once the formal introductions were over. "Boy, which way did your father go?" he asked.

"Down this path," the boy said, pointing in the direction made obvious by the wagon-ruts. Then he paused, a worried look in his eyes. "Are you going to leave me, too?"

For answer, Sir Hanson picked up the boy and plunked him down astraddle Bessie's rump, then remounted. "I am called Sir Hanson the Hawk-eyed. Let's find this errant father of yours, lad," he said with a backward glance.

"Bardric," the boy said.

"All right, your father Bardric. I'm sure we can—"

"My father's name is Wulfram the goldsmith," the boy cut in. "*My* name is Bardric. Or were you going to call me 'lad' and 'boy' and 'hey, you' all the time?"

As Sir Hanson and his newfound companion trotted on down the road, they passed more and more abandoned carts. The graveyard of derelict vehicles presented a more chilling tableau than any set-piece of gnarled and sinister trees, their bare branches like black claws, their lightning-blasted limbs home to birds of ill- or somewhat-under-the-weather omen.

"This likes me not," said Sir Hanson. Bessie stopped dead in her tracks, turned, and gave him one of those equine *Oh, please!* looks such as she always dispensed whenever he assumed the mantle of pretentious parlance so dear to his blue-blooded paladin peers. "What I mean to say—" Sir Hanson gave the sarcastic steed a killing look. "—is this smells funny."

"No, it doesn't," Bardric said, his nose twitching like a squirrel's. "It smells like gingerbread."

Indeed it did, and after navigating her way through an especially nasty bottleneck of forsaken carts, Bessie brought Sir Hanson and the boy out of the Dark Woods and into a bright clearing whose centerpiece was a wonderful cottage made all of gingerbread and decorated with lashings of sweetmeats and candy.

"Wow!" Sir Hanson exclaimed in astonishment. Unluckily, Bessie took "Wow!" for "Whoa!" and pulled up short. The surprise of this sudden stop sent the unready knight toppling from the saddle, landing flat on his back on the ground.

The ground was lumpy. The ground was talkative.

"Hey! Get offa me, you big clod! I'm workin' here!"

Sir Hanson rolled himself over quickly and pushed himself up on his forearms, then stared in astonishment at the wee goblin who'd broken his fall. The creature wore a crisp peppermint-striped tunic emblazoned with an embroidered badge bearing the name *Drogo*. Beneath it was a brass pin with the words *Employee of the Month*.

Sir Hanson stood up and bowed to the goblin. "My apologies, good monsterling. It was an accident."

"Yeah, that's what they all say." The goblin clambered to his feet and brushed loam off his livery. "'Specially the cheapskates what leave their carts parked back in the woods so's they won't hafta tip a poor, honest, hard-workin' goblin." He spat to emphasize his contempt for such niggardly highpockets. "So you want I should take care of the horse or you wanna stand there yapping all day? No skin off my scales, either way." Then he glanced up and caught sight of the boy, still holding onto Bessie's back. A cloud crossed Drogo's grotesque visage. "Hey, wassa matter, you don't know the regs? No kids allowed!"

Sir Hanson calmly drew his sword and leveled it at the goblin's wrinkled throat. "That, sir, is no child. That is Malagendron, the most puissant wizard in seven kingdoms. He has taken a fancy to view the world through a child's eyes, and who am I to argue with a sorcerer who has the capability to summon up a legion of fiends at the drop of a hat? Goblin-eating fiends," he clarified.

Drogo gave "Malagendron" a dubious look, but between Sir Hanson's persuasive steel-edged argument and the cardinal rule of You-never-can-tell-with-wizards, he decided to err on the side of cowardice.

"Oooookay, buddy, he's a wizard, have it your way." He cut a brief bow to "Malagendron," then turned back to Sir Hanson and said, "So you want valet parking or not?"

"WOW," SAID BARDRIC, his eyes growing wide and wider as he took in the scene that burst upon his senses the instant he and Sir Hanson passed through the gingerbread cottage's door. "This is— It doesn't make sense that— It's impossible for—" He gave up trying to put his astonishment into words and merely whistled, low and long.

Sir Hanson agreed with him on all counts, including that whistle. "This is beyond belief. How can a simple, woodland cottage hold a hall like this, clearly at least three storeys high and the length of ten such huts? How could it contain so many people making so much noise, yet we heard not one hint of this commotion on *that* side of the door?" He made a sweeping gesture, wishing to indicate the humble pastry portal.

The door was gone, and in its place there stood a woman of surpassing allure, clad in a gown of rich carmine velvet. She must have paid a pretty penny for it, though a shrewd consumer would point out that she'd been short-changed as far as upper body coverage. The neckline swooped so low that for all intents she wore a skirt with sleeves.

Sir Hanson's dramatic gesture wound up lodged warmly between her bared bosoms. He gasped and jerked back his hand, blushing. The woman gave him a smile that dripped piquant knowledge.

"Have we met?" she purred, fingers playing idly with her thick black curls.

"Er, no," Sir Hanson managed to say. "I'm new."

"Wouldn't you rather be used?"

"I beg your pardon?"

The lady laughed. "Never mind. Welcome, good sir knight. I am Bezique the enchantress. Your pleasure is my sole concern, however—" She cast a sidelong look at Bardric. The boy was gazing rapturously at her cleavage with the single-mindedness of a cat regarding an unattended anchovy. "Hmm. I was about to say that we do not permit children on the premises, but given the way this one's staring—"

"He's not a child, he's a wizard, and we're only staying long enough to find his father," a flustered Sir Hanson blurted.

Bezique lifted one shapely eyebrow. "Do tell. Very well, then. Welcome, O mighty wizard." She curtseyed low before Bardric, who almost choked on his own tongue as a result of the view. "What name do men employ who speak of thee?"

Poor Bardric uttered a series of hormone-hampered squeaks and gurgles before managing to gasp: "'S Murgedandron— Rhododendron— Didjamindron— *Bob*!"

"Oh, ho, ho, my powerful wizard, you jest with the lady," Sir Hanson cried in haste, slapping Bardric on the back. Grinning stiffly at Bezique he added: "This is *Malagendron*, just as we told that likely little goblin out there who parked my horse Bess— Barbelindo."

"I see." The enchantress laid a finger to her soft lips. "And who are you, apart from being the third-handsomest Knight I've ever seen?"

"I am called Sir Hanson the Hawk-eyed," he replied.

"Sir Hanson—" Bezique looked pensive. "There's something about you that reminds me of— No matter: You didn't come here to chat with me, much as I'd like that. The games await, and I'm certain that Lady Luck perches on your shoulder, eager to show you that you're her special darling. What would you prefer to play, good sir?"

"Er, what do you offer?" Sir Hanson hedged.

"Wouldn't *you* like to know?" The lady's throaty laugh made the ruby necklace resting on her bosoms bounce, which sent poor Bardric rocketing into puberty on the spot.

Shortly thereafter, her hands resting on her guests' shoulders, Bezique guided the newcomers on a grand tour of the gingerbread cottage's many attractions.

"Now over there you have the card tables—your choice of Dragon's Grandma, Sixty-two Ogres, Over-Under-Up-Me-Jerkin, and of course everyone's favorite, The Dwarf's Drawers. And *there* we have the dicing tables, if you fancy a game of Fewmets instead. You'll notice that our older customers prefer the one-armed brigands, over by the far wall—"

"Oooh! I wanna try that!" Bardric tugged on Bezique's arm and pointed to where many men were gathered around a long table with a large wheel in the center. "It looks like fun!"

As the boy spoke, the ogre in charge of the game gave the wheel a forceful spin, then reached into the cage at his elbow, plucked out a hamster, and tossed it onto the reeling wheel. The little creature's cry was midway between terror and delight as it went whirling and bouncing around and around before falling into one of the many numbered hollows on the wheel's perimeter.

"My apologies, great Malagendron," Bezique said smoothly. "The Great Wheel is off-limits to wizards. All of our equipment is proof against any magical attempts at cheating, but the hamsters themselves are susceptible to sorcerous influence." She steered them away, toward a different part of the hall.

The heady reek of ale and stronger waters made Sir Hanson's head spin as Bezique conducted him and Bardric up to the bar. The tapster, a troll of dour aspect, leaned one warty elbow on the sleek mahogany counter top and rumbled, "What'll it be?"

"Give these men whatever they like, Thrombo," Bezique said.

"Oh no, I couldn't possibly—" Sir Hanson began.

"Shurrup'n drink!" the troll roared, slamming down a monstrously huge tankard. "The first one's always free."

With the cool assurance of one who knows nothing of alcohol, but has heard it being ordered just so, time after time, by the grownups in his life, young Bardric rapped out: "I'll have a Wyvern's Revenge, straight up, with a twist, and don't bruise the gin."

"You'll do no such thing!"

A big-bellied, broad-shouldered man came charging up to the bar, grabbed Bardric by the back of his tunic, and hoisted him off his feet. "What are you doing *here* when I told you to stay *there*? And who told you that you could drink, scamp?" he bawled in the boy's face while Bardric kicked wildly and impotently. "At your age? Your mother would have my skin if she found out that— *Argh!*"

The man's tirade was brought to an unexpected halt by Sir Hanson's brawny hand closing on the back of *his* tunic and jerking him backwards so hard that he dropped Bardric. "And what part of your pathetic anatomy do you think that good woman would have if she found out you deserted the lad *there*, in the middle of the Dark Woods?" The knight gave his captive a brusque shake to emphasize his point, then let him go.

The man staggered a few steps off, turned, and assumed an air of wounded dignity. "How dare you, sirrah!" he huffed. "Do you know who I am?"

"Apart from a bad father?" Sir Hanson replied. "You're Wulfram the goldsmith, and a 'special' friend of Good King Donald's, unless I miss my guess."

"That's *Master* Wulfram to you, O Sir Paltry of Penniless," the goldsmith thundered. "And how do you know of the favor our beloved king has given me?"

"Because, *Master* Wulfram," Sir Hanson said coldly, "I am the one whom our beloved king saddled with the quest of finding out what became of you and a dozen or so more of His Majesty's most generous 'friends'." He cast a look over the varied delights of the enchanted cottage, recognizing more than a few of the missing merchants at the bar and the gaming tables. "Now I know."

"By my broomstick!" Bezique exclaimed, staring at Sir Hanson. "And now *I* know where I've seen such a prissy, self-righteous face before! You've a father named Hansel, perchance? And an Aunt Gretel, too?"

Sir Hanson gave the enchantress a somewhat baffled look. "Even so, m'lady. How did you—?" It came to him. "You're *that* witch?" He gave her a closer look. "I must say, you've aged well, for a dead crone."

Bezique slapped his face with dispassionate competence. "So hale, so handsome, so hearty, and yet— so hamheaded. Pity.

Did you ever stop to think that I might have had a *mother*? Or that I'd consult my crystal to conjure up a vision of her doom?"

"Very resourceful of you, m'lady," Sir Hanson said. "And much as I apologize for my father and aunt having killed your mother—" (Here he drew his sword.) "—I'd appreciate it if you didn't force me to do the same to you."

He did not hold the sword like a man who means business, for he acted most reluctantly. Though he found Bezique both charming and attractive, he had his knightly duty to perform.

"I am sent here to return these men to the bosoms of their loving families," he declared. "Clearly your spells are both the vile lure and the unsavory bond keeping them tethered here. On peril of your life, release them from your toils, O sorceress!"

Bezique, the troll barkeep, Master Wulfram, and every other merchant and employee in the general vicinity stared at Sir Hanson for about three heartbeats. Then they all burst out laughing.

Only little Bardric refrained from shaming his rescuer with such raucous mockery. The boy gazed up at the knight, gently touched his sword arm, and said: "There's no spells to break, Sir Hanson. They come here 'cause they *want* to."

"Have *you* fallen under some enchantment while I wasn't looking?" Sir Hanson demanded of the lad. "What power on earth would compel sensible, prosperous men to dare the heart of the Dark Woods, abandoning carts, kine, and kids en route? What power if not the blackest magic?"

"Well, I don't know about anyone else here," Master Wulfram spoke up. "But I had to come back and try to break

4

even. If the wife finds out I lost all my gold and trade-goods again, *plus* another pair of oxen, she'll kill me."

Sir Hanson's mouth hung open like a dropped drawbridge. "You all came here because you *wanted* to?"

"Who wouldn't?" one of the other merchants spoke up. "There's gold to be won by easier means than our daily toil."

"The one-armed brigand I played this morning just spewed out five hundred silver pieces!" another man announced, to loud cheers. Neither he nor his audience considered the fact that he'd fed the machine over five *thousand* of those same bits of silver.

"The hamsters love me!" a third merchant shouted from his place beside the Great Wheel.

Bezique laid her graceful hands upon Sir Hanson's arm and gently coaxed him to re-sheath his sword, then steered the stunned knight to a small table in the most intimate corner of the bar. A buxom wood-sprite clad in a pair of maple-seed pasties and a whisper of ivy-trimmed panties set two glasses and a pitcher of something green between them before flying off again.

"You see, after Mother died—" Bezique began.

"I can't beg your forgiveness for that enough, m'lady," Sir Hanson broke in. "I vow upon my honor as a knight, I will make full restitution for every coin my father and aunt stole from her!"

Bezique waved away his impassioned offer. "Water under the troll-infested bridge," she said. "Mother knew the risks of the profession. It was her own fault for letting her gambling addiction get the better of her." She absent-mindedly dug two huge chunks of spicy cake out of the wall beside her and passed him one. "Here. On the house."

Between bites of gingerbread, she continued: "Some years after Mother died, I took over this location. The other woodland witches were very helpful when it came to reconstructing the old place. Did you know that with gingerbread cottages you need permits from the Building Inspector *and* a reputable baker? But alas, soon after that, your *dear* King Donald built that blasted Dark Woods Bypass."

"I understand your feelings, m'lady, but understand ours," Sir Hanson said. "The Dark Woods teems with anthropophagous perils. A worthy king must look to the welfare of his subjects."

Bezique sipped her drink languidly. "And building a road that charges ruinous tolls that go straight into the Royal Treasury is *so* magnanimous," she drawled.

As little as he personally cared for Good King Donald, Sir Hanson felt impelled by his oath of knighthood to defend his sovereign. "All good citizens of this realm must stand ready to make sacrifices in the name of security," he intoned. "If the king had not built the Dark Woods Bypass, toll road or no, the child-devouring witches would have already won."

Bezique laughed. "Do you believe *everything* you're told? Eat children? Gah! Do you have any idea how hard they are to *clean*? To say nothing of the calories, or choosing the proper wine. And don't you *dare* mention Chianti!"

"You can't mean to say you exist on gingerbread," Sir Hanson protested.

"We almost existed on nothing, thanks to your precious king," Bezique shot back. "Do you know how badly his stupid toll-road impacted the local economy? When you call something a bypass, simple folk presume it's shielding them from something they *should* pass by! No more moony swains and lasses came to see us for love potions, no more harried husbands sought cures for their wives' peevish fits, nor peeved wives sought something to make their less-than-lusty mates a bit more *manly*, if you follow me."

Sir Hanson wore the look of one who has awakened from a bad dream into a substandard reality. "Is that all you did?" he asked. "Sell potions to the peasants?"

"Peasants?" Bezique showed her teeth in a feral grin. "Just ask Good Queen Ivana why it took her ten years to produce the crown prince, and then only after she made a trip into the Dark Woods."

Sir Hanson slumped back in his chair. "I'm dead," he announced.

Bezique stood up, leaned across the table in a most scenic manner, took his face in both her hands, and gave him a long, deep kiss. He responded eagerly, and when at last she broke their embrace she observed, "You don't kiss like a corpse. Why claim kinship?"

"Because my mission hither was to bring back the errant merchants. It doesn't look like they'll come willingly, and I can't force all of them. Good King Donald has little use for knights who fail him."

"Bother Good King Donald. Stay here, sir knight, and serve us."

"'Us'?"

The enchantress spread her arms wide, indicating the flash and glitter of the vast gambling den. "Does this *look* like a one-witch operation? We woodland sorceresses formed a corporation, once we realized what Good King Donald had done to us. We reasoned that if the public no longer had any *need* to enter the Dark Woods, perhaps we should make them *want* to do so."

Sir Hanson shook his head sadly. "Fair lady, I'd gladly stay here and turn my sword to your service, but if I return a failure, King Donald will imprison me for a false knight, and force my father to ruin himself with my ransom. And if I don't return at all, Good King Donald will declare me a traitor and confiscate my father's property to the last crumb."

"We could fake your death," Bezique suggested. "I'd really like to take you on as my new chief of security. In fact, I'd really just like to take you on." She licked her lips.

Sir Hanson shook his head. "As I would like to serve you, in all ways possible, and in one or two that might not be possible but that it would be a lot of fun to try anyway. However, if I'm reported dead, it would break my parents' hearts, and then there's Good King Donald's death-tax to be paid, and— and— and—" He sighed. "And even if I could evade all those consequences, I wouldn't have long to enjoy my new life here. Mark me, the king will order knight after knight into the Dark Woods until he finally learns about the riches gathered here, and then he'll send an army here to take 'em from you. That man loves gold like a pig loves slop, and there's only so much that witchery can do to ward off cold steel."

"Do you sense a *unifying theme* to the woes confronting you and me and all this kingdom?" the enchantress asked grimly. "Have you never thought how . . . *pleasant* things might be, were we rid of such rapacious royalty?"

"*Kill* him?" Sir Hanson was aghast. No matter his personal feelings about Good King Donald, he was still an honorable knight. As such, he could not countenance the summary snuffing of his liege lord, and he said so. "Besides, the regal wretch has always got at least fifty guards protecting his miserable royal hide at all times," he concluded.

Bezique leaned across the table and traced titillating patterns on Sir Hanson's dampening palms. "Oh, I wasn't going to suggest that *we* kill him," she said.

"A TRAIL OF CRUMBS, is it?" Good King Donald lowered his voice until it was barely audible and darted his eyes to left and right, vigilant against prying eyes. He and Sir Hanson were barricaded together in a secret chamber in the topmost turret of the castle, but the king wasn't taking any chances. He'd commanded his guards to leave him alone with the man (following the ceremonial weapons-removal-and-strip-search, of course). The news this knight had brought back from his quest more than made up for the fact that he'd failed to fetch the missing merchants.

"Aye, crumbs," said Sir Hanson, reaching into the little pouch at his belt. "Like these I first showed you." He sprinkled a pinch of gold bits across the tabletop.

The king's eyes lit up like bonfires into which he flung all caution. "You left a whole *trail* of them behind you?"

Sir Hanson nodded solemnly. "Not all the way to the castle, nor even all the way to the edge of the Dark Woods, lest uninvited eyes catch sight of them and deprive you, my king, of a treasure trove that's yours by right. No birds will gobble crumbs like these; the route back to the dragon's cavern will remain well-blazed. There was such plentiful store of gold in that cave that I could safely squander as much as I needed to mark the path."

"And you say that the dragon in whose cavern you found this fortune is—?"

"The cave is filled with dragon bones, Sire," Sir Hanson replied. "And so much gold that even if you were to take your fifty stout guardsmen with you, there'd be more than enough for all of them to have a share."

"Share. . ." The king repeated the word as though it were coined in some foreign tongue. He pursed his lips in thought, then asked: "Is gold very heavy, good Sir Hanson the Hawk-eyed?"

"Heavy enough, but not so heavy that one man, alone and unassisted, couldn't carry off a fortune in his bare hands. And if he took an ox-cart with him, the beasts could bear away enough to purchase an empire or two. So if you bring your guards, they would be able to carry—"

"Never mind about my guards," said the king. "Go get me some oxen, good Duke Hanson the *Silent*."

"*HE'S* THE ONE who jumped to conclusions," said the newly-made duke to his sorcerous sweetheart. They were closeted together in her bedchamber, just off the casino floor, whither she'd dragged him the instant he returned to inform her of the success of his errand. "It wasn't as if I lied."

"Of course you didn't," Bezique replied dreamily, doing magical things with her hands.

"The trail *was* well-blazed. He could have followed it out again easily enough."

"Mmmm."

"And the cavern *did* hold just as much gold as I told him. I saw the same vision in your crystal that you did."

"Such a clever boy. Hold still. Stupid armor. Where's my monkey wrench?"

But conscience would not allow Duke Hanson to enjoy Bezique's attentions. He sat up and exclaimed: "And the cave *was* filled with dragon bones, just as I said! Is it *my* fault that there was still a living dragon wrapped around them?"

"Found it!" cried Bezique, brandishing the wrench.

Some time later, a loud whoop rang through the raisin-studded rafters of the gaming hall. At the joyful sound, Master Wulfram looked up glumly from his losing hand of Sixty-Two Ogres.

"'Bout time *someone* got lucky in here," he grumbled.

"Shut up and play cards, Pa," said Bardric, raking in the pot.

This story originally appeared in the *Fantasy Gone Wrong* anthology, DAW, 2006.

Nebula Award winner **Esther Friesner** is the author of over 40 novels and almost 200 short stories. She is also a poet, a playwright, and the editor of several anthologies. The best known of these is the Chicks in Chainmail series that she created and edits for Baen Books. The sixth book, *Chicks and Balances*, appeared in July 2015. *Deception's Pawn,* the latest title in her popular Princesses of Myth series of Young Adult novels from Random House, was published in April 2015.

Esther is married, a mother of two, grandmother of one, harbors cats, and lives in Connecticut. She has a fondness for bittersweet chocolate, graphic novels, manga, travel, and jewelry. There is no truth to the rumor that her family motto is "Oooooh, SHINY!"

Her super-power is the ability to winnow her bookshelves without whining about it. Much.

FELLOW TRAVELER

DONALD J. BINGLE

CORBIN HAD ALWAYS said that he would rather walk barefoot over broken pottery shards behind a donkey with diarrhea while wearing his scratchy winter great coat on the fiercest, breezeless mid-summer afternoon with a squabbling, squirming, and overweight six-year old under each arm, than travel with barbarians. And he had always gotten a laugh when he said it.

So what had he done?

He had decided to travel with barbarians.

It had seemed like a good idea at the time. He wanted to go from here to there, but there were rumors of brigands and boogens and marauding disobeyers of civil authority and . . . and he had little to no ability to defend himself or, frankly, anything or anyone else.

After all, back when he was known as Corey the Comedian, working bars with a traveling troupe of performers, he had never needed fighting skills and he had never feared the open road. The troupe's manager always hired itinerant warriors to protect the players and their wagons full of costumes, props, and magic items. Consequently, neither he nor any of the various actors, comedians, or attractive and comely dancers and singers had any worries of ambush or other unseemly encounters. Indeed, one of the ways he had convinced his mom to let him go on the open road as a teenager years ago was that he promised always to use protection.

"No worries of ickiness," he had intoned. He'd always had a way with words.

Unfortunately, even though he was well protected in his travels by moonlighting city guards and heroes for hire, he was not quite so well protected from the vagaries and vicissitudes of life. In short, his career had not flourished. He was, he had been forced to admit after constant and rude reminders from his dwindling audiences, a not-particularly-funny comedian. The manager of the troupe had not only noticed this vocational flaw, he had joined in the heckling. Corey could live with that, but when the manager "forgot" to mention once that the troupe was leaving town early the next morning, Corey had taken it as a possible indicator that he was not indispensable to the troupe's performances.

Corey had, of course, wished to stay with the troupe and did his best to help in other ways, but he did not have a good enough memory to transform himself into a teller of epic tales and was insufficiently coordinated to become a juggler. He had tried to sing a time or two, but really wasn't fond enough of vegetables to continue that particular career path. He was useless, even behind the scenes. He couldn't remember what props went where and nobody liked his cooking, including him.

When you came right down to it, Corey was only part of an itinerant troupe of players because he liked staying up late and hanging around bars. In the end, he was reduced to playing the part of any corpse that was needed in the group's various dramatic performances. Even this was problematic, as he had an unfortunate tendency to squirm uncontrollably when he lay on his back too long. It was in an attempt to improve his corpse portrayals that he discovered his new calling.

He convinced a mage who was riding the same circuit of miserable hamlets and villages as his troupe to teach him a magical spell that allowed him to feign death. Magicians, of course, don't like to give out their secrets, but feigning death is not really one of those "wow" spells that everyone clamored to know. Corey was sufficiently adept or appreciative or, perhaps, annoying that the magician, Magnifico the Magnificent Mage, went on to teach him a few more of the lesser spells.

His change in profession was just in the small, bleeding gash of time, as Corey was fired just a fortnight later . . . or, at least, the troupe moved out to another, undisclosed town under the cover of darkness, without him being informed.

That's how he came to be traveling alone to the west while the troupe and its mercenary guards traveled east . . . or north . . . or south . . . or southeast . . . or north-northeast . . . or some other direction, for all he knew. No one was talking. Even the street urchins and panhandlers had apparently been paid off.

Having been spurned by the troupe, Corey decided to take his magic act on a solo tour of the smallest and least sophisticated hamlets and hovels he could find. His new moniker was Corbinico the Comedic Conjurer. Of course, in a fortnight, he had not learned much magic. And, in a decade, he had not learned much comedy. But he believed that he had learned just enough spells and just the right spells to punctuate his otherwise uneven comedic monologue and amuse an audience of simple folk with simple minds and not enough wealth to waste vegetables as projectiles.

He could make someone hear a whisper. He could make someone sneeze or make them itch in an embarrassing spot. He could give someone a bit of a zap—causing pain, but not really much damage. He could untie simple knots, no matter how tight, without using his hands. And he could feign death.

Not really much of a routine, but he would work that out as he walked. All he had to do was get to the farm country, where the roads were safe and the inhabitants guileless. The immediate problem was that his magical abilities did not provide much in the way of offensive or defensive fighting power and the road west to the farmlands was risky.

That's why he needed protection.

That's why he decided to travel with the barbarians. He didn't have the money to hire professional, or even semi-professional, guards. But he figured if he just traveled along with the barbarians, he would be safe. They were known as fierce fighters, especially when attacked from downwind. They were skilled with the various blood-encrusted bladed weapons they carried with them, they were too stupid to retreat, and they generally carried no treasure worth stealing.

That made them the perfect companions for a lone traveler seeking protection, except, of course, for the stench, the lack of intelligent conversation, the inedible trail food, and the lack of any rest stops along the way. (Horses peed while they walked; why should barbarians do any different?)

Oh, and the fact that barbarians hate magic and will kill a magician without a moment's thought should they run across one.

Corey wasn't stupid, just unemployable, so he omitted mentioning that he was a magician when he conversed with his would-be companions about their upcoming travels. It was pretty easy to avoid the topic. The conversation went something like this:

"We go toward setting sun. Go far," said Torg, the largest and smelliest of the breed. Torg had one bright blue eye and one green eye that was clouded over and oozing pus.

"Me go with you," said Corey, stifling a gag. "Be friends. Share food. Be strong,"

Torg looked him over and said something rude to Barack and Kindo, his two lackeys and partners in slime. "You little. No strong. We eat food yours. We be strong. We go toward setting sun."

"Yeah, whatever," said Corey, smiling broadly and nodding like an idiot.

IT ALL MIGHT have worked out alright, traveling west together, with the brute barbarian beasts not knowing of Corey's magical proclivities, if Corey's troupe hadn't also traveled west . . . and left a squad of professional mercenaries behind to make sure that Corey didn't follow. That might have made for considerable excitement and gratuitous bloodshed, except for the fact that barbarians are so fierce, they don't think they need to set a watch for the night.

Instead, as the dawn rose in the east, Corey, Torg, Barack, and Kindo woke-up . . . well, gained consciousness . . . each with a large lump on his head. Each was tied firmly to his own tree trunk, his face turned toward the burning rays of the sun. After the appropriate amount of confusion, swearing, straining ineffectively at their bonds, and finger-pointing (without actually being able to use fingers), a sullen silence set in. The foursome actually might have stayed in such position for some time, but the barbarians let loose with their morning pee and Corey was downwind. Something snapped and he did something incredibly useful and stupid.

He muttered a few magical phrases and the ropes tying them to the trees began to untie themselves.

Each of the constituent members of the barbarian horde (any group of two or more barbarians technically qualifies as a horde, etymologically speaking, though there is some dispute as to whether the term "horde" actually is an abbreviation for the word "horrid") looked at the ropes, then looked at Corey, then looked at one another, then looked at their weapons piled next to where the campfire had been, then looked at Corey, then smiled (not in a friendly "thanks for the help, good buddy" way, but in a drooling, toothy "I get his intestines" kind of way), then tried to engage in what appeared to be a barbarian variant of rock-paper-scissors, except that they couldn't see each other's hands, so Torg just growled and the others looked down (as if to agree that he not only got the intestines, but the brain as well).

Things didn't look good. The pee-soaked, battle-lusting barbarians certainly didn't look good. And Corey, what with being knocked out and tied to a tree and not having had an opportunity to take care of his morning biological functions, and being so concerned about being sliced in half that he was about to imitate the barbarian peeing-on-oneself practice, he didn't look so good, either. Here he was, about to be killed for being a magician and he was barely even a magician apprentice wannabe, who had cast less than a half-dozen miserable, puny little spells in his entire adult life. It wasn't as if he was a threat to the barbarian horde, or all barbarian hordes, or their women, or, more importantly, their goats. It's not like he was the most powerful mage in all the world. Of course, they didn't know that.

Of course! *They* didn't know that.

Corey extricated himself from his loosening bonds and leapt between the group of three barbarians, still in the midst of stepping out of their now-untied bonds, and their trusty, crusty weapons. He took up an exaggerated fighting/casting stance that he had seen one of the more flamboyant actors use in a performance of *The Veiled Threat of Seven Parts* and, in the deepest voice he could muster, shouted: "I am the greatest magician in all the world. I am Corbin the Conqueror. I have the power of Life and Death in my hands."

Well, that started a lot of barbarian yammering and various slit-eyed looks as the horde either discussed his claim or tried to figure out what the hell he was saying. Finally, Torg pushed Barack forward. The barbarian underling began to edge toward Corbin the Conqueror and the stash of weapons behind him.

"Death will come to you," shouted Corbin, looking sternly at the more tremulously trepidatious than intrepid tribesman before uttering a few arcane phrases. The words "Death, death, death will come to you," whispered in Barack's ear. The barbarian lackey backed off, twisting about like a dog chasing its tail to see who or what had whispered in his ear until he got dizzy and fell down.

Kindo made a minor move next, but yet another muttering by Corbin caused the maneuver to abort, as Kindo grabbed at his suddenly itching privates, even more than he had the night before.

Torg spat at the ground in disgust, then pushed his underlings to either side, and strode forward, as manfully as one can with urine-soaked goat skin breeches. "You no strong. Torg strong."

"Fair warning," sneered Corbin. "I have the power of Life and Death in my hands." He gazed quickly about the sky and saw a buzzard lazing overhead, no doubt waiting to get in on the leftovers of any violent encounter. Corbin pointed at the bird. "I show you."

With as much showiness and force as he could muster, Corbin gesticulated broadly and shouted magical phrases in basso profundo, ending with his hands and his eyes pointed straight at the innocent scavenger. "Death to you," added the magician, as his minor zap spell sprang from the tips of his stubby fingers heavenward toward the unsuspecting fowl.

The bird screeched in pain and fell from the sky, dead (maybe from the zap or maybe from the fall; Corbin wasn't picky, he was just grateful).

Corbin smirked crookedly and looked Torg straight in the eye (the blue one). "I can do that ten thousand times a day." He waggled his little finger to discharge the static that always clung after a 'zap' spell, sending a minor spark into Torg's snot-encrusted nose. "Do not anger me, puny one. I am the most powerful mage the world has ever known."

The barbarians bought it, muck, slime, and stinker. Their eyes widened, then cast downward. They fell to their knees. They wrung their hands in supplication. They bowed in obeisance. They quivered in fear when they weren't quavering in awe.

The trip went much better after that. They rested when Corey wanted them to rest. They allowed him to walk where he wanted (upwind). They offered him the largest, moldiest portions of what he was sure they believed were fine cheeses. They even bathed, at his direction, in a river-rapids they were crossing, scouring away months of grime and replacing their usual stench with the smell of wet goat-hair, at least for awhile.

Corbin almost thought things would work out until it came time to camp for the night. Oh, the horde was obedient and helpful: stoking the fire; cooking up fish for him that they usually ate raw (without cleaning them first); mounding up dry grass for a mattress; and more. But Corbin saw the gleam in Torg's good eye (he avoided looking at the pus in the bad eye) and realized that the barbarian would come for him in the night (and not in the "gee, we don't have any goats here" way). Suddenly, things looked a lot darker, and not just because the sun had set.

Corbin was right. At the darkest hour, Torg came for him. Corbin couldn't see him, of course. There was no moon. But he could smell him. So he did the only thing he could do when faced with a superior fighting foe. He leapt up, screamed like a little girl, tried his best to duck as he heard the swish of a weapon aimed for him, and collapsed to the ground, feigning death.

In case you've never tried it, feigning death is pretty cool . . . especially to the touch. You can hear and see and smell normally, but you appear to be completely dead. No pulse, no apparent breathing, no reaction to stimuli. Skin cold and clammy. Corbin worried a bit that Torg might mutilate his corpse in rage or celebration, but the brute only nudged him a few times with a heavily-calloused toe with a frighteningly long toenail.

Torg hooted in victory, waking both of the rest of the horde, and jumped up and down a few times. Then he clapped his companions on the head for being inferior to their fearsome leader and everyone went to sleep. Corbin dozed himself.

The horde was just about to decamp the next morning, when Corbin calmly canceled the spell and sat up, refreshed and unharmed. He looked squarely at Torg. "I hold the power of Life as well as Death. The next time someone from your tribe kills me, I will rise again and kill not only you, but all of your women . . . and all of your goats."

And, so it was that Corey the Comedian became the God-King of the barbarian horde (I mean the full horde; not just the three guys he had traveled with). Torg became the high priest of the acolytes of Corbin, the Conqueror of Life and Death. Barack and Kindo carried Corbin around in a litter. He was fed the best goat and the best berries and offered the best women the barbarians had to offer. Life was good. And Corbin didn't just take advantage; he was an enlightened leader who instituted wise policies, like cooking fish and peeing in the bushes instead of on oneself.

For quite a few months, it seemed as if it really had been a good idea to travel with barbarians.

And then came the armed legions of the king.

Soon, and apparently for the rest of their lives, the horde was surrounded by ten thousand armored soldiers, a force that had been assembled to rid the kingdom of the pestilent scourge of the barbarians. And everyone in the horde, every man, woman, and goat, looked to Corbin and cried in unison the phrase he had used at the beginning of every speech, every judicial pronouncement, every greeting he had ever made since becoming the God-King of the Horde: "I am Corbin, the Conqueror of Life and Death. I can kill ten thousand times a day. And I can rise from the dead to do it again tomorrow."

You have to admit, it's a good line. But, of course, that's what the horde was looking for him to do. Kill ten thousand times. The king's legion, of course, had no such expectation. Accordingly, the knights bugled their charge, lowered their lances, and came at the tribesmen. The horde didn't even bother to pick up their weapons, such was their faith in Corbin the Conqueror . . . their stupid, misguided faith.

It was going to be a slaughter.

Suddenly, traveling with barbarians didn't seem like it had been a good idea after all. So Corbin did the only thing he could do.

He feigned death.

Maybe Corey the Comedian could entertain the troops after the slaughter.

This story originally appeared in the *Fantasy Gone Wrong* anthology, DAW, 2006.

Donald J. Bingle, the world's top-ranked player of classic role-playing game tournaments for fifteen years, is the author of five books and about fifty short stories in the thriller, horror, fantasy, science fiction, mystery, steampunk, romance, comedy, and memoir genres. Many of his previously published stories are reprinted in his Writer on Demand series, including: *Tales of Gamers and Gaming; Tales of Humorous Horror; Tales Out of Time; Grim, Fair e-Tales; Tales of an Altered Past Powered by Romance, Horror, and Steam; Not-So-Heroic Fantasy;* and *Shadow Realities.* His latest novel, *The Love-Haight Case Files,* co-authored with Jean Rabe, is, according to *New York Times* best-selling author William C. Dietz, "... *a comedy, locked within a mystery, hidden in a horror story... Wonderfully clever, stylish, and ghoulish. Delightfully twisted fun!"* More about Don and his writing can be found at www.donaldjbingle.com.

A FISH STORY
SARAH TOTTON

IN THE VALE of Brecon where the fishermen hunt their game amid deep and succulent cloud, where the yaks are pink, and where the maidens are all beautiful (with some exceptions) lived the grand old dowager, Lydia Batterfly.

Lydia Batterfly's greatest regret in life was her niece, Dagmar. Dagmar was neither inclined toward the practice of womanly etiquette, nor suffiently attractive to be forgiven her disinclinations. Despite attendance at finishing school for two full years, she stubbornly refused to act like a lady. Worse was her tendency to make a spectacle of herself over the most inappropriate things, most recently and deplorably "that awful tower boy," as the dowager Batterfly referred to him.

"I don't know why you bother with him," said the dowager.

"His name is Henry," said Dagmar, "and I bother because he is *superb*."

"Not by *our* standards," said Lydia, by which she meant the standards of any sensible woman of good breeding and taste.

Henry, the bell tower boy, was nearly seventeen with limbs as long as a spider monkey's and hair so short it barely colored his scalp. He went about town in simple white clothes, displaying no familial colors—the shameful apparel of a bastard. Henry's job was to climb the tower and play the fish until their echoes rang from the valley walls. There were five fish in the tower, caught from the Sonorous River, in the days when fish swam in rivers, by one Martidel Bayliss, the greatest fisherman in Brecon history. His enormous catches had been bronzed for posterity and hung in the tower where they were twice daily made to clatter amongst themselves in a semblance of music. Henry, the current bell tower boy, was recognized as one of the better practitioners of the art of fish-clattering. Dagmar had been in love with him from the moment she'd first seen him, trousers rolled up to his knees in the Friday Bog with a frog clutched in his fist, squeezing it just hard enough to make its eyes protrude.

The greatest disappointment in Dagmar's life was that Henry did not appear to be likewise infatuated with her. She ascribed this, given her deceptively unremarkable appearance, to his simply not having noticed her. She set about to remedy this.

On the eve of the coldest night of the year, just after the last murmur of the fish jangles had died away, Dagmar stationed herself below the tower looking up at the fish chamber fifty feet above. In her hands, she held her uncle's bangy-wurdle, salvaged from the dowager Batterfly's lumber room. Bangy-wurdles were the instruments of the insane, the bizarrely eccentric and the lower classes of society. No one of good breeding would even admit to owning one. The instrument produced a music often described as "a din of iniquity."

Practicing in secret, Dagmar had spent the summer learning to master the instrument. She reasoned it thusly: a piano was too difficult to drag to the town square, and a clarinet didn't allow for singing. And sing she did. She sang a song she had composed for her love, amidst daydreams of his froggy hands, his simian limbs and his days at play among the shining fish. At the close of the second verse, as she launched into the chorus, she saw a white face thrust out from the tower window.

"What's that fuss?" said Henry. "Are you ill?"

She finished the chorus and shouted up to him, "A song professing my love for you, dear Henry. Sit back and enjoy while I serenade you." And she continued to play what was later described by the town wag as "the musical equivalent of a cat caught under a pram wheel."

Despite several pleas from around the square for Dagmar to hold her peace, she played on, singing of Henry's attributes.

"My what?" Henry shouted. "What are you saying?"

"Your glorious shining fingers," she shouted back.

There were some hoots of laughter from one of the nearby houses.

"Clear off," said Henry. "People will hear you."

"You are the most desirable man in the Vale of Brecon, and I am not going to stop until everyone knows it." Dagmar continued to play. She had not quite finished her fourth turn through the chorus when Henry, desperate to shut her up, emptied a water pail out of the tower window. The air was so cold that the cascade had nearly crystallized by the time it broke over Dagmar's head. Dagmar squeaked in shock and almost dropped the bangy-wurdle on the cobblestones.

"Now go home!" said Henry. And he banged the tower shutters closed.

Dagmar took a few moments to collect her wits, shaking the beads of ice from her coat and brushing them from the bangy-wurdle. Her hair was now frozen into points.

Lydia Batterfly's house abutted the square, and Dagmar retreated to it. There was no point in further stating her suit if Henry had closed the window. Unfortunately, as soon as she tried to open the front door, her wet hand froze fast to the metal knob. Try as she might, she could not get it free. Her shouts for assistance were met with answering shouts to shut up. Eventually, though, they drew her fondest friend Eora, the duchess' daughter, from the house next door. Eora was of that sensible type who are really quite wonderful in a pinch, though they tend to be dull and full of advice for living a good life at other times. On this occasion, Eora, who'd watched the entire spectacle from her bedroom window, came prepared carrying a bowl full of hot water from the kettle. The bowl had contained some exotic fruits which were now dumped over her mother's oak dining table. Eora proceeded to pour the steaming contents of the bowl over Dagmar's hand in an attempt to loosen it from the doorknob. The major difficulty being to stop herself laughing so hard that she dropped it.

"Yes, all right, all right," said Dagmar peeling her hand from the door handle. "It isn't funny. I mean, you have no idea what love does to a person. You'll see."

Though really, Dagmar thought, Eora was the sort of person who would fall in love—or something respectably close to it—with a suitable gentleman approved by her mother the duchess, and they would be wed in a ghastly ceremony in which Dagmar would be forced to attend in some abominable dress. Dagmar loathed dresses.

WORD GETS ABOUT in small places, and it wasn't long before Eora's mother, the Duchess, was informing Lydia Batterfly of what Dagmar had been up to while she had been out of town.

"She's sending me back to finishing school," said Dagmar to Eora that afternoon.

"Not again! That's what...The fourth time? What are you going to do?"

"Third, and I think she's going to find that Madame Loge will have nothing to do with me. She doesn't like to be reminded of her failings. They're so few and far between. As to what I'm going to do, I've thought of another plan."

"Plan?"

"To win Henry."

Eora stared at Dagmar and said nothing. Perhaps it was a tactful omission of words. When at last she spoke, she said, "What are you going to do?"

"Come with me and see," said Dagmar. She led the way down the center of the street, down the narrower alleyways of Brecon town, to Tyrone's Fishing Tackle Emporium.

"What on Earth?" Eora muttered.

Dagmar went inside and accosted the shop's proprietor. "I would like your best and strongest rod, please."

"Yes, madam," said the proprietor. "We have a variety of—"

"The longest one you've got."

"Oh," said the merchant, and he led her to the window of the shop from which he pulled a small brass cylinder.

"That doesn't look very large, man," said Dagmar.

"If you would come outside." The merchant stepped out into the street and proceeded to extend the rod. The mechanism was a telescopic one. The merchant pulled each joint out, lengthening it until it stretched the entire length of the alley and protruded out over the High Street sidewalk. Curious onlookers peered at it warily and walked around it.

"Well?" said the merchant.

"I suppose if that's the longest one you've got, it will have to do," said Dagmar. "How much is it?"

"Oh, madam, workmanship like this... This is a one-of-a-kind, made on the Gwyntog Coast and designed after the one used by Martidel Bayliss who once fished with it in the ocean. It is the most beautiful piece of wo—"

"I'm amazed you're willing to part with it."

"I could be coerced," said the merchant. "But it would take a king's ransom."

"Far be it from me to part a man from his beloved rod. We'll look elsewhere, thanks."

"You will not find a larger or better rod in the entire Vale of Brecon."

"That's as may be, but I haven't got a king to ransom."

"Perhaps we could negotiate."

A price was settled, though the merchant claimed he would go bankrupt, and Dagmar claimed she would have no dowry, "Though without this, there would be no need for a dowry."

"Why, Dagmar?" said Eora. "What are you going to do?"

"I," said Dagmar, "am going to catch the Barbary Fish, and then—"

"You're out of your mind!" said the merchant. "You?! The best fisherman in the history of Brecon spent his entire career trying, and even he couldn't catch the Barbary Fish."

"Please," said Dagmar. "You interrupted me. As I was saying. I am going to catch the Barbary Fish and present him to Henry the tower boy as a token of my love."

"Dagmar..." said Eora.

"I know," said Dagmar. "I'll need bait."

Dagmar strode off waving her rod, now telescoped down to a more manageable twelve inches. Eora was forced to run to keep up with her. Dagmar led her to the fishing grounds at Leechfield. The day was gloriously clear, and there were several fishermen sprawled amid the long grasses, eyes following the spiderfloss of their fishing lines which disappeared into the sky, ending at their lures glinting from colorful balloons. High above them, the braver fishermen rode in baskets beneath larger balloons, harpoons held at the ready, sighting along the Vale for the cloud-wisps of fish-spoor.

Dagmar made straight for the oldest and raggedest of the veteran fishermen at Leechfield and without preamble, said, "If you were to try for the Barbary Fish, where would you set your line and how would you bait your hook?"

The man looked at Dagmar and snorted. "Five miles of golden spiderfloss, four of silver. And for a lure, the blue stained glass from the window of Epiphany. And everyone knows the Barbary Fish frequents the hills at Devil's End."

"You've never tried to catch him yourself?"

"I'm not mad."

"Well then, thank you, sir," said Dagmar.

That night, someone broke the Epiphany window. It was later determined that a stone had been thrown through it. Three days after this Dagmar's aunt found the family tapestry bundled up in the cupboard under the stairs. Half of it had been unravelled, and the gold and silver threads had all been pulled out. None of the servants would own up to doing it.

Shortly afterwards, Dagmar became suddenly attentive at her macramé and crochet lessons. Madam Loge began to entertain cautious hopes for her reform.

Ten days later, Dagmar appeared dripping wet at Eora's door. "You'll have to help me," said Dagmar. She led her friend to Leechfield where a gathering of fishermen were ringed around the convex, glittering side of an enormous fish.

"Is that the Barbary—?"

"Well, no actually," said Dagmar. "But it's quite a respectable one I think. It dragged me across Leechfield and all along the Sonorous River. Do you see this?" Dagmar proudly displayed a missing tooth. "Came out when I hit the Bridge. No one warned me it might take me up. Anyway, it dropped me in the sea and I suppose it expected me to let go, but I wasn't going to give it the satisfaction. I worried it about a bit, then it seemed to tire, enough that I could wind it in close enough to start biffing and kicking it. It got the message and went to ground here. Which was lucky, as I didn't fancy landing in the quarry."

"What are you going to do with it?" said Eora.

"Have it bronzed, of course. It's easily bigger than any of the ones in the tower now."

Eora's eyes grew wide, but she didn't comment. The look of fanatical determination in Dagmar's eyes stilled her tongue.

HENRY, AS IT happened, was neither pleased nor impressed when Dagmar, accompanied by a parade of dancing acrobats and men in military costume, presented the bronzed fish to him at the door of the tower.

"That won't fit up the steps," he said.

"We'll hoist it from outside," said Dagmar. "This is a gift to you, a token of my esteem."

"Look," said Henry. He glanced at the acrobats somersaulting crosswise in front of him and lowered his voice. "Stop doing this."

"Doing what?"

"Giving me things, publicly declaring your feelings for me."

"Martidel Bayliss didn't stop trying to catch the Barbary fish and look at him."

"Right, but he never caught it, though, did he?" said Henry.

"No, but he spent his *entire life* trying. Isn't that utterly marvelous? That is dedication, Henry, as I am dedicated in my love for you."

"But I don't love you. I don't even like you. What you're doing... It's embarrassing me. It's insulting. Stop it."

Dagmar's face fell, and her brow furrowed in thought. "Very well." She bowed. "But take the fish."

"SO, YOU HAVE seen sense at last," said Eora as they sipped wine in the conservatory.

Dagmar shrugged. "If you mean have I given up, then no. Not at all."

"But he ordered you to leave him alone."

"Ah, yes. And that is because I have not done enough to earn his love. I have not sacrificed enough, I have not suffered enough."

"And you think he has not suffered enough either." Eora sighed. "This is fatuous. It's senseless."

"No. Senseless is in the country of Giving Up. What is the purpose of living if I can't pursue him? If I stopped, it would mean I didn't really love him. And I do."

"He says he doesn't love you."

"If he really believes that..."

"Yes?" Eora leaned closer.

"...then I haven't been trying hard enough."

Exasperated, Eora proclaimed, "A woman pursuing a man is a scandal. I think you are doing it to mortify your Aunt Lydia."

"I am doing it for the glory," said Dagmar. "A glory most women are afraid to taste."

FOR A FEW WEEKS nothing new transpired, except that Dagmar began to pay rapt attention to her art instructor. Then one morning, a large mural was found covering the front of Dagmar's house. It depicted a man, endowed with yak-like proportions, strutting atop an enormous tower from which a golden fish hung.

The next day, Henry of the bell tower asked the swineherd's daughter to marry him.

"Now, even you must admit defeat," said Eora.

"Not at all," said Dagmar. "This girl, what do you know about her?"

"She's very beautiful."

"Ah," said Dagmar, "But did she earn her beauty, or did she happen upon it by way of the womb? What has she done to be worthy of Henry?"

"Well, nothing," said Eora, "except I suppose that he likes her. And perhaps she was patient enough to let him make up his own mind about that, and doesn't wake him at midnight singing his praises, or drop uninvited fish and acrobats in his lap."

"No," said Dagmar. "It can't be that simple. If he truly believes he loves her, then it's because I haven't tried hard enough."

EORA HAPPENED TO meet Henry in Evelyn Street the next afternoon. They greeted each other cordially, if cautiously, like two people who share an embarrassing complaint.

"It won't work," said Eora. "I mean, if that's why you've done it."

"What?"

"Proposing to another girl. In fact, I think you've spurred her on to try even harder to win you."

"Tell her from me that she can go to hell," Henry muttered. "Tell her I'll send her there myself if she doesn't stop it." He stalked off.

Eora went off to do as he asked, but at the door to Dagmar's house, she stopped. Her hand, lifted to tap on the door, dropped to her side, and she regarded it pensively. What was the use talking to Dagmar? She wouldn't listen to reason.

A FEW DAYS LATER, Dagmar was sitting on the bank of the Sonorous River, working out a plot to stop Henry's wedding.

She was planning the speech she would make when the minister asked if there were any objections to the wedding. Of course there were. Anyone could see that Henry had become engaged solely to annoy her and not because he loved this other girl.

Dagmar was deep in thought writing her speech when a shadow fell across the parchment. She looked up, but instead of an obtrusive cloud, she saw a man looming over her.

"You're in my light," said Dagmar. "Move off."

"*You* are my light," said the man.

Dagmar, whose head had bowed to the task of writing almost before the words were out of her mouth looked up suddenly. "What?"

"Lady for whose sake alone I breathe, listen while I tell you that I adore you."

It was the fisherman from Leechfield. The old, ragged man who'd told her about baiting hooks.

"You're cracked!" said Dagmar. "You're twice my age for a start. And anyway, in case you hadn't noticed, and you must be deaf, mad and stupid if you haven't, I'm in love with Henry the tower boy."

"Henry is engaged to the swineherd's daughter."

"That's what he thinks," said Dagmar, standing up and brushing the heads of grasses from her cloak.

"He is betrothed," said the fisherman. "Whereas I am not. We are better suited to each other." He began to follow Dagmar as she made her way back to the square.

"Don't you have fish to catch?" said Dagmar.

"None more beautiful than you, and none more sly and worthy than you." As they walked, the fisherman's voice rose so that people in the square turned to watch them.

"Look," said Dagmar, rounding on him, "Look here, back off. I've told you to go. Everyone knows where my heart belongs."

The fisherman fell to his knees. "Most glorious girl, listen to me while I declare my love for you in front of these people, for no one could be more worthy of a fisherman's love than the woman who tried for the Barbary Fish."

"Yes, yes, all right. Everyone knows I didn't get him, but thanks for bringing it to their attention. Now clear off."

The fisherman grabbed hold of the hem of Dagmar's cloak so that she had to jerk it free. She turned and stalked off.

The fisherman followed her, tossing glass-glazed fish scales over her head. "A tribute," he said.

Someone nearby sniggered. Dagmar had to make an undignified run to her house, slamming and bolting the door behind her.

"IT ISN'T FUNNY, EORA," said Dagmar. She had to raise her voice to be heard over the wailing coming from below the window as the Leechfield fisherman serenaded her.

"I think it's romantic," said Eora. "Why don't you consider him?"

"Look, Eora, there are two kinds of people in the world. The Pursuers and the Pursued. And the Pursuers neither like nor wish to be pursued. It is an insult to their nature."

"I heard that Henry proposed to the swineherd's daughter," said Eora. "She didn't pursue him at all."

Dagmar frowned. "Do you know, that man is singing off-key. I didn't sing off-key when I serenaded Henry...did I?"

Eora shrugged. "I couldn't really tell over Henry's shouting at you to shut up."

"And at least I composed an original song," said Dagmar. "This raving nit is borrowing an old chestnut and trotting it out like it's the latest thing. He's doing a poor job of it all around." Dagmar shot to her feet and marched to the bathroom, filled a tub with the coldest water she could manage and wrestled it back to the window. She tipped the water out of the window onto the singing fisherman.

"Hmmm," she said. "Perhaps I ought to learn from my own mishaps."

Eora brightened. "Yes!"

Then Dagmar picked up the potted plant next to the window and tipped out over the ledge as well. "Yes, the water makes the soil stick quite well," she said, peering down. "It *does* pay to learn from one's mistakes."

THE NEXT DAY in church, the Leechfield fisherman presented Dagmar with a garland of the finest cerise yak's hair. Yak's hair garlands were considered *de rigueur* at the time. Dagmar stood up in the pew and shouted, "Stop! I cannot think of anything more annoying, more aggravating, more infuriating than your pursuit of me when I have clearly told you that I am not interested. You are an ass. An ass' ass, and your attention to me is insulting." As she said this, her eyes happened upon Henry who was standing by the door to the tower, about to ring his fish to signify the end of the service.

Dagmar's cheeks turned a shade reminiscent of the most fashionable yak's hair, and she walked out.

Henry married the swineherd's daughter without incident and they lived in comfortable married squabblehood, his wife being unencumbered with the notion that she had married a perfect man.

Dagmar failed finishing school in spectacular fashion for the third time and finished up a merry spinster, living on the outskirts of town. On fine days, she can sometimes be seen using her famous brass rod. She has yet to catch the Barbary Fish.

The Leechfield fisherman moved to the City where he bought a suite of rooms in one of the city towers from which the trawling was more rewarding than from his former, cheaper lodgings in a down-to-earth bungalow. It was an expensive purchase, but affordable to one who has benefited from the dowry of a duchess' daughter.

The fish served at Eora's wedding fed six hundred people.

This story originally appeared in *Realms of Fantasy* magazine, 2006.

Sarah Totton's short fiction has appeared in various anthologies and magazines including *Black Static Magazine*, *The Year's Best Dark Fantasy & Horror 2011* (Prime Books), *Fantasy: The Best of the Year 2007* (Prime), and *Writers of the Future XXII* (Galaxy Press). In 2007 she was named the Regional Winner (for Canada & the Caribbean) in the Commonwealth Short Story Competition. Her debut short story collection, *Animythical Tales*, was published in 2010 by Fantastic Books.

ANOTHER END OF THE EMPIRE
TIM PRATT

THE DARK LORD MOGRASH descended to his deepest basement, below the lower dungeons, below the magma reactors, below the well-warded and unquiet family crypts. He traveled down a spiraling path cut by a rockworm grown to enormous size by the Excessive Mining research and development division, and brooded as he went.

Visits with the sibyl of the depths never ended well. Such consultations had heralded the end of his father's life, and his grandfather's, and his great-grandfather's, and even the ancient half-giant forebear who'd founded their rapacious lineage. The old creature only brought ill tidings, but there were dire prophecies regarding the consequences of even easing her into retirement, let alone killing her and dumping her in a slither-pit somewhere.

Mogrash bashed open the door, scattering the heap of the knickknacks and souvenirs from conquered shores his ancestors had brought as gifts to the crone. As if keeping her happy with trifles might spare them her grim visions. He stepped over a pottery tortoise and a miniature hut woven of grasses and knelt in the alcove where the sibyl made her pronouncements.

Greasy torches flickered into life, casting the room in long shadows. The blood-smeared curtain before him twitched aside, revealing darkness and the twin blue sparks of the sibyl's eyes. "You were summoned, and you came," she rasped. Family lore said in her youth she'd had a euphonious voice, which had made the dread pronouncements even worse to hear. The rasp was more fitting.

"I am here," Mogrash said. "Give me the bad news."

"A child dwells in the village of Misery Chin, in the mountain provinces to the east. If allowed to grow to manhood, he will take over your empire, overthrow your ways and means, and send you from the halls of your palace forever."

Mogrash relaxed. This was, at least, not an immediate threat—not like the pronouncement of metastasized bone cancer she'd given his grandfather. He sighed. "So I'm expected to send my Fell Rangers to the mountains, raze the village, leave no stone upon a stone, enslave the women, and kill all the younglings to stop this dire prophecy from coming to pass."

"It's what your father would have done."

"Yes, but I'm more modern than he was. Besides, we've seen this happen a thousand times—the attempt to *stop* the prophecy will make it come to pass, won't it? We'll think all the children are dead, but one will have been spirited away, or maybe he'll just be off in the woods gathering mushrooms. He'll be so traumatized by the destruction of all he holds dear that he'll vow to avenge his family and dedicate himself to my downfall, learning the subtle arts of the marsh witches and the blatant arts of axecraft. And in ten or fifteen years he'll have my head on a pike, am I right?"

"Maybe," she said.

"Unacceptable." Mogrash shook his head, clacking together the tiny skulls of pixie-mages dangling from his braids. "No, I'll find another way. The key here is *innovation.*"

THE IMPERIAL SURVEYORS arrived in Misery Chin, a village of subsistence farmers and foresters whose women had a brisk sideline in making protective fetishes of hit-or-miss efficacy for the miners who labored over the next ridge. The surveyors answered no questions, but proceeded to demolish the timbered central meeting hall. The villagers huddled in their hovels and waited for their inevitable deportation, drafting, or human sacrifice, all of which were known to occur regularly closer to the center of the empire. If the surveyors were here, that meant the Lord had some use for the village, and it probably wouldn't involve the inhabitants living there. Everyone had heard what happened over in Ragged Ledge not two decades past.

Instead, the surveyors and their fabrication wizards built a beautiful new airy domelike meeting hall of lightweight silver metal and sheets of something like glass that could be darkened or made transparent at a custodian's command. A man the surveyors claimed was Lord Mogrash himself—though that was patently absurd, he'd never travel all the way out here, he must be a lowly official in disguise—addressed the crowd at the dedication ceremony.

"This new community center is just the beginning of the changes I'm bringing to Misery Chin, beginning with the name itself: this place will hereafter be known as Progress Village. I have chosen your fair hamlet as the new experimental model for the perfect imperial society, and we will be building schools—of the practical, magical, and piratical arts—and providing job training for all." The ersatz Lord chuckled. "I see the worry on your faces, but fear not—none of the retraining is compulsory. Apart from having homes that are better insulated and meals with something other than weevils for protein, your lives won't change unless you want them to. The old are set in their ways, I understand. The new advances are really meant for the children."

He grinned, and the people in the front row said his teeth were carved into tiny skulls, so perhaps it *was* the Lord himself. "Attendance at school will, of course, be mandatory. It's important for children to learn." He waved a gauntleted fist toward the crowd of officials at his left. "Address any questions or concerns to the overseers. But rest assured, I will be visiting from time to time to check in on the progress of the darling little ones."

And thus began the Golden Age of Plenty in Progress Village.

THERE WERE ONLY thirty children in the village, ranging in age from still-suckling to fifteen, which was the Lord's cutoff age. Anyone over fifteen wasn't a child anymore, but someone with the rights and responsibilities of an adult, as even the sibyl conceded. "And the girls can be dismissed, since you let slip the 'he' pronoun in your original prophecy," Mogrash mused. "One of those fourteen boys will be my downfall, then. I shall get to know them all wonderfully well."

"You could just kill them," the sibyl grumbled. "Nobody has any respect for tradition anymore."

"Yes, but we both know the executioner would go soft and bring me lamb hearts instead of the hearts of children to prove he'd done the deed. Even if I went in myself, wielding my mighty Trepanner"—his enchanted battle pickax—"there'd be some mistake, or the boy would turn out to be a changeling, with the *real* child living among the wood-whimsies, or *something*. No, better to keep them all under my eyes. The probability witches say this approach has the best chance of neutralizing negative results."

"Probability witches," the sibyl sneered. She'd emerged from her alcove to have tea, and she looked remarkably good for a creature countless centuries old—not a maiden, but not the crone he'd imagined, either. "As if you can tell the future with beads on strings and counting the chimes of bells and tossing dice endlessly in the air. You need blood and guts to get the attention of the gods."

"I prefer my gods inattentive," Mogrash said. "I'll bring you a jar of the local honey when I return from my next visit to the village. It's really quite good."

THINGS WENT WELL in Progress Village that first year. The people were prosperous, and having enough to eat and decent homes strangely made them work *harder*—violating the premise of motivation-through-privation on which most of the empire ran. Mogrash gradually rolled out similar model villages throughout the empire, focusing on the provinces where unrest was most common. He even made sure the slaves got enough to eat, and the need for extreme suppressions dropped by seventy percent. He had to put half the Slavering Corps on indefinite leave, and sent most of the rest to clear the ancient discredited swamp deities out of the jungles. So far, the dire prophecy wasn't proving all that dire, though Mogrash imagined that would change when one of the clever children tried to put a dirk into his eye and steal his crown away.

THE OLDEST CHILDREN graduated from an accelerated course in management and were sent off to cushy apprenticeships in the imperial city, once the probability witches determined none of them were the prophesied threats. The algorithms used by the witches were slow but implacable, and the Dark Lord had no doubt they'd eventually home in on the specific threat. As the years passed, Mogrash spent more and more time visiting the village, usually without his retinue of monsterish bodyguards—they made the locals nervous—and even had a residence built there, only slightly grander than the mayor's house. Occasionally he would go to the school as a guest lecturer and teach classes on geography (he'd been everywhere), history (he'd witnessed much of it), political science (he'd reinvented it), and mathematics (though his examples tended to involve numbers like troop strength and ration supplies).

Eventually the probability witches narrowed the suspects down to three children: Meph, a pale and moody boy of twelve who enjoyed shooting birds from trees with a slingshot and excelled at anatomy; Zander, a studious ten-year-old with some Wispfolk blood in his heritage, to judge from his faintly luminous eyes and his skills at gardening; and Khalil, a dark-complected child of eleven with a gaze that penetrated like acid-dipped arrows, who wanted to know *everything*. Mogrash spent weeks at a time in the village, running a special class consisting only of those three children, putting about the rumor that he was grooming them for positions high in the empire.

He grew fond of all three children, though Zander's pacifism was simultaneously irksome and reassuring (a boy who refused to learn the combative arts was unlikely to kill him, true, but Mogrash had trouble comprehending the mindset). Meph had a fondness for setting fires and vivisecting small animals and some of the local semi-sentients, so Mogrash tailored his curriculum to the destructive arts and the empirical sciences, while Khalil devoured history and statecraft books insatiably.

One day in a round-table seminar, as they were discussing the social experiment of Progress Village and its sister settlements, Khalil cleared his throat. "After careful consideration, my lord, I have a proposal: you should immediately abolish slavery."

"*What?*" Mogrash bellowed. "That's madness! Slavery is the backbone of our economy!"

"Ah, but my lord, if you'll look over these figures," he said, pulling out a slate and making rapid chalk marks, "you'll see that if you simply pay them low wages, institute a company store, and offer loans with, say, twenty percent interest compounded annually, you'll give your slaves freedom—something many of them clamor for—and save wear-and-tear from whipping, while still retaining them in the workforce and even making a profit from the usury."

Mogrash pondered. His family had gotten their start as slavers, but times changed, didn't they? He sent Khalil's proposal to the empirical accountants—the theoretical accountants would have rejected it out of hand—and was only slightly surprised when they found the projections sound. Mogrash abolished slavery, re-tasked the overseers as floor-, mine- and site-managers, and set up an account for Khalil to receive a fraction of a percentage of the interest from the company stores as a reward.

Before the boy was fifteen, he was richer than many of Mogrash's under-lords.

"You might've told me I couldn't have children." Mogrash was drunk, leaning against a wall in the sibyl's chamber, gulping from a jug of imported fermented woolbeast milk. "I married fifteen wives before my personal physician dared to suggest the trouble might be *mine*." He held his face in his hands and wept.

The sibyl sniffed from her shadows. "I foresaw that giving you *more* bad news would make you fill in the passage to my cavern with concrete."

"*This* will be the doom of the empire, not your prophecy. I have no successor!"

"Fool," the sibyl said, almost fondly. "As if you've never heard of adoption."

* * *

MEPH, KHALIL, AND ZANDER were all from poor families, and their parents were happy to let the Dark Lord adopt their sons, not that they would have said anything if they'd disapproved.

Mogrash told the boys they were moving to the imperial city. Khalil barely looked up from his figures, just nodding briefly; Zander asked excitedly if the gardens were as grand as everyone said; and Meph asked how old you had to be to start pit-fighting. Mogrash, to his surprise, enjoyed answering their questions and extolling the many virtues of the city that bore his name, and even Khalil seemed interested by the time the troop convoy drake landed on leathery wings to bear them away.

THE PROBABILITY WITCHES hit an impasse. Even after a year living in the palace, with the boys studying their passions with the greatest tutors and access to the greatest libraries in the world, they couldn't tell which one was the prophesied threat. Mogrash went to visit the sibyl, for the first time since embarrassing himself by crying in her presence. "Why can't they figure it out?" he demanded. "Which of my sons will betray me?"

"Hard to say," she said. "I see several paths—it's possible this is a dynamic destiny, that it could be *any* of them. Kill two of them and whichever one remains will be your undoing."

"Your continued comfort and your collection of trinkets depend on *my* largesse," he said, putting on his most threatening countenance, which had sent barbarian chieftains and effete overseas ambassadors alike into paroxysms of trouser-soaking terror. "You *will* give me guidance."

"Make sure none of them have any reason to do you ill," she said. "Just exactly what you've *been* doing. It won't neutralize the prophecy, but it may continue to push back the moment of betrayal until a point after you've died in some other less destiny-entangled way. It's the best I can do, my lord."

"Fine," he said, glowering. "I'll keep making their dreams come true."

THE BOYS GREW UP. Zander spent almost all his time among the floating gardens, and fell in love with a Wispwoman, which seemed somewhat inevitable in retrospect. Meph trained with the most dangerous members of the Slavering Corps, and by all accounts held his own admirably well; when he wasn't studying the martial arts he was in the basement with the anatomists, delving into the secrets of life and death; and when he wasn't doing *that*, he was breaking the hearts of beautiful young men in the duelists'. quarter. Khalil sat in with different magisters, surveyors, and advisors, learning the ins and outs of empire management, always near Mogrash's right hand. Khalil made many good, practical contributions to running the empire—there were Progress Villages all over by now, running different social experiments in parallel, with positive techniques exported empire-wide—though the Dark Lord preferred the company of Meph, and they often went hunting and whoring (albeit in different wings of the brothels) together.

When the boys attained their manhood and majority, the time came to give them formal posts. Mogrash went to the sibyl again, pacing in her chamber and pondering possibilities.

"Meph seems the most likely to attempt a coup. He hungers for conquest. I fear he may be the one who turns on me."

"You haven't conquered the *entire* world," the sibyl said. "Give him something to do."

Mogrash called Meph to his war chamber. "How would you like to sail across the sea and conquer the jewel-rich lands of Lloqupul? It's a long journey, and there may be no coming back soon, as the barrier leviathans only sink below the waves and open a passage every few years."

"They have strange martial arts there, don't they?" Meph said. "I've heard they can make a man's testicles recede permanently just by poking two fingers into a nerve cluster." He flexed his hands experimentally. "I wouldn't mind learning that."

"Conquer them and they'll teach you whatever you like. And I'll make you governor-general of any lands you take."

Meph embraced him. "I'll pack my bags."

"Take Trepanner," Mogrash said, tears threatening to rise for the second time in the decade. "I hear the skulls in Lloqupul are thick."

"AND WHAT OF ZANDER? I can see him turning on me, too. He disapproves of the ravages of empire—he's already pushed me to stop strip mining, replant forests, release the Wispfolk from their ancient bindings. . . . He won't attack me directly, but he might poison me, or send deadly venomous insects against me, or have his girlfriend attempt to possess me."

"There hasn't been a life-tree in the empire since your great-great-grandfather's day," the sibyl remarked.

Mogrash called Zander to his rooftop garden, and among the fragrant carnivorous plants, embraced him. "My son. In the central plains, before my ancestors charred out the tree-dwelling natives, there was a sacred tree, and the whole of the plains were lush. Perhaps some seedling yet remains among the ashes. Would you be the equal of finding such a thing, and tending it to health?"

"I think it must be the work I was meant for, Father," Zander said, eyes shining more than usual. Mogrash had no family heirloom to give him, but he gave Zander's Wispform lover full citizenship status as a going-away present.

"AND KHALIL. KHALIL, KHALIL. He is so full of *ideas*."

"Alas," the sibyl said. "I have no ideas about what to offer *him*."

Mogrash called Khalil to his throne room. "My son. Would you like to be a diplomat? Head of the secret intelligence services? Tell me your desire."

"I wish only to implement the vision of a better empire you introduced with Progress Village, Father." Khalil's voice was full of reverent respect. "Your great experiments are glorious things."

I only instituted the programs to keep you and your brothers from killing me, Mogrash thought, but he nodded. "Prime minister, then? We've never had one, but I think you'd fit the job. Is there anything I can offer you, as a gift for making an old man proud?"

"Only sufficient funding, Father," he said, and Mogrash had to smile.

* * *

AND SO MOGRASH ruled, though in practice Khalil did most of the ruling. After a few years of relative boredom, Mogrash gave Khalil his proxy and visited Meph in the ruins of the Lloqupulian capital, where they got drunk together and pissed on the floor of the Senate, singing bawdy songs. They harrowed the contested areas for a while, which Mogrash found more exhausting then he'd remembered, until the barrier leviathans opened another passage and Mogrash said his farewells and returned home. When he got back to the imperial city three years later, things were running more smoothly than ever. Khalil had granted all the Wispform people citizenship, banished the demonic engines below the Spiral Mountains and replaced them with coal-fired plants, and instituted other, even vaster reforms. "I apologize, Father," he said at their first meeting. "I knew my projections were sound, and that these changes would lead to greater prosperity, but I was afraid you wouldn't agree if I proposed them while you were here. . . Forgive me?"

Mogrash considered splitting Khalil's skull for the presumption, but he couldn't ignore the results; the empire was richer than ever. "I gave you my proxy," Mogrash said. "You are my son." Khalil's way was not the family way, but perhaps, unbelievably, it was better.

He visited the sibyl, who had not aged a day while he was gone. "It's the succession I fear," he said, having brooded over the subject during the long sea voyage. "Brother against brother, the empire thrown into chaos, all my work undone. Meph's warlike tendencies, Zander's gradually expanding zone of peace and green in the center of the empire, Khalil's philosophical underpinnings . . . they're bound to collide."

"So talk to them," the sibyl said. "Unlike every man of line Mogrash before them, your sons are good at talking." She paused. "Except Meph, but he'll manage."

WITH THE HELP OF his witches, he called up images of Meph and Zander from their distant locales, and sat with Khalil in the throne room. "I will not rule forever, and I do not wish to see my sons kill one another—"

"Oh, we've worked all that out," Zander said. "I don't want to run the empire. I'm happy with my trees. We've got two new seedlings this week."

"There's precious little killing to do back home," Meph said, raising his voice to be heard over the sounds of battle behind him. "I'm content here, where there are still frontiers. Let Khalil run things there."

"This is so . . . civilized," Mogrash said, unsure whether to be proud or disturbed.

"I will rule only with your blessing, Father," Khalil said.

"You have it, of course."

Khalil cleared his throat. "When do you think you might want to, ah, retire, Father?"

"Retire? No Lord Mogrash has ever retired! We've always ended in blood and glory! Or at least blood."

"Well," Khalil said. "I respect the precedent, but . . . do you *want* to end that way, Father? None of us wish you pain."

"I don't know what I want anymore," Mogrash said, and went away to think on it for a while.

* * *

"I WAS SURE I'd die in battle," the former Dark Lord said, sitting on the stone floor in the cold bleakness of the sibyl's chamber. "Or at least be assassinated, or possessed by a bodiless horror from the hell-world next door. Something more traditional. Instead, this—peaceful regime change? And no more slavery, no more strip mines, no more necromantic factories fueled by human suffering? I thought I was modern, but Khalil. . . . Great-grandfather must be twirling in his crypt."

"I have heard rather more noise than usual from up there," the sibyl said. "What will you do now, Sirid?"

He hadn't heard his given name in decades, and rather liked the sound of it. "Khalil says I'm welcome to stay here—he loves me, the beast—but I'd feel useless. All these years, I thought I'd outsmarted you, found a way around your prophecies, but you were right. That child *did* take my empire away from me, he did overthrow my ways and means, and he will indeed see me leave these halls behind forever."

"Where will you go?"

"I don't know. I thought of going to the provinces, raising an army of snake men and omniphages and trying to overthrow Khalil, just to keep myself occupied . . . but the empire is better under his leadership, and I think I'm too old to lead monstermen. And the worst of it is, I don't even mind being sidelined."

"I understand. I'm leaving, too," the sibyl said.

Mogrash blinked. "You've been down here since this place was just a crack in the earth!"

"Yes, but I can see the future, in glimpses, and in those glimpses, I am no longer consulted. Khalil doesn't need me. He has probability witches and the surveying corps and ten-year plans. My time is done. And you know, I have all these souvenirs from the world beyond, but I haven't *been* anywhere. I was thinking of going to one of the little islands in the Lambent Sea, where you can hear the chanting of the dead sailors under the waves and watch the witchlights in the water each evening. I think I might have come from there, originally."

"You don't remember?"

"I see the future, betimes, but the past is mostly lost to me."

Mogrash felt his hand creep across the floor, almost of its own volition, and touch the sibyl's long delicate fingers. "I've always liked the islands. A simple house, among the palms. It sounds . . . pleasant."

"It will be," the sibyl said, entwining her fingers with his.

This story originally appeared in *Strange Horizons*, 2009.

Tim Pratt is the author of over twenty novels, most recently *The Deep Woods* and *Heirs of Grace*, and many short stories. His work has appeared in *The Best American Short Stories, The Year's Best Fantasy, The Mammoth Book of Best New Horror*, and other nice places. He's a Hugo Award winner, and has been a finalist for World Fantasy, Sturgeon, Stoker, Mythopoetic, and Nebula Awards, among others. He lives in Berkeley, CA and works as a senior editor at *Locus*, a trade magazine devoted to science fiction and fantasy publishing. He tweets a lot as @timpratt, and his website is www.timpratt.org.

GIANTKILLER

G. SCOTT HUGGINS

It is presumed by the simple that we legends know no fear, that we are born into our roles, and take to them as easily as stud bulls, who leap to their duties knowing only boundless energy and excitement. Those who know only the Giantkiller's record may be pardoned, of course. But before there was the Giantkiller, there was a man called Jack...

- From Chapter 1: "The Map's Greatest Legend." *A Man Called Jack: The Early Years.* with Cleave Custer. Singing Harp Press: Happy Valley, MDCXVIII.

"AND YOU BEST NOT get taken, boy! You hear me? You just best not!" The shrieks of Jack's mother followed him up the road with the rising sun. Briefly, Jack's brow creased in puzzlement; he gazed at the rope in his hand. To his utter lack of surprise, it looped around the neck of their cow, Milky-White. Milky-White stared back at him with an arch look of contempt. Yes, he was taking the cow to market. The cow was behind him; he was not behind the cow. Therefore, Jack was doing the taking. Dismissing his mother, Jack continued toward the market. Milky-White had stopped living up to the first half of her name earlier in the week. It was all very simple: a lovely day's walk in the sun. Sell the cow. A lovely day's walk back. It was all very simple until, just a mile from their door, they ran into Jack and his cow.

Meeting a double of myself on the road was the first inkling I had that things had gone wrong. Following the lessons my instructors had drilled into me, I stepped forward, using every ounce of the cold-steel nerves the gods had granted me to stand there with a dumbfounded expression on my face and greet my doubles as if I hadn't noticed a thing.

- From Chapter 2: "The Naïve K.N.A.V.E." *A Man Called Jack*

"HOWDY, STRANGERS," Jack called out. He stuck his hand in his pouch. There was some cheese with hardly any mold on it, and it cost nothing to be generous. Or was that, 'it costs nothing to be friendly?' Jack often got the two confused. The strangers looked awfully familiar, but Jack couldn't place them. The cow especially looked as if he should know it. Suddenly, he realized what it was.

"Hey," he said to the man. "We're wearing the same clothes!"

The stranger stared, and then said, pityingly, "Most people do, Jack. Roughspun is pretty much roughspun, no matter how you tailor it." He looked behind Jack at Milky-White. "All right, Bulganova, we've found you. Are you going to come quietly?"

Jack looked at the man. He'd heard of people talking to cows, or even walls when they were drunk, but those people tended to fall down more. "Who are you talking to? Say, did you notice we're the same height, too?"

"Just your cow, Jack." The stranger smiled reassuringly. "Bulganova there is an excellent cow, and I'd really like her to have this fine cowbell." He pulled one from his pouch. Attached to a silver mesh collar, it *was* a fine cowbell, and the stranger advanced. Milky-White backed away from him. Tugging Jack. Jack set his heels in the dirt, but Milky-White tugged harder, pulling him off the road.

Milky-White is pulling me, now. She's taking me off the road. I'm getting taken by a cow, Jack thought. In desperate terror of abject poverty and drastically upset mother, Jack heaved with all his strength on the rope. Abruptly, Milky-White reversed, cannoned forward past Jack, and lunged at the stranger with her horns. He howled in pain.

Jack reacted with the speed of a farmer. "Bad cow!" he cried, hitting Milky-White in the shoulder with his full weight. She staggered away. Jack picked up the silver bell in one hand, still holding the rope. "He only wanted to give you a present." Jack smoothly fastened the bell around Milky-White's neck. She bellowed, jerking to her feet, horns leveled, and then suddenly stood looking blankly behind him, completely motionless.

Jack tried to help the stranger, and found his path blocked by the other cow. Who, he now realized, looked exactly the same as Milky-White. But this cow glared at him in a fury. "Haven't you done enough?" she said.

Before Jack could react, another voice said, "I think you've all done rather enough."

Emerging from the hedge was a dwarf. A dwarf with a wicked-looking hand crossbow, pointed straight at Jack. Jack had never had a weapon pointed at him before. Jack had never seen a weapon before.

"Don't move, boy," said the dwarf. He looked down at the stranger. "So, the great James Nulsieben. At last, defenseless. And Bulganova, too. One of our greatest agents. I congratulate your double; I've never seen Bulganova enspelled before, though many tried. You almost got her. I always hoped I'd kill you." His grin widened. "But I never dreamed I'd get to do it twice."

The stranger—James—breathed in labored gasps, blood staining the road. "The boy knows nothing," he got out. "Do you, boy? I knew you were our enemy, Rumpel. But I never thought you'd betray your own kind by siding with giants."

"Really?" said the dwarf. "And why do you think they call me the Stilts' kin? The Giants will make me taller than any of you dream. But enough of this." He pointed the bow at Jack's heart. "Will you die honorably, or will you further insult my intelligence by pleading that you know nothing and only wish to wake up from this nightmare?"

"Oh, no," said Jack. "Pleading isn't much use in nightmares, and that must be what this is, because I can't see how there could be two Milky-Whites, and even if there could, I don't reckon there's ever been a hedge by this crossroad in real life."

The dwarf turned in surprise. Then vines looped from the hedge, gripping the bow, his hand, and his neck. There was a brief contraction of foliage, and the dwarf dropped limply. The hedge contracted, collapsed in on itself and became a dark green figure with long, flowing hair.

Jack stepped forward on quaking feet and addressed the dryad. "Thank you, Miss."

"What do you mean, miss?" the figure said in a brassy tenor. He knelt by James. "Sorry, Jim. Didn't see it coming." He gave the cows a glance. "Well, well. Bulganova. So nice to see you. When were you going to lose the spare, here?" his chin gave a jerk toward Jack.

Milky-White simply mooed.

"Don't play dumb with me!" He picked up the lead and looped a tendril of vine over the cow's neck. "I know that little enchanted bell won't let you move much, but you can talk just fine."

"What are we going to do?" asked the other cow.

"Don't worry, she's not for hamburger. We'll find out everything she knows. We don't often get a chance to interrogate a deep-cover cow."

"Not her," said the other cow, "the mission!"

"What mission?"

"That's on a Things Man Was Not Meant To Know basis!" the cow snapped.

"James is a man. I'm not," he replied.

"You can't replace him," she sneered. "Our contact is expecting something that looks vaguely human, not a half-a-dryad."

"That's 'hamadryad,'" said the green man, his voice going cold. "And look who's talking about human."

James coughed and both their eyes fell on him. "I believe that the watchword of the agency," he labored, his own eyes falling on Jack, "has always been 'improvisation?'"

No one would have believed in the last years of the XVIIth century that this world was being watched keenly and closely by intelligences tinier than man and yet with bodies twice the size of a bull elephant; curiously as a drooling toddler might scrutinize maggots squirming on a heap of garbage and wonder if they would be fun to eat. Or, failing that, to step on.

- From Chapter 3: "The Lore of the Worlds." *A Man Called Jack*

"BUT WHY," SAID JACK, as the hamadryad and Milky-White, with James tied securely atop her, vanished into the distance, "did we have to trade you Milky-White for real Milky-White?"

"Bulganova," corrected the cow. "We traded me for Bulganova, because she's working for the Giants. Plus, she's quite a deadly fighter. Hey, keep your hand out of that pouch."

Jack had traded pouches with James as well as cows. It was no improvement. James had not packed any cheese. The cow went on. "We saved your life back there, in case you hadn't noticed. So stay out of the pouch until I tell you."

Jack said nothing, partly because the cow was right, but partly because he was trying to think whether pointing out that he had captured Bulganova would be a good idea.

"All right, other Milky-White."

"And stop that," the cow snorted. "I have a name. It's Philomila." At the sight of Jack screwing up his mouth to perform hitherto unimagined feats of polysyllabic speech, she said, "Phil will do."

"All right, Phil." After a pause, Jack said, "How much do you suppose the butcher will pay for a cow like you, Phil?"

Phil just stared. "You know," she finally said, "just about any other man, discovering himself to be in the company of a talking cow would say something like, 'How does a cow learn to talk?' or 'I wonder what the circus would pay for a talking cow?' Yet you're thinking of the butcher. Why do you suppose that is?"

"Because my Mum said to sell the cow to the butcher." Faintly, Jack also thought, *and Mum also said not to get taken, and there's Phil ahead of me.*

"We're not selling me to the butcher," said Phil.

"Then how much will the circus..."

"Or the circus."

"How much then?" asked Jack.

"Four beans. Haggle. Try to make it five. We don't want him to be suspicious."

"I should take five beans from the man we sell you to," repeated Jack. "And then he will not be suspicious?"

"Not if Bulganova's intercepted reports are any indication," sighed Phil. "Five, four, three, two..."

"What giants?" said Jack. "And why were you counting backwards?"

"Never mind, Jack," said Phil. "Have you ever noticed how, on most days, there are great white clouds in the sky that look like castles on the top of mountains, floating above the valley?"

"Yes!" said Jack, "They look like towers, and hills, and houses..."

"And have you ever wondered why that is?"

Jack wrinkled his head in thought. It seemed an easy question. "That's where the giants live?"

Phil stopped dead in the street. "Yes, Jack. It is." She cocked her head, a difficult thing for a cow. "Our local half-a-dryad, pain though he is, did help us stop Bulganova from contacting her agent."

"Why do you call him a half-a-dryad?" asked Jack.

"Because he is," said Phil. "Mom was a dryad; Dad was a man who didn't mind splinters. Cross a tree and a man, and you get a hedge. He's a bit sensitive."

"Oh," said Jack. "Are you sensitive about being a cow?"

"No," said Phil. "It's not that much different from life as a princess. Men still drool at the sight of you. On the plus side, it's in the fresh air, and if they do catch you, it's a quicker and less painful way to go."

"Oh, good," said Jack.

"Irony is just the taste of nails in your mouth to you, isn't it, Jack?" asked Phil. "Anyway, we don't know why Bulganova was meeting her contact, but he's sure to figure out that I'm not her once we're alone. That'll be the dangerous part. Hopefully, you'll be away with the beans by then; you won't get hurt."

Until I bring Mum home five beans in trade for the cow, Jack thought.

"Oh, hell," said Phil. They were rounding the corner and the village lay before them. "I'm not sure it matters anyway. The giants may invade no matter what we do. Sure as hell we'd invade them if we thought we had a chance."

"Why?"

"Jack," Phil sighed. "You know those mountains in the sky we were discussing?"

"Yes?"

"When the sun sets, what color do they turn?"

"Gold," said Jack. "Oh."

"Just as well we can't get up there. It would be easier for the giants to get down than for us to get up."

"But you can get there, can't you?" Jack said. "Mum told me how a cow jumped over the moon!"

Phil gave him a withering look. "No, Jack."

"No?"

"That was a prototype model, and she burned up on re-entry anyway."

"Where were you princess of, then?" asked Jack.

Phil looked up at him. "You know, Jack, just when I think you're going to forget how to breathe and topple over in the road, you say something that makes me suspect there's a brain in there." She sighed. "It was an enchantment a long time ago and it makes an even longer story. Besides, the witch is dead. And we don't have the time. We have a mission, which means trading me for these beans: that's the only thing we know about this man Bulganova was meeting. He has beans. Unless...?" she looked up at Jack.

"Unless what?" he asked.

"Jack," Phil said in a low tone. "You're standing in the lane with an princess who's been bewitched into the form of a cow. She likes strong young guys with a lot of learning potential, and doesn't particularly want to finish a mission that could result in her being turned into prime rib." Phil paused. "Princess. Enchantment. Transformation. Happily Ever After." She stuck her muzzle up into his face and whispered, "Does that suggest a course of action to you?"

Jack leaned down, his lips moving towards hers.

"Like what?" he whispered back.

I knew that kissing her would have broken the enchantment right then, of course. Had I known Phil then as I know her now—the half-elf assassin acrobat with nerves of mithril and skin of alabaster, whose sheer sexual magnetism reveals her in a city simply from the way the statues of the local fertility gods are pointing—I might have done it. But only as a cow could she impersonate Bulganova and fool the Bean Man.

- From Chapter 5: "Cow of the Wild." *A Man Called Jack*

"IF YOU DON'T MIND," said Jack, "I'd like to have a few words with my cow."

"Sssure, kid," said the man. His face was completely obscured by the hood of his cloak, his voice born of the darkness within. The large beans he'd handed Jack gave off a heady green smell; he kept feeling they ought to move when he touched them. Jack led Phil a slight distance away and knelt down.

"Good work, Jack. Now slip one of those beans inside my collar. We'll get the Technical Section to work on it after I've escaped."

Jack did. "Will you be all right?"

"Oh," Phil tossed off lightly, "sure, Jack. I've been in lots of worse places than this. Well, at least once."

"What do I do with the rest of the beans?"

Phil shrugged, insofar as that was possible for a cow. "Just hide them where no one will find them," she said. "Whatever they are, they're dangerous."

"Are you sure you'll be all right?" Jack asked. "I don't like the Bean Man. Are you sure he isn't one of those Things That Man Was Not Meant To Know?"

Phil glanced at him. "I doubt it," she finally said. "Probably just an engineer selling company secrets. They don't get out much. Now, Jack, you're well clear of this. Go home and Forget That Any Of This Ever Happened." Those last words took on a special resonance, as if they'd been spoken in a large, invisible cave enclosing just the two of them. Jack nodded, handed Phil's lead over to the Bean Man, and then went home. He felt uneasy at leaving Phil with the Bean Man. But even if he was a Thing Man Was Not Meant To Know, Phil wasn't a man, and there probably weren't many Things Cow Was Not Meant To Know, so Phil was unlikely to come to harm.

The walk home was a blur, as if the morning had been a dream. There was something very important he had to remember, and he did eventually remember it. This was because being beaten systematically by an enraged farmwife who has just discovered that you have traded her only cow for four really odd-looking beans focused even Jack's attention.

He did remember that he was supposed to hide the beans where no one would ever find them. So, reasoning that only an idiot would plant crops slap up against the side of the house, he buried them there. Sore and aching, his mind even blurrier than usual, Jack went to sleep.

I can truly say that the planting of the Beanstalk is the foundation on which my entire character as an operative rests. Those who accuse me of rashness or (poor fools) being under the influence of some enchantment, have simply failed to think the matter through. An agent like Bulganova would never put her masters' invasion route in proximity to her lair. She must have reckoned with the chance, however small, that some sharp K.N.A.V.E. would recognize her; she could be compromised, the Beanstalk could not. Therefore, this was the one spot in which no Giant would ever expect the Beanstalk to be raised. As Bulganova's absence might at any time be noticed, I could not contact my superiors; only my bold action would save the day. And though I would be called many things during the course of my career, I would never be called a coward.

- From Chapter 7: "Jack of All Raids." *A Man Called Jack*

"JACK, WHAT IN the name of St. Ignatz' blessed balls did you do?" The cow's head leaned in through the window as far as it would go.

Jack awoke and knew he was dreaming, because he'd sold Milky-White the day before, or at least he must have, because he'd been going to. Things after that were a bit fuzzy. But at any rate, cows didn't talk.

"Hello, Milky-White. Are you in cow heaven yet?"

"Cow heaven?" cried Milky-White. "Cow heaven? I'm in Special Agent Ninth Circle of Bloody Hell! The one with the Parliamentary Inquiry of Eternity and The Expense Auditor With A Thousand Briefcases! What have you done, Jack?"

Jack looked around. Yes, he was still in bed, and it was still dark. "Sleeping, Milky-White."

"Don't start that again! I'm Phil, remember?"

"No, Phil," said Jack.

"What did you do before you went to sleep?"

Jack remembered that, a feat he thought he could be quite proud of, considering that he was being awakened by an angry talking cow in the middle of the night. "I hid the beans, Phil."

Jack couldn't see very well, but it occurred to him that sunlight had never streamed through holes in the roof while it was pitch dark out before.

"You hid the..?" Phil broke off in a splutter. "Oh, gods. You didn't. You did. This is all your fault. It's all *my* fault! And you don't even remember because of my spell. You planted the beans right in their top agent's safe house! I should have told you to *swallow* the bloody things! You'd be dead, but I'd feel better!"

Slowly, Jack arose and walked to where Phil's head poked through the window. The rest of the window was opaque blackness. He had heard of 'darkness so thick you could cut it,' but he never had pictured the darkness as being green. Nor with little veins running up the side.

"Jack," said Phil, in tones of dead calm. "Come outside." She withdrew her head, and sunlight burst through the space she had been. The green surface curved away outside.

The snores from the other room of the house told him his mother was still asleep as he went out, which Jack considered all for the best.

The Beanstalk obscured a great portion of Jack's personal sky before it disappeared into the clouds. Half the house's roof was missing, pushed aside by the lowest leaves. Jack stared in, mouth hanging open.

"There's a bean sitting in the dungeons of the Emperor," said Phil in a dead voice. "It's being studied by archmages, alchemists, and the wisest of the wise. It could have been planted in secret, where the giants would never have known. Better still, we could have learned how to kill it, just in case they ever planted one."

With visible effort, she pulled herself together. "All right, Jack. Our only chance is surprise. You have to climb up there and see whether the Giants have assembled an invasion force."

"How will I know it's an invasion force?"

Phil frothed at the mouth. "Because they'll be forty feet tall and have swords the size of castle gatehouse towers! An invasion force of Giants is not a clan-bloody-destine operation!" Phil visibly calmed herself. "If they have, then just get back down here; you can't do anything. I'll run back to town and see if I can raise the local garrison. We may be able to delay them." She sighed.

"But if they haven't, Jack, it's time for you to be a hero. Well, to try, at least. What makes the Giants really dangerous is that they..."

"Are forty feet tall and have swords the size of gatehouse towers?"

"Yes, *besides* that. They have the Golden Harp."

"The Golden Harp?" Jack asked fearfully.

"The Golden Harp unifies the Giants. Alone, they're dangerous brutes. Marching to the Harp, they're actually an effective army. We don't know why."

Jack struggled to think. "But why do the Giants want to invade us? Don't they have all the gold?"

"Food," Phil said, chillingly.

"But couldn't we just trade them, say, beef for gold?"

"Not if I have anything to say about it," said Phil. "Now climb up there."

"Climb? To the land of the Giants?" Jack was not completely familiar with the territory of fear, as the entrance requirements generally included more imagination than he possessed, but this disturbed him. "I don't think that's a good idea. The roof will need fixing; Mum's dead set on roofs for houses..."

Phil's horn struck so fast Jack wasn't really aware of pain. He simply found that he'd levitated ten feet in the air and was grasping a vine frantically with one hand and rubbing himself somewhat lower with the other.

Further down, he saw Phil, horns pointed skyward and looking determined as only a cow can look. He considered what loomed above. He considered what waited below. He heard stirring from the house.

One thing to be said for the Land of Giants, Jack considered as he climbed. Mum wasn't in it.

The Giants were asleep, just as I had predicted they would be; beings that massive could never shed enough heat to function in daylight. It did not take long to spot their headquarters. The problem of navigating the land of the Giants lies not in the intellect, but in the sheer size. Pressing on toward the castle, any room of which could have housed a wing of the Imperial Palace, I stole through the day.

- From Chapter 9: "Robbing the Giants' Kingdom: A Knight in their Fief." *A Man Called Jack*

TO JACK'S SURPRISE, the only giants he saw outside the palace, the two doorwards, were asleep. Their spears, each fashioned from a redwood tree, leaned against the wall, their snoring muffling any sounds Jack might have made.

Jack had been relieved not to find a Giantish invasion force ready to cook *him* in lieu of all the cows roaming the plains below. So relieved that he had almost slid down the vine to tell Phil. But the twinge in his left buttock told him this might be unwise. He now found himself wandering through the courtyard of the castle, asking himself, "If I were a Giant, where would I keep a Golden Harp?"

Trembling with fear, he set his feet down as if they were made of glass, or cymbals, or both. It was almost a letdown when Jack, entering the smaller courtyard of the central keep and ready to be seized and eaten at any time by armed giants, found himself confronted by a large woman in a plaid dress.

"Are you lost, little boy?" said the woman.

Jack stared. She was hardly a Giant at all, no more than twice his size. Jack's rustic manners took over in the absence of conscious direction. "No, Ma'am," he said, though his fright made it come out more like, "Nuh, Mum."

"Well, I'm hardly your Mum, little boy. But she must be worried. Why are you wandering about the palace at this hour of the day? Don't you know that the King has set a curfew? Are you lost?"

"Yes, Mu...Ma'a... milady."

"Oh, don't start that," said the woman. "It's bad enough going around all night hearing 'Your Majesty' this and 'Your Grace' that, as if we were those ant-folk down below with their kings and such. 'Mathilda' will do, and I'll just call you 'lad,' as is proper for young Giants whose parents haven't thought up a name for them yet, which yours can't have done, young as you are. Come along, and we'll have a midday snack together."

Jack followed Mathilda, who looked enough like his mother that he found it hard not to flinch respectfully in her presence, through the castle's deserted corridors until they came to a great room. The ceiling was sixty feet high, hung with an iron chandelier that could have enclosed an arena. A pair of small bonfires roared in the lamps, and the table was a long trestle, made from sequoia halves sanded flat. The benches along it were as high as Jack could reach. Mathilda reached down and lifted Jack up to one of them. "Now run along to my seat on the end there, and I'll bring you some nice bread and cheese."

It wasn't hard to find Mathilda's chair. It was set next to the biggest chair in the room, a great iron monstrosity that looked as though it had been made out of a thousand sword blades. Blunted, of course, because not even giants are that stupid. Mathilda's bronze chair was different. It was piled with cushions, and had steps leading up to it. Jack ascended the chair, and found it no great feat to stand on the table.

In the center of the table was a great bowl of fruit, with grapes the size of watermelons and an apple Jack might have used as a closet. Flanking the bowl, apparently asleep, sat two golden shapes.

The first was a great golden hen, with rose gold crest and yellow-gold feathers. She was about half the size of Phil.

The other shape could only be the Golden Harp.

Golden it was, a floor harp of the kind played at Imperial banquets. Jack would barely be able to lift it. To a Giant, it was a simple handharp. Or would have been had the Harp not already possessed hands. And feet. And the body between them.

The woman was not chained to the harp. She flowed into it, her golden skin blending into the gold of the harp until it was impossible to tell the two apart. Only her hair was not golden; a mass of ebony that curled around her body. She, too, was asleep.

Jack was not familiar with the term "exotic beauty," having been born and raised in country where heavy farm work meant that beards were the most reliable way of telling genders apart. But he was dimly aware that here was magic of a sort that sang in the blood. He felt a pounding in his chest.

It took him a moment to realize he also felt the pounding in the soles of his feet, in the planks of the table, and the very air around him. He just had time to sprint the length of the table and glimpse the harp and the hen come awake before he dived into the fruit bowl.

From his place under the grapes, Jack saw the Giant King. On his head was a crown of gold, crudely incised with Giant pictograms. His beard was long and black, and twice Jack's length.

"Queen," roared the Giant King. "What's that I smell? Are you having a man for a snack without me?"

"No, dear," answered Mathilda's voice. "It's just my perfume. Go back to sleep; it's still daylight."

"I must count my hen's golden eggs," declared the Giant King. The pounding footsteps came closer. Jack got a far more intimate experience with Giant morning breath than he ever wanted as the Giant King leaned over the hen and lifted her in one Jack-sized fist.

"Three, four, five, one!" He counted the golden eggs, each the size of Jack's head. Then he sniffed.

"I smell the blood of an Englishman!" he roared.

"No you don't, dear," said Mathilda, reappearing with a plate of rolls and sliced cheese. "We don't do men the English way anymore; all that batter gives you heartburn."

"There is only one egg from this lazy hen, my Queen," said the Giant King. He lifted a knife with a blade as long as Jack and fingered the edge, looking at the hen.

"That's four eggs, dear," said Mathilda. "I explained counting before. You always mix up the numbers."

The Giant King growled.

"Would you care to join me for cheese?" asked Mathilda. "If not, please go to bed. And don't shout; you'll wake up the troops and they'll be all cross for tomorrow's invasion."

The King scowled and stomped off to bed.

"You can come out now, lad," said Mathilda.

Jack climbed out of the bowl, and walked across the table to Mathilda's plate, where he picked up a cube of cheese half the size of his head.

"The invasion makes him grumpy. I figure that cow really sold him a bill of goods when she promised a beanstalk that would let him climb down to the Land of Men below and have all the cows he wanted if he'd only let her go." She shook her head. "Between that and the Golden Harp there, it's been a madhouse. Once that thing started playing, all of a sudden caves in the hillsides weren't good enough. No, we had to have palaces and armies and a foreign policy."

G. SCOTT HUGGINS

"What is a foreign policy?" asked Jack.

"If it's smaller than you and moves, squash it," said Mathilda promptly. "That's good enough for giants. All this human cleverness has caused such trouble. As if we need to compete with vermin. If we move down there, they'll infest everything in no time."

"What does the King need golden eggs for if the mountains here are made of it?"

"Gold?" laughed Mathilda. "You've been hearing a bit of Miss Harp's propaganda, there. Ask your parents when they last saw gold. Not bad enough giving my husband delusions of royalty," Mathilda sighed, flicking a lump of cheese at the quiescent harp, "she has to corrupt the young, too." Mathilda rose. "You wait here, lad, and I'll make us some tea to wash this down."

Mathilda left.

Behind him, Jack heard, "Hey. Hey, boy."

Jack turned, and found two pairs of eyes, one demi-human and one avian, regarding him expectantly.

"Time to go, boy," said the hen. "Take me and go. Now, while you've distracted her."

"Don't be ridiculous," said the Harp, her voice like honeyed thunder. "It is I who am your salvation. Carry me away from here, and you shall be King."

"I'd rather not, thanks," said Jack. "The King isn't very nice. But he likes you both. Why shouldn't you stay?"

"You thick or something?" said the hen. "That monster loves my eggs. And he can't even count them. He thinks I'm drying up! Any day now he'll decide he can get them all by doing a bit of amateur surgery!"

"And the King loves only the power I grant him," said the harp darkly. "You would not be like him, I am sure." She smiled, and Jack felt himself go weak.

"Phil said I was to take the Harp," he said, uncertainly.

"Harpy," said the hen. "He said Harpy, I'm sure. That's me!"

The Harp turned on the hen, discord in her voice. "You liar! You are not a harpy. A harpy is half-bird, half-woman!"

"Yep," cackled the hen. "So I am!"

"Which part is the woman, then?" asked Jack.

The hen slapped him across the face. "La. How dare you be fresh, sir."

"Boy," said the Harp, turning her voice sweet again. "Take me with you and I can command all men to your desire."

"But obviously not women," said the hen. "You never got Mathilda under your spell, did you?"

"Shut up!" snapped the Harp. "And what are you doing?"

"Part woman!" crowed the hen. "See?" There were two bulges just below her neckline.

"You've got two of those grapes stuffed under your feathers, you colossal pervert!" screamed the Harp.

Jack became uncomfortably aware of how loud the Harp's voice was.

"What's all the ruckus in there?" Mathilda's voice came from the kitchen.

"Look, boy," said the hen. "It's no secret to us you're here from the Land of Men. You can carry one of us. Now which is going to be better received by your people down there? Gold?

Or a beautiful woman who can't charm other women worth a damn?"

Jack and the hen were accelerating through the main courtyard before the Harp even managed to get the soldiers stirring.

I confess that the run to the Beanstalk is now a blur in the haze of memory. Goldenharp, the first double agent I would ever turn, and the only one I would ever love, had stayed behind to undermine the Giants from within. But in drawing the wrath of the Giant King upon myself, I had run no small risk. However, overheated by the chase in the strong sun of the afternoon, his judgment fatally compromised by rage, he plunged headlong onto the Beanstalk, where Phil's company of sappers waited with their Greataxe directional mines affixed to its stalk. The threat was ended; the Giant King no more than fertilizer strewn over that corner of the Empire.

Tragically, James would never recover from the venom Bulganova had dosed him with. It was a sad end to a great man's career, and it was my honor to have worked with him on his last mission. Until now, my oath of secrecy to the Empire has kept me from telling the true story of the Beanstalk, and the official record would always show that I did not truly become a K.N.A.V.E. agent for another three years.

Of course, the Land of the Giants would hold many more adventures, the rescue of Goldenharp not least among them, but that is a story for another time. And by then, the story of another man. The man codenamed: Giantkiller.

- From Epilogue: "The Giant's Leap." *A Man Called Jack*

This story originally appeared in the *Heroes in Training* anthology, DAW, 2007.

G. Scott Huggins grew up in the American Midwest and has lived there all his life, except for interludes in the European Midwest (Germany) and East (Russia). He is currently responsible for securing America's future by teaching its past to high school students, many of whom learn things before going to college. His preferred method of teaching and examination is strategic warfare. He loves to read high fantasy, space opera, and parodies of the same. He has a theology column in the magazine *Sci Phi Journal*. He wants to be a hybrid of G. K. Chesterton and Terry Pratchett when he counteracts the effects of having grown up. When he is not teaching or writing, he devotes himself to his wife, their three children, and his cat. He loves good bourbon, bacon, and pie, and will gladly put his writing talents to use reviewing samples of any recipe featuring one or more of them. You can read his ramblings and rants (with bibliography) at scotthuggins.wordpress.com.

A MILD CASE OF DEATH

DAVID GERROLD

DEATH—AFTER THE FACT—feels just like a bell, like a great giant gong struck with a silver hammer. Bdooonnnggg!!

While I stood there wondering just what the hell had happened, a voice materialized beside me.

IT'S TIME TO GO, DAVE.

"Dave's not here, man—" I said it without thinking.

PLEASE DON'T MAKE TROUBLE, DAVE.

I turned to look at the intruder. "Who are you and what the hell—" The rest of the sentence died in my throat. Or what would have been my throat, if I had still had a throat. But yes, it died.

To tell the truth, I felt disappointed. I had expected, hoped that Death would appear as a tall sepulchral figure in a black hood and cloak, carrying a transparent scythe of mysterious power. If I squinted just right, I could sort of imagine Death as that kind of figure, but mostly he manifested as a polite blurry darkness.

IT'S TIME TO GO, DAVE.

"I already told you, Dave's not here."

The figure hesitated, appeared to check its PDA, or maybe a clipboard. I said it was blurry.

THE SCHEDULE SAYS DAVE. 11:37, SUNDAY EVENING.

"And I told you twice already, Dave's not here."

YOU'RE DAVE.

"No, I'm not."

YOU'RE HERE. IT IS 11:37, SUNDAY EVENING. 11:38 NOW.

"But I'm not Dave. Dave doesn't even live here. He was supposed to stop by earlier, but he never showed. He didn't call either. I don't know what happened to him. Tell you what, if he calls I'll tell him you're looking for him—"

THE SCHEDULE SAYS DAVE. 11:37, PACIFIC STANDARD TIME. AND HERE I AM AND HERE YOU ARE, SO YOU MUST BE DAVE.

"I'm not Dave."

ARE YOU SURE?

"I'm sure."

The figure hesitated. It's hard for a blur to look confused, but it did.

"What's the problem?"

YOU'RE TRYING TO FOOL ME, AREN'T YOU?

"No, I'm not. I'm not Dave. You made a mistake."

NO, I DIDN'T. YOU'RE DAVE.

"Listen, it's all right. Everybody makes mistakes—"

Death checked its clipboard again. I HAVE A SCHEDULE TO KEEP. I HAVE OTHER APPOINTMENTS. WHY DON'T YOU JUST PRETEND YOU'RE DAVE AND COME ALONG LIKE A NICE CHAP. THAT WILL SAVE US BOTH A LOT OF TROUBLE.

"No, I don't think so. That doesn't sound like a good idea to me."

BUT I'VE ALREADY COLLECTED YOU.

"You did *what?*"

LOOK DOWN.

"Eh? Is that me?"

NO. THAT'S YOUR BODY. YOU'RE RIGHT HERE. NOW IF YOU'LL JUST TELL THEM THAT YOU'RE DAVE, EVERYTHING WILL BE ALL RIGHT FOR BOTH OF US.

"No, wait a minute—!! I know how Dave lived. He was a liar, a thief, a cheat, a fraud. He was a television producer, for god's sake. If I tell them I'm Dave, they'll send me to the bad place—"

IT'S NOT THAT BAD. IN FACT, IT CAN BE QUITE PLEASANT. EXCEPT FOR THE COMPANY, OF COURSE.

"You've been there?"

NO. BUT I'VE READ THE BROCHURES.

"It's full of lawyers, isn't it?"

NOT AS MANY AS MOST PEOPLE THINK. THEY DON'T LET LAWYERS IN, BECAUSE THEY BRING DOWN THE PROPERTY VALUES. BUT THERE ARE A

LOT OF TELEMARKETERS, EVANGELISTS, USED CAR SALESMEN, AND BARRY MANILOW FANS.

"Barry Manilow?"

Death sighed. IT'S A LONG STORY.

"Like we don't have all eternity...? Look, can I ask you something?"

YES?

"Do you have to talk like that?"

LIKE HOW?

"Like that."

OH, THAT.

"Yes."

"Well, not really. But it's sort of expected, so—well, you know."

"That's better. Listen—you seem like a nice fellow, a hard worker, just trying to do the best job you can. I'm sure you call your mom regularly, floss your teeth every day, you don't jaywalk, right?"

"Well—"

"But you get my point. So, why don't you just put me back and let me get on with the rest of my life and I tell you what— if you'll give me your pager number, as soon as I can track down Dave, I'll beep you, okay?"

"I can't do that—"

"Sure you can—"

"No, I can't. I don't know how."

"You don't know how?"

"We don't do reinsertions. Once you're decanted, well— that's pretty much it."

"Decanted? Like you can't get toothpaste back in the tube, eh?"

"Actually, you can get toothpaste back in the tube. Would you like me to show you how it's done?"

"Toothpaste you can do. People, you can't."

"Yes, that's right."

I felt like I should sit down and sink my head into my hands and feel something. Anger? Outrage? Grief? Except I couldn't feel anything. Dead people don't have feelings. Great. Just great.

"Y'know, this is really crappy. All that exercise, all that healthy living, all those goddamn pills and herbs, look at me, I'm so goddamn healthy, vitamins take me. Look at what I missed. All those cheeseburgers and fries and Cokes, all the beer and pizza I never put away. All the booze and dope and fatty foods. This is not fair." I turned to the blur, realizing I towered over it, well maybe not *towered*, but I had at least a good two inches, maybe three. "Do you have a supervisor?"

"Yes, but it won't do you any good."

"Why not?"

"He's on vacation."

"I'll wait. Right here."

"That's probably not a good idea."

"Why not?"

"Because, well—do you really think you'll want to be reinserted after two weeks?"

"This is a done deal, isn't it?"

"Pretty much."

"Somebody owes me, big time."

"You're very convincing, you know."

"Thank you."

"You even had me going there for a minute. Now, come along, Dave."

"I'm not Dave."

"Have it your way." The blur gathered itself together. IT'S TIME TO GO NOW. Then it added politely, DAVE.

"I'm not Dave."

DON'T BE DIFFICULT. YOU'RE DAVE NOW.

"I will too be difficult. I'll be any damn thing I want. I'm going to tell them I'm not Dave."

IT WON'T DO ANY GOOD.

"Why not?"

HUMANS SAY ANYTHING TO AVOID THE CONSEQUENCES OF THEIR ACTIONS. THEY WON'T BELIEVE YOU. IF I SAY THAT YOU'RE DAVE, YOU'RE DAVE.

"This isn't fair—!"

DEATH HAS NEVER BEEN FAIR.

"But I'm not Dave!"

THIS WAY, PLEASE. MIND THE STEP—

It was a long step. Down.

Down?

"Excuse me?"

WHAT?

"Down?"

YES, DOWN.

"This is really not right. I mean it. You got the wrong guy and now you're taking me to the wrong place."

THEY ALL SAY THAT.

"Would you please stop talking like *that*?"

IT'S PART OF THE JOB.

"Well, it's freaking me out, and I'm already freaked out enough."

EXIT THROUGH THE GIFT SHOP, PLEASE.

"The what—?"

Souvenirs

"HELLO, WELCOME to the gift shop!"

The young man was as bright and smiley as a high school cheerleader, and every bit as cute—bubble-butt and all. He wore a crisp red and white uniform. The insignia was shaped like a Star Trek badge. His name badge identified him as Michael.

Great, just great.

"Where am I? Is this—?"

"This is the gift shop, of course. There's always a gift shop at the end of the ride, so you can pick out souvenirs."

"Souvenirs—?"

"Of course!" he sparkled. "You don't want to leave life empty-handed. Take your time, look around. You'll find all kinds of wonderful mementos—"

"Mementos…?"

Michael gestured proudly, pointing with his whole hand. His posture, his smile, everything—he'd obviously been trained by Disney. "Over here, to your right, we have action figures. And over here, to your left—" Another open-palm gesture. A wall of screens.

"Here we have a display of photos taken at all the most surprising moments in your life—here's where you pooped your pants in first grade, *that* was embarrassing, you look like you're going to cry, what a cutie you were. Oh, I like this— here's one of you learning how to masturbate, looks like you were having a lot of fun there, humping your pillow while watching the Mouseketeers. And here's that auto accident where you were almost killed, that was a close one, look at how scared you were, that's such a great expression! Oh, here's my favorite—your first time having sex with another person—oh my, he was handsome, wasn't he? Look at how amazed you were when he took off his underwear. Let me suggest that you order the whole collection, it comes in a beautiful red leather folder with your name engraved in gold, plus your birth and death dates, no extra charge. Oh—and look, here's your death already—ooh, that's a much better expression than most people make. That's quite nice. You should have that one framed—"

"I, um—okay, this wasn't what I was expecting."

"Yes, I understand. You were on the ride a long time, longer than most—we're seeing that more and more these days, a lot of guests are staying on the ride for decades, sometimes as long as a century. Getting off so suddenly can be a little disorienting." He brightened. "Maybe you'd like to see the action figures—?"

He led me across the aisle, where the racks were filled with stacks and stacks of boxes, each with a different figure, each one appropriately dressed—each of them attached to a colorful cardboard backing, all of them posed and mounted behind form-fitted, stiff transparent plastic. "On this rack, most of these just have you typing, there's a lot of those—but over here, there's even more of you just sitting and staring out the window, I guess you were thinking, right?"

"So those are the *in*action figures....?"

Michael shook his head disapprovingly. "Oh no. We would never insult the guest. Those might have been your most interesting moments—that's when you did your best imagining—"

I was already moving to the next counter. "Hey? What are these—?" I held up a couple boxes. "I was never in the Navy. Not the Army either. And what the hell is this? I was never a drag queen. I never did drag in my entire life—I would have looked like my mother."

Michael hurried over to explain, "Oh, those are your alternate lives—who you could have been, what you could have done. I'm afraid you were a disappointingly good person— okay, there's a little shoplifting when you were a kid, some tax evasion as an adult, but those hardly count. Some people, their alternate lives—they've been drunks, abusers, junkies, child molesters, thieves, televangelists, and a lot more murderers than you would believe—but that's a contextual possibility as much as a personality thing—"

Michael indicated the shelves with another of those professional gestures. "But you—the worst you'll find on the Bad Lives Shelf is lying to your parents, a little bit of early plagiarism—you covered that one well, I'll give you credit for that—and that time you went out driving drunk and stoned and whiplashed that old lady. Tsk tsk. But that's hardly very exciting, I mean, compared to some of the things you could have been—"

"So, all the bad things I've done are—?"

Michael waved it off. "Negligible in context. Compared to some people who've come through here—never mind, that would be tattling."

I looked around. "Is there a Good Lives Shelf? Are there better lives I could have had?"

Michael shook his head. "Well, yes and no—there are better lives you could have had, but you don't need to see them. Some people find them depressing. And in your case, oh my, yes. We don't want you breaking down and crying, collapsing in anguish, smashing things in rage—it disturbs the other guests."

"I'm not that kind of person."

"No, but you could be."

"Really? That's the first piece of good news I've gotten here—"

Michael said, "The whole point of the Alternate Lives Section—to show you some of the other possibilities of the ride. For the next time you do it."

"The next time?"

"Oh yes. Just go around to your right—"

"Uh, no. I don't think so. Not right now. Which way is the exit?"

Michael pointed to the left. "Right out there. Remember, the afterlife is the happiest place after life." He twinkled at me. "Would you like a pair of complimentary wings and a halo?"

"Not really."

"Well, some people expect it, so we make it an option—" He handed me a pair of sunglasses. "But do put these on. It can get pretty bright out there. It's full of stars."

* * *

After Life

EVENTUALLY, I FOUND myself in a room.

Well, not a room. A space. Not very well defined. In fact, not defined at all. So I wasn't sure how I knew it was a *space*. But I knew.

There was a person here. Sitting behind a desk. There was nothing on the desk except a thin black vase with three white lilies sticking out of it. The person behind the desk was indeterminate, dressed in something that could have been white, or maybe gray, but wasn't quite enough of either.

"Please sit down. Be comfortable."

"Sit where?" I looked behind me. There was a chair there. Now. I sat. It was neither hard nor soft. Neither comfortable nor un-.

"Excuse me?" I said.

"Yes?"

"Is it necessary for this whole place to be so ... so indeterminate?"

"Mm, yes. I see your point. Just a moment. Is this better?" The space was now identifiably a room. Bare blank walls. No door.

"Um, no. It isn't."

"Something wrong?"

"It's—it's very stark. Institutional. Not very comfortable."

"You think this place should be comfortable?"

"Is there any reason why it shouldn't be? And you did tell me to be comfortable."

"Point taken. How's this?"

I looked around. Now the space was defined by Grecian pillars that stretched infinitely upward. Long silky-white drapes wafted in a soft breeze. Beyond, summer-blue sky with soft cumulus pillows here and there. "Nice," I admitted. "A little bit of a cliché, very Warner Brothers, but—"

"I can change it, if you wish—"

"No, no thanks. This will do."

"You're sure."

"Quite."

"Can I get you something? Water? A soft drink? Iced tea?"

"No, I'm fine. Really."

"Good."

I waited. He waited. We waited. He still seemed indeterminate.

Finally, I asked, "Are you God?"

"I'm an aspect of the universe."

"You don't look like an aspect."

"Oh? How do you think an aspect should look?"

"I don't know. Like God, I guess."

"And what does God look like?"

I shrugged. "Like God. Unmistakeable."

"I see. Do you prefer the George Burns or the Morgan Freeman iteration? Or perhaps something more in the Charlton Heston or Michelangelo mold? Or maybe Hattie McDaniel?"

"Hattie McDaniel?"

"A very popular aspect."

"Um, no. I just—"

"How's this?" Gregory Peck. The Atticus Finch version. "Will this do?"

"Yes. That's fine."

Gregory Peck looked at me across the desk. "Is there anything else?"

"Is this where I get judged?"

"No."

"I get judged somewhere else?"

"No."

"Well, where *do* I get judged—?"

"Being judged is important to you?"

"No. Yes. I mean, I thought it was part of the deal."

"No, it isn't."

"No judgment at all?"

"No. Are you disappointed?"

"Well, sort of. I thought I did pretty good. Didn't I?"

"I don't know. Why don't you tell me—"

That stopped me for a moment. "I have to tell you?"

"It's a start."

"Oh, I see. This is all self-service. Like a cafeteria. I'm supposed to sort it out for myself, argue both sides of the case, all my good works versus all my sins, right? I get to undertake a self-examination of my entire life, however long as it takes, and then finally pronounce my own judgment. Right?"

"No," said Gregory Peck.

"No...?"

"No."

We waited some more. He waited while I sorted it out in my head. No judgment. But if there's no judgment, then what is this place? What am I doing here?

"Is this Heaven? Or Hell?"

"What do you want it to be?"

"Look, you're the aspect. You're the one who knows what's going on. Not me. So could we just get on with it?"

"We are getting on with it. This is it."

"This is it? *This* is it? This is *it?*"

"Yes."

"What about eternal reward? Eternal punishment? Judgment day? Heaven? Hell? God? St. Peter? Pearly Gates? Satan? Fiery pits of agonizing brimstone? Demons? Pitchforks? Are you telling me none of that is here? If it's not here, where is it?"

"Is that what you want?"

"No, I don't—"

"What is it you want?"

"I want an explanation. I think I deserve an explanation, don't you?"

"What I think is irrelevant. This is *your* space."

"Did I end up in some kind of purgatory? Limbo? Is that it? This is a waiting place, isn't it? How long do I have to wait? Ten thousand years? A million? That really doesn't seem fair. I only had 72 years on Earth. Why should all of eternity be determined by a mere flick of time? I didn't even have enough time to—to live a whole life, to learn enough to—to be wise. I didn't have enough time to do all the things I planned to do."

"You had 72 years, 4 months, 3 days, 22 hours, 14 minutes, 33 seconds. Wasn't that enough?"

"No, it wasn't."

"It was a lot more than most people get. And you had your health."

"Fat lot of good that does me here."

We waited some more.

"So okay, fine. I get it. What happens next?"

"Nothing."

"Nothing?"

"That's right."

I inhaled. I exhaled. Mostly for effect. That was interesting. I could breathe here. I did it again. "Nothing," I repeated.

"That's right," said Gregory Peck. "Is there something you would like to have happen?"

"Can I ask you something?"

"Ask anything you want."

"Will you answer honestly?"

"Of course."

"How long does this go on?"

"As long as you want."

"Where is God?"

"God is here."

"Here?"

"Yes."

"Where?"

"Here."

"Do I get to meet God?"

"If you wish."

"When?"

"Whenever you wish."

"How about now?" I said.

"All right."

Nothing happened.

I looked across at Gregory Peck. He did not seem antagonistic. In fact, he seemed very nice. He wasn't doing this deliberately.

"So, where is God?"

"God is here."

"Are you God?"

"I'm an aspect."

"Yeah. I got that part. So, let's see. There's no Heaven. There's no Hell. There's no Day of Judgment. There's no reward, no punishment."

"Do you want any of those things?"

"No, I don't." I got up from the chair, went to the edge of the room—the *space*—and stared out into the eternal blue. I scratched behind my ear.

"Is it this way for everybody?" I asked.

Behind me, the aspect answered. "No. It's this way for you."

"Hm." Well, that was useful. The afterlife was a personal experience. A puzzle that each person had to solve for himself. "So how much time do I have here?"

"As much as you want. We create it as we need it."

"Yes, of course. I should have known. Thank you."

"You're welcome. Are you sure I can't get you anything? Water? A soft drink? Iced tea?"

Something went click. Or *klunk*. Or whatever sound a small epiphany makes inside your head—if you have a head.

But I was starting to figure it out. I walked back to the chair and sat down at the desk. The aspect sat across from me. He waited patiently.

"You work for me, don't you?"

"Yes, I do."

"You didn't tell me that."

"You didn't want me to. You wanted to see how long it would take for you to figure it out for yourself."

"Well, this is embarrassing."

"Every time."

"Right." I scratched behind my ear again. An interesting sensation. I'd have to remember that one.

"I like playing jokes on myself, don't I?"

"Yes, sir, you do. Who else do you have to play jokes on?"

"Yes, there is that."

"That was a good one with the redhead, though. Nicely orchestrated."

"Yes and no. It didn't seem like fun from the inside."

"I guess not."

"I'll have a cappuccino, please."

"Right away—"

And there it was. Coffee was one of my better ideas. Almost as good as sex. I put the mug back down on the desk. "So," I said. "I guess I'm ready for the next life."

"Very good, sir. What would you like to try this time?"

"Well, I'm just brainstorming here, but how about this—"

This story originally appeared in *Galaxy's Edge*, 2015.

David Gerrold has been writing science fiction for half a century. His novels include *When Harlie Was One*, *The Man Who Folded Himself*, the *Dingilliad* series for young adults, and the *Star Wolf* series. He's currently editing book five of his seven-book *War Against the Chtorr* trilogy. David Gerrold has written for many different television series, including *Twilight Zone*, *Land of the Lost*, *Babylon 5*, *Tales from the Darkside*, *Sliders* and *The Real Ghostbusters*. He also wrote scripts for *Star Trek Animated* and *Star Trek: The Original Series*.

FAIRY DEBT

GAIL CARRIGER

"I WON'T DO IT, I tell you!" I was mad, and I had a right to be.

Aunt Twill sighed dramatically and swished about where she sat in the lake shallows. Aunt Twill did most things dramatically. She was the naiad of the Woodle River, and it was a bit of a dramatic river, full of small but excitable waterfalls.

"Unfortunately it's your debt to pay."

I crossed my arms and glared at her.

She explained as though to a child, "Your mother was rescued from *certain death* by a human King. That's a great debt of honor for a fairy to endure."

"Yes, but these things are easily taken care of," I insisted. "All mamma had to do was show up at the christening of the King's firstborn and grant it something humans care about." I tried to come up with examples. "You know—beauty, boxing, bee keeping. That sort of thing."

My aunt fluttered her webbed fingers about her face in exasperation. "Yes, but your mother missed the christening and, most inconveniently, died."

I sighed. I was only a nestling when she died, so I didn't remember. They say it had to do with a golden barbell and a frog with a steroid addiction but it was all kept very hush-hush.

Aunt Twill reached down and gathered a few water lilies about her. "So the princess has no fairy godmother and you can't grow wings." She began braiding the lilies into a chain with her magic. "An honor debt warps wings. Especially in the young."

I fluttered my four stubby wings angrily in reply. They weren't any use to me, but I liked to flap them for effect.

"Debts carry forward to the next generation." My aunt draped the water lilies about her neck. "You owe the princess."

"But I've no working magic without working wings. Nothing to pay her with."

"You have your Child Wishes."

I snorted. A fairy's Child Wishes had power over only one thing, usually to do with human domestic life. Evolutionarily speaking, this ensured that mankind would always find value in sheltering fairy offspring. My cousin, Effernshimerlon, could manufacture safety pins as needed. My Wishes improved baked goods. For a fairy potluck I once made banana puff cupcakes so delicious they caused a visiting earth dragon to cry. Earth dragons are fond of cupcakes. They have notorious (and very large pointy) sweet-tooths.

"What could I do with my Wishes?" I asked Aunt Twill. "Ensure that the castle's bread rises perfectly for the next one hundred years?"

I was being facetious, but my aunt took me seriously. She bobbed about in the lake and the lily chain fell from her neck.

"No, I don't think that's enough. Not unless the castle's bread is cursed."

I raised my eyebrows at her. "What do you suggest, then? I can't be fairy godmother to the princess, she's my age, that'd be ridiculous." I felt as though everywhere I looked there was a troll with a club pointed at me, and no troll-pacifying porridge in sight. Was there no way to pay off mother's debt? "What do I do?"

Aunt Twill shut her damp old eyes. I could practically hear her thoughts sliding about in her head, like water over pebbles. Very slow water over very large pebbles.

"You'll have to pay it back the hard way."

"Oh and what's that?"

"Old-fashioned servitude."

I PACKED UP and trekked west, away from the Woodle River, toward the Small Principality of Smickled-on-Twee. There lived a king who'd once rescued my mother from certain death.

What else was I to do? I wanted wings. What good is a fairy without wings?

I'm tall for a fairy (all that naiad blood) but really very short for a human. I come up to the knees of the average adult male. With stunted wings tucked under a tunic I looked like a hunchback. There's only one role at a royal court for a short hunchback: jester.

I knew it would all end in tears the moment I saw the hat.

"Do I have to wear it?" I asked the Most Jester in shock, staring at the ghastly thing.

He jiggled his own at me. A four-pronged confection of red, blue, and green plaid tipped with silver bells. "Required uniform, I'm afraid," he replied. Clearly he'd gone into the profession out of physical necessity as well. He was extremely tall and decidedly skinny with a great beaked nose and a very deep voice.

His hat was elegant compared to the one presented to me. Mine had only three prongs and was worn so that one prong always fell directly in front of the eyes. One of the prongs was yellow with pink spots and the other two were purple with white stripes. Mankind may have made uglier hats but I doubt it. Don't even get me started on the subject of the bells. The darn thing was covered in them.

I put it on, and the accompanying checked green pumpkin pants and doublet (which, next to the hat, seemed quite somber), and slouched after the Most Jester toward the Throne Room.

"Your Majesty," the Most Jester bowed low to the king. Too low, for he toppled forward, stumbled and sprawled flat on the floor. The assembled courtiers laughed appreciatively. "May I introduce our new Least Jester?" He waved a spade-like hand in my direction from his prone position.

I had fairy grace at my disposal even if I didn't have working wings. So I did a flip and two somersaults to end in a bow at the king's feet.

The king nodded at me happily, and the princess clapped. Not every court was lucky enough to have a tumbling jester.

"Why," said the princess, looking at me closely, "you can't be much older than me."

I looked up at the human who held my fate in her hands. She didn't seem all that bad—a little chubby for a princess and rather graceless. Hadn't she been given *any* fairy gifts at all? I know my mother fell down on the job, as it were, but this poor thing was practically ordinary! She seemed to know it, too. She slid off her throne in the most humble manner, and bent down in order to properly introduce herself to me.

"Princess Anastasia Clementina Lanagoob. How do you do?"

I came out of my bow. Standing upright my head ended just below her waist. I reached up and shook her pudgy hand with my tiny one. "Bella Fugglecups," I replied. I couldn't give her my fairy name, of course, too recognizable. Aunt Twill had invented this one as an alternative. It was silly, but so was my hat.

"I shall call you Cups," announced the princess.

"Only if I can call you Goob," I retorted.

The king seemed appalled by this impertinence, but the princess was clearly delighted. The statement made her laugh. Which is, after all, a jester's job.

"Done," she said, letting go of my hand. "Will you teach me how to tumble?"

I looked dubiously at her full white skirts covered in gold beads and silver embroidery.

"Now? If you insist, but I hope your under-things are as attractive as your outer ones."

The princess laughed again. The rest of the court gasped in shock. The Most Jester made a frantic sawing motion across his neck. I had no idea what he was on about.

"Anastasia Clementina, I forbid such an undertaking!" The king rose from his throne and glowered down at the two of us. He was a large sort of human, full of hair, and prone to some kind of disease that made his face go all red and splotchy. It was doing so now.

"Please, Daddy," the princess turned big muddy brown eyes on her father. Cow eyes. "I'll change my outfit."

The king sighed.

What I didn't know then was that the princess rarely took an interest in, or asked for, anything. When she did, her requests carried more power. It's a good approach to life, generally gets one what one wants. (So long as one doesn't "want" too often.) I would come to appreciate this character trait over the course of my association with Princess Goob, for all too often we fairies are on the receiving end of demanding humans. Take Cinderella for example—with her gown, and her coach, and her glass slippers, and on and on. I mean, really! But, I digress.

"Very well." The king ceded defeat. He looked at me. "You don't mind?"

I tilted my head way back. "It is my honor to serve, Your Majesty." What else could I have said?

I did a back bend, kicked my heels up, and walked away from the two royals on my hands until I'd rejoined the Most Jester. Then I flipped to standing.

The princess clapped delightedly.

I bowed to them both.

"Tomorrow at noon, Cups," she ordered.

"Noon, Princess Goob." I agreed, and followed the Most Jester out of the audience chamber.

"DO YOU THINK it's enough of a service?" I asked Aunt Twill that evening through a small cup of tea.

Her image wiggled in the brown liquid. Normally tea talking is a delicate spell requiring both parties use bone china, Earl Grey, and silver stirring spoons. But Aunt Twill had a contract with the tea daemons that allowed her conversational access (between the afternoon hours of half-past three and five o'clock, of course) to any cup in the kingdom. It's a naiad gossip thing.

My aunt extracted a small gudgeon fish from her hair and ruminated. "I doubt teaching a princess acrobatics constitutes proper repayment of an honor debt. Though it is a nice thing to do. Why would she want to learn, do you think? It certainly isn't normal princess-y behavior."

I shrugged. "She isn't a normal princess. More like a normal dairymaid. Poor thing."

Aunt Twill nodded. "Plain ones happen sometimes. I'll do a little research and get back to you on the tumbling. Until then, I'd proceed as though this were *not* the answer."

I sighed. "Very well, Aunt Twill."

"Oh, and niece," I looked up, "that's a hideous hat."

I stuck my tongue out at her and lifted up the bone china cup. Her face wavered in the brown liquid as I drank down the tea. Fairies invented tea, did you know that? It was one of our best collective spells, until the daemons stole it, and humans got in on the idea. Still, it explains my Child Wishes: baked goods go very well with tea.

THERE WASN'T MUCH for the jester contingent to do during the daytime at court. Most of our entertaining work was done at night, or at feasts, or at festivals. The rest of the time we were left pretty much to our own devices.

I spent the first few weeks poking about looking for spells or curses I could break—princes disguised as dung beetles or the odd evil loom weight. Nothing. Not a single enchanted sausage. Smickled-on-Twee had to be the most boring principality in the entire province of fairy-kind. The princess was painfully average. The queen had died a perfectly respectable death (by plague). The only thing out of the ordinary the king had done, in his long and uninteresting career as ruler, was rescue my mother. And he didn't seem to remember doing that.

Princess Goob and I became fast friends. She was hopeless at tumbling—far, far too clumsy. But I soon realized the lessons were only an excuse. What she really wanted was the company of someone her own age, and to get out of the castle once in a while. In keeping with these two desires, I announced that we really must practice on a mossy lawn every afternoon, so took her through the castle gates and over the drawbridge to a sheep pasture near the moat. There I pretended to show her handstands, cartwheels, and flips. She pretended to try and learn them. Mostly we lounged about and chatted.

"I always wanted to be a shepherdess," she confided in me one afternoon. "I think I'd be better suited to that kind of life."

I looked at her from my supine pose on the grass. She wore a very plain dress, borrowed from one of her maids, and long brown bloomers underneath, which were supposed to be for riding. She'd tucked the skirt of the dress up on each side and tied a kerchief about her hair. She looked very like a shepherdess.

"I think the role would suit you."

"That's what I like about you, Cups. No silly pandering or hedging. Everyone else secretly agrees when I say such things, but they all pretend to be shocked. Or worse, tell me what a perfect princess I am."

She flipped onto her stomach and began picking at the grass. "I never had a fairy godmother, you heard by now, I suppose? Shocking thing. Dad spent a good deal of time trying to find and rescue fairies in his youth, hoping to gather honor debt, but it didn't work. So I got nothing."

"You're probably better off that way. I always felt that princesses with all those boosts in looks and manners had no idea how real people felt. How can anyone be a good ruler if they have no understanding of those they rule?"

The princess looked at me and nodded. "You're absolutely right, and I want you to arrange it for me."

I sat up, wondering what I'd gotten myself into—small fairy, big mouth.

"What?" I asked, nervous.

"This 'understanding.' Since I can't learn acrobatics during our afternoons together, I should learn something useful. What better thing is there to learn than the lives of my people?"

I squinted at her. She might look nothing like a princess, but she certainly spoke like one. If she kept her mouth shut, we should do all right. It was a bit like the enchanted leading the enchanted though. The only person less likely to know about the common lives of humans than a princess was a fairy. But an order was an order.

So our afternoon tumbling sessions turned into afternoon field trips. First we visited the shepherdesses (because she really *was* interested), and then the dairymaids. Then we called on the stable hands and the goose-girls, the portrait painters and the gatekeepers. I learned a lot on these journeys. I found the lower class humans far more interesting than the nobility.

Eventually we ended up in the castle kitchens.

My Child Wishes made us quite the popular visitors there. The princess liked it too. Even without my help she seemed to have a natural talent for cooking. She invented a roasted peacock dish, stuffed with dates and sage, slathered in thick gravy with wild mushrooms and cubed ham, that caused the king to give the entire kitchen staff a raise.

Of course, the staff all knew she was the princess, but they pretended not to, and that seemed to work well for everyone.

Me, on the other hand, they called their Lucky Least, as whenever I was around pastries and breads seemed to turn out moister, chewier, fluffier, and more delicious than when I was away.

"Why is that, Cups?" the princess asked me, dusting flour-covered hands on pure silk petticoats.

"I like baking, so I'm good at it."

"But you don't actually touch anything. You're too short to reach."

I shrugged, a movement made very odd by my hump of hidden wings. "I keep an eye on things. Make sure they don't mess up."

Princess Goob looked at me skeptically, but she left it at that. She'd learned if she questioned me closely I got all philosophical so it was better to stop before things got epistemologically out of hand.

I'D BEEN THERE nearly a year, and was no closer to repaying my debt, when the peace of Smickled-on-Twee was finally disturbed by something terrible.

It was festival day and everyone was sitting down for high tea. We jesters were gallivanting about jestering, when an earth dragon waddled into the main banquet hall.

He was a smallish, fat sort of dragon, only about two horses long and probably that many wide, with muddy bronze scales, six sad little horns, lots of sharp teeth, and a sour expression.

Still he was an *earth dragon*, and as such, terrifying to humans. Earth dragons take food seriously, you see. They collect interesting recipes and bags of fizzy lemon candies to stash deep in the recesses of their muddy caves. They also consider humans crunchy little treats of meaty goodness. Other dragons don't care a jot for such things. Air dragons eat birds and collect kites as a general rule, while water dragons eat algae and collect fishing tackle. Fire dragons are the ones who hoard gold. No one is quite sure what *they* eat, though they have a nasty reputation. Difficult to get close enough to find out.

As a fairy, I don't mind earth dragons all that much, but then I'm a fairy. Magic in the blood makes us far too spicy for consumption.

This particular dragon headed straight for the high table. There he squatted across from the royals and gave Princess Goob a very toothy grin. Princesses tend to be succulent—well fed and soft-skinned. It was earth dragons that started the whole "kidnapping of princesses" policy. They like to steal them away and keep them around for late night attacks of the munchies.

The king knew this and panicked. His face went redder than I'd ever seen it, and he began to sputter like an over-filled teakettle.

I snuck under the table to sit at the princess's feet. I could touch the dragon's baby toe from there. It was about the size of my head.

I touched the princess's toe instead. She twitched slightly. I touched it again. She lifted the edge of the tablecloth up and looked down at me.

"Tell your father," I said, "that the only way to get out of being eaten by an earth dragon is to serve it a high tea far better than the one *you* would be."

The princess nodded and her head vanished.

A moment later I heard the king bang hard on the table and call for service.

This dragon was unlikely to be particularly impressed with the king's tea. Smickled-on-Twee was a small principality and not precisely prosperous. The honey glazed whole pig with thyme and raisins was not as big as it would have been in the Bugdoon-near-Schmoo. Nor were the mounds of tiny new potatoes drizzled in melted butter and sprinkled with mint quite as delicate or as minty as they would have been in Schmoo itself. But the bread was certainly up to par; I'd been lounging about wasting Child Wishes on it all morning. There were huge crispy brown loaves shaped like tortoises and filled with sweetmeats; small round honey-soaked buns rolled in cinnamon; and long skinny cheese encrusted baguettes. The dragon ate sixteen loaves in all, and I had to sneak away to the kitchen to make sure the second batch came out as good as the first.

The dragon consumed three of the princess's famous peacock dishes, eight racks of lamb smeared with roasted garlic and rosemary, two platters of pork sausage with hot mustard, and several spit-roasted pheasants. Between each course the dragon picked up his teacup and gazed deeply into the murky depths. The fifth time that he did this the princess stopped me when I came from a bread check and asked me about it.

"He's doing what?" I said.

"Talking dragoonish into his teacup."

I looked at the dragon. At that moment he was stuffing his face with a trencher of bacon-and-tomato stuffed quail. I was suspicious. So far as I knew, only naiads and daemons used the teacup network. What was this dragon up to?

I examined the huge beast. There was something oddly familiar about his markings. Had we met before? I crinkled my forehead in thought. Then I remembered. Once, long ago, an earth dragon had turned up at a fairy potluck. Could this possibly be the same one? I squinted at him—six horns, sour expression . . . yes, it must be. And if this dragon was talking into his teacup, I bet I knew who he was talking to.

I snuck a cup of tea off of the high table myself and retreated into a corner of the room.

"Aunt Twill," I hissed into the cup.

The surface of the tea shivered slightly and Aunt Twill's wrinkled face appeared in the dark brown liquid, looking harried.

"Aunt Twill, what are you up to?"

"Add a little milk will you, dearie? You know the spell is easier in milky tea."

I ignored her and said firmly, "Aunt Twill!"

My aunt had the good grace to look slightly guilty. "He's been asking about your banana puff cupcakes for ages. So I thought, why not send him along?"

I was shocked. "Aunt Twill!"

Aunt Twill straightened her spine. "Now don't go taking that tone with me, nestling. This is quite the opportunity. The princess is at risk, the castle in danger, and you and your Child's Wishes can save the day."

Just then, behind me, the dragon sent up a great roar and tipped over the high table. There was a cacophony of sound as plates, platters, knives, and teacups slid to the floor.

"Gotta go," I said, drinking the tea unceremoniously.

I turned and rushed toward the chaos.

The dragon was yelling in dragoonish—a sort of rolling fuzzy language. I don't speak it well myself, but I gathered he wasn't entirely pleased with the meal.

I ran up to Princess Goob. "Stay out of his reach as much as possible and keep feeding him bread. It's very filling." She looked at me with wide eyes and I could tell she really wanted to ask how I knew so much about dragons. But instead she just nodded.

I turned to run back to the kitchens.

"Where are you going?" asked the Princess in a panic.

"I have to make banana puff cupcakes! Your life may depend upon it."

Strange as that statement was, Princess Goob merely nodded again. That's what I liked about that girl, no silly interfering when there's work to be done.

Once in the kitchen I marched straight up to the Most Cook.

"I need to make banana puff cupcakes."

The cook looked at me in a harried kind of way. He had about a hundred desserts all going at once. "At the moment," he said, "the needs of the Least Jester don't particularly concern me."

I stared up at him. "The princess's life depends upon it."

The thing I've learned about humans is, if you make a bizarre enough statement, they simply don't know what to do. In this case, it was easier for the Most Cook not to argue with me. He pointed at a small oven and a bit of counter space in one corner and I went off to find myself a stepping stool so I could use both.

With the help of Ernest, one of the Least Cooks, who was very tall and liked assisting me, I managed to gather all the ingredients and get to work. There were only six small bananas, almost completely black and very sad, so I used every last Child's Wish I had on that one batch of cupcakes. I decided to let the earth dragon eat up as much of the other desserts as possible first so that he had very little room left. That way my cupcakes would come as a kind of crowning glory to the whole high tea experience.

Eventually evening rolled around, which signified the end of tea. All the cooks were looking exhausted, there was very little food left in the storage cellars, and servants began to slink down to hide in the kitchen away from the dragon.

I removed my banana puff cupcakes from the oven, popped them out of the pan, sprinkled them with cinnamon and sugar and arranged them on a platter, using up the very last of my Wishes to make sure they were as perfect as they could possibly be.

Then I whisked them up onto one shoulder and carried them into the banquet hall. A hush had descended upon the room in my absence. Everyone was looking at the dragon, who was polishing off the last of the raspberry parfait and muttering into his teacup between bites.

"Where are they?" I heard him grumble into his tea.

I inched up beside him and slid the cupcake platter onto the table in front of him.

The dragon sniffed and looked up.

He poked a claw into one of the puffy yellow cakes and delicately popped the confection into his mouth. He chewed for a moment, swallowed thoughtfully. Then he closed his eyes and sighed.

"Just as I remember," he muttered to the teacup in dragoonish. The teacup chirruped back at him in the dulcet tones of my Aunt Twill. I couldn't hear exactly what she said but the dragon nodded vigorously and replied, "You have a deal."

He poked a cupcake onto each of his front claws, leaving one behind on the platter for Mr. Manners. Then he turned away from the table and slithered awkwardly out the front entrance, on his elbows to keep the cupcakes from dragging on the floor.

He turned at the door to look back.

"I await my Wishes, little fairy," he said, looking directly at me.

I realized what Aunt Twill had done. When a fairy reaches adulthood and trades in child's magic for the real thing, she has a choice as to who gets to keep her Wishes. (How else do you think human wizards got magic in the first place?) Obviously, Aunt Twill had promised my Wishes to this earth dragon.

He left, moving awkwardly across the cobbled stone bailey, out the barbican and over the moat. Soon he was out of sight.

The courtiers heaved a collective sigh, and then everyone, including the king and the princess, stared at me.

I wasn't paying attention because something very strange was happening to my wings. I took off the jester's hat in order to concentrate. Then I found I had to take off my whole uniform as my wings were starting to push against it. It was a good thing I always wore fairy garb underneath.

Sure enough, in a very short space of time, there I stood in front of the whole court—with fully grown wings!

I looked at the king. He was staring at me in wonder.

"You saved my mother once," I said, "but she died without repayment. So I've been serving your daughter in secret in her stead." I flapped my wings experimentally and they lifted me easily into the air. I was a little wobbly, but I could stay up and that was the important part. It was nice to look down on people for a change. "My cupcakes have saved your daughter from certain death, so my debt to you is fulfilled."

I looked down at the princess fondly. "Goodbye, Princess Goob."

She grinned up at me. "Goodbye, Cups."

"But wait," said the king, "Don't you have to stay? Be her fairy godmother, make her beautiful and graceful and stuff like that?"

I shook my head. "I could choose to stay if I thought she needed my help. But I think she'll do perfectly fine without me." I thought about all the gatekeepers' daughters Goob and I had met, and the millers' sons we'd laughed with, and the servants who'd helped us in the kitchen, and the goose-girls who'd gossiped with us. "I think there are others who need fairy godmothers far more than princesses," I said. And with one more wave to Princess Goob, I flew out of the castle and away into the forest.

I sent the earth dragon my Child's Wishes by butterfly post the very next day. I also sent him the recipe for banana puff cupcakes. I understand he grew even fatter.

I kept in touch with Princess Goob. Right up through the time when she became Queen Goob. She'd married by then. A nice young writer-fellow I found for her, named Adolphus Grimm. They had two children, both boys. I became a kind of adopted aunt, since I had far too many fairy godmother gigs by then to take on them as well. I did tell them about my exploits though, usually over Sunday tea. Fairy-tales, the boys called them. I had no idea they would write them all down. But that's another story.

This story originally appeared in *Sword & Sorceress 22,* Marion Zimmer Bradley Literary Works Trust, 2007.

Gail Carriger writes comedic steampunk mixed with urbane fantasy. Her books include the *Parasol Protectorate* and *Custard Protocol* series for adults, and the *Finishing School* series for young adults. She is published in 18 different languages and has thirteen *New York Times* bestsellers via seven different lists (including #1 in Manga). She was once an archaeologist and is overly fond of shoes, octopuses, and tea. Her website is www.gailcarriger.com.

A VERY SPECIAL GIRL
MIKE RESNICK

A HARRY THE BOOK STORY

I AM READING the *Racing Form* in my temporary office, which is the third booth at Joey Chicago's 3-Star Tavern, and coming to the conclusion that six trillion to one on Flyaway in the 5th at Saratoga is a bit of an underlay, as there is no way this horse gets within twenty lengths of the winner on a fast track, a slow track, or a muddy track, and I have my doubts that even a rain of toads moves him up more than two lengths. I conclude that this horse cannot beat a blind sea slug at equal weights even if he has the inside post position. Suddenly a strange odor strikes my nostrils, and without looking up I say, "Hi, Dead End", because one whiff tells me that it is Dead End Dugan, who simply cannot hide the fact that he is a zombie.

He also is an occasional employee that I use when some goniff does not wish to honor his marker, and indeed he has just returned from Longshot Lamont's, where I have sent him to collect the three large that Longshot Lamont bet on Auntie's Panties to come in first, and indeed the filly does come in first by seven lengths, but she comes in first in the 8th race after she goes to the post in the 7th race thirty minutes earlier.

"So do you pick up the three large that Harry the Book is owed?" asks Benny Fifth Street.

"Of course he picks it up," says Gently Gently Dawkins. "After all, he is half as big as a mountain, and is covered by almost as much dirt, and how much can three large weigh anyway?"

They immediately get into one of their arguments, Gently Gently saying that a three thousand dollar diamond weighs less than a cigarette, and Benny replying that it all depends who is manning the scales, and that his cousin is the clerk of scales at Belmont and has been weighing Flyboy Billy Tuesday in at 120 pounds every day for years, even though the Flyboy has not topped 108 pounds since eating some bad chili three years ago. This drives Joey Chicago, who has been standing behind the bar, wild, because he has been betting against Flyboy Billy Tuesday's horses all year, and now he learns that they've been carrying twelve pounds less than they should, but Benny points out that it's okay, because 108 pounds of Billy Tuesday is more of a handicap to a horse than 130 pounds of most jockeys, and Joey Chicago has no answer for this, so he goes back to cleaning the bar around Dead End Dugan, which requires cleaning every time Dugan moves.

"So does Longshot Lamont pay with a smile?" I ask Dugan.

He gives me that puzzled expression – he doesn't think as clearly as he used to before he became a zombie – and says, "I thought you wanted money, Harry."

"Money is even better than smiles," I say to comfort him, and because it is also true. "I trust you have it with you?"

"Well, I *had* it," says Dugan. I was going to say "says Dugan uncomfortably" but the fact of the matter is that nothing makes him more uncomfortable than being dead, which is a permanent if not a stationary condition.

"If you do not have it any more, you had better tell me where it is and why it is not in my hand right now," I say.

"I am in love," says Dugan. "I meet the most wonderful girl this afternoon on my way back from Longshot Lamont's."

"Is this not a bit early in the relationship for an exchange of three thousand dollar gifts?" asks Gently Gently.

"Do not be so fast to misinterpret," replies Dugan. "This girl is just half a step short of perfection."

"Then she will understand that that was not your money to give, and she will be happy to hand it over to me," I say.

"Uh...*that* is the half a step I was referring to," says Dugan, brushing away the flies that are starting to play field hockey on his face, as they always do when he stands in one place for a few minutes.

I decide to be the reasoning father figure, partially because I am a saint among men, and primarily because I have not yet figured out how to threaten a man who is already dead, and I say, "Tell us about this remarkable lady who has won your heart."

"She has left my heart right where it has always been," answers Dugan. "She is much more interested in my brain and my soul."

"I can't imagine why," says Benny. "You never use the one, and you are no longer in possession of the other."

"She is kind of a collector," explains Dugan, and it is the first time in my life I ever see a zombie swallow uneasily, or swallow at all for that matter.

"What does she collect, brains or souls?" asks Benny, who has a healthy curiosity about such things.

"I get the impression that she is not all that choosy," answers Dugan.

"Where do you meet her?" I ask.

"I am passing Creepy Conrad's Curiosity Shop, and I see her through the window, nibbling on a little snack in a feminine way, and it is love at first sight."

"What kind of snack?" asks Gently Gently, who at 350 pounds and counting has a serious interest in such things.

"I cannot see through the window," replies Dugan, "but it is wiggling its tail just before she swallows it."

"But she swallows it in a feminine way," I say, though my sarcasm is lost on Dugan.

"Yes," he says. "She is just beautiful. And very precise. Why, she drains an entire fifth of Comrade Terrorist vodka and does not spill so much as a drop."

"I figure the tail accompanies both ears of whatever it was as a prize for her feminine appetite," says Benny.

"She should skip the Olympics and go pro," adds Gently Gently.

"Does she eat anything else we should know about?" I ask.

"Like what?" asks Dugan.

"Like small children," I say. "Or even big ones."

"You are speaking of the woman I love!" says Dugan heatedly.

"I am speaking of the woman who is holding three large that belongs to me," I say. "Maybe you should introduce me to both of them."

"Both?" asks Dugan.

"Your girl and my money," I say. "I will take it from there."

"All right," says Dugan. "I am dying to see her again anyway."

"Poor choice of words," notes Joey Chicago from behind the bar.

"But you have to approach her gently, Harry," continues Dugan, ignoring Joey's unfeeling if accurate remark. "She is a sensitive thing and takes offense easily."

"I will approach her so gently she will hardly know I am there," I assure him.

"She will know," he assures me. "She is very perceptive." He pauses. "I think it is the extra pair of eyes."

"She has four eyes?" I say.

"At the very least," says Dugan.

"Has she got four of anything else important?" asks Benny, suddenly interested.

"She comes equipped with all kinds of extras," says Dugan. "This is why I have fallen in love with her. She is unique, even among women, who are all unique, each in their own alien way."

"What kind of extras?" I ask.

"Teeth," says Dugan. "Claws. Eyes. Tails. Well, it is only one tail, but compared to everyone else it is extra."

"I cannot argue with that," agrees Benny.

"And how many women can lift an entire car?" says Dugan proudly.

"Six cylinders or eight?" asks Gently Gently.

"Why would she lift a car?" chimes in Benny.

"It is a very tight parking space, so she just walks out, picks up the car, driver and all, and sets it down in the empty space." Dugan smiles wistfully. "And she does not even break a sweat."

"I agree that she is unique among all the women of my acquaintance," I say. "Right up to the incident with the car she is running neck and neck with a redhead named Thelma, but she has sprinted into the lead."

"That is nothing," says Dugan. "You should see her fly."

"Probably I shouldn't," I say. "I have enough trouble falling asleep as it is."

"She just flaps her arms and flies away?" asks Benny.

Dugan smiles. It is maybe the first smile anyone has seen on him since he came back from the grave. "Nobody can flap their arms and fly," he says. "She flaps her wings."

"Does she imbibe anything besides vodka while you are with her?" I ask suddenly.

"Like what?" says Dugan.

"Like blood," I say.

"I will not dignify such a crude question with a response," replies Dugan.

"I doubt that there can be more than one of her," I say, "but just in case God has been asleep at the switch and there are two or more, what is she wearing so I will be able identify her?"

"I will be right alongside you, Harry," he replies.

"True, but you are still a relative newcomer to the zombie trade, and what if you suddenly decide you don't like it? If I am to present a moldering corpse to the lady of your dreams, I at least should be sure I have the right lady. So what is she wearing?"

"I don't know," says Dugan. "I am so enraptured by her face, I never notice."

"Now I know for sure he's a zombie," says Benny.

"All right," I say, trying to hide my annoyance. "What color is her hair?"

"That's kind of difficult to say."

"How hard can it be?" I persist. "It is blonde, brunette, or possibly red."

"Well, it wriggles and hisses a lot, and it keeps changing colors under the lights," answers Dugan. "Sometimes it is red and sometimes it is green. I do not think it is ever blonde, but I could be wrong."

"Are you saying she is a Medusa?" I ask.

"No, I am not saying any such a thing," answers Dugan. "For one thing, her hair is friendly."

"How can hair be friendly?" asks Gently Gently.

"It chats with me, and it sings '99 Bottles of Beer on the Wall' while she is drinking the vodka."

"You talk to her hair?" says Benny disbelievingly.

"No," answers Dugan.

"Then you just made that up?" says Benny.

"I made nothing up," says Dugan sharply. "Her hair chats with me, just like I say. But I do not talk to it, because I am shy and tongue-tied in her presence."

"So she has extra eyes and teeth, and comes equipped with wings and a cold-blooded hairdo," I say. "I hope you will not take it askance, Dugan, but I think I am going to bring a little protection along."

"A gun?" he asks.

I shake my head. "I have a feeling that a hail of bullets would just annoy her," I say. "No, I will take Big-Hearted Milton."

"I do not see him," says Dugan, looking around.

"That is because you are not looking in his office," I say. "I will go and fetch him."

And with that, I walk to the men's room and enter it, and there is Big-Hearted Milton, my personal mage, sitting in his usual spot on the tile floor, surrounded by five black candles which have all burned down to nubs.

"Hi, Harry," he says. "Be with you in a minute." He mutters a spell that has very little melody and even less vowels. As he says the last word of it, all five candles go out. "That'll show her," he says with a satisfied smile.

"What will show who?"

"Mitzi McSweeney," says Milton. "I take her to dinner last night, and just because I play a little itsy-bitsy-spider on her thigh under the table she throws her soup in my face and walks out." He glowers furiously. "And I do not even like chicken gumbo."

"What have you done to the poor girl?" I ask.

"When she steps on the scale this morning, vain creature that she is, she will find out that she is ten pounds heavier than last night, and nothing will take the weight off except an apologetic phone call to me."

I decide not to point out that Mitzi is bordering on anorexic anyway and an extra ten pounds will fill her out nicely. I especially decide not to mention that she can probably pack more of a wallop at 115 pounds than at 105.

"Okay, Milton," I say, "if you are done with your just and terrible vengeance, I have need of your services."

"I am the best there is at my trade," he says. "I put Morris the Mage in the shade. Spellsinger Sol cannot hold a candle to me. But I tell you up front, Harry, that even *I* cannot bring Flyaway home a winner at Saratoga tomorrow. I could put a saddle on *you* and you could spot him eight lengths and still beat him by daylight."

"That is not the particular service I need," I say. "It seems that Dead End Dugan has fallen in love, and has given his ladyfriend the three large that he picked up for me from Longshot Lamont. It is my intention to retrieve it."

"And you need my help taking your money back from a girl?" laughs Milton.

"Anything is possible," I say.

"Oh, well, I have not been out of my office since I show up to wash the soup off my face last night," he says. "A little fresh air will do me good. And getting your money back should be like taking candy from a baby."

I resist the urge to ask him a baby *what*, and a moment later we emerge from the men's room into the bar, and pick up Dead End Dugan, Benny Fifth Street, and Gently Gently

Dawkins, and we are about to walk out the door when Milton asks Dugan what the name of the lady we are about to visit might be.

"Anna," he says.

"And her last name is Conda, right?" says Milton, laughing at his own joke.

"How did you know?" asks Dugan.

CREEPY CONRAD'S CURIOSITY SHOP is easy to find. You just see where all the terrified women and children are running away from, and follow the screaming to its source. On the day we go there Conrad is having a sale on shrunken heads, but these differ from every other shrunken head I have ever seen in that they are still alive and are attached to non-shrunken bodies. They spend most of their time eating, because their mouths are so small and their bodies are so big.

Because he is on the outskirts of an Italian neighborhood, Conrad also sells a lot of full-sized wooden crosses, with or without hammers and nails. His vinyl record section – he has not yet made the jump to CDs – sells mood music, providing that your mood is either morbid or panic-stricken. He is also having a special on surplus dialysis machines, and three pale lean gentlemen, each wearing a velvet cape, are examining them.

The rest of the merchandise is *really* esoteric, especially the part that is still alive, but we have not come to enjoy a pleasant afternoon browsing through Conrad's stock. We have come for Anna Conda and my three thousand dollars, but as I look around there is no morsel of femininity to be seen, nor is there anyone who answers to Anna's description.

Finally Creepy Conrad emerges from a back room. He is missing one eye, and his left cheekbone protrudes through the skin, and those few teeth he still possesses are filed and miscolored, and the nails on his hands are about an inch long and curve like those of a leopard, but aside from that he looks every bit as normal as Dead End Dugan, which is perhaps not really an apt comparison as Dugan still possesses his hair.

"Well, curse my soul if it isn't Harry the Book and his retainers," says Conrad. "What may I do for you fine gentlemen today? Could I perhaps interest the illustrious Mr. Dugan in a coffin?"

"You couldn't interest me no matter where you were," says Dugan. "We have come to see the delectable Anna Conda."

"Well, there is an Anna Conda on the premises," answers Conrad. "But a delectable one? Possibly you want Madame Bonne Ami's House of Exotic Comforts for the Recently Departed. They might have one."

"Watch your step, sir," says Dugan, drawing himself up to his full height. "You are speaking of the woman I love."

"Now, why would the woman you love be working for Madame Bonne Ami?" muses Conrad.

"Keep a civil tongue in your head," says Dugan ominously.

"I already have one," says Conrad, sticking his tongue out at us. "It belonged to a little old lady who only used it in church on Sundays."

"Where is she?" demands Dugan.

"The little old lady?" says Conrad. "She is long gone."

"Where is Anna Conda?" says Dugan.

"I heard you mention my name," says a voice which sounds kind of like a wire-haired terrier being combed against the grain, and a moment later Anna Conda steps out from one of the back rooms.

She is everything Dugan says she is, but Dugan does not say the half of it. He never mentions the cold reptilian eyes, the pointed ears, the reticulated greenish skin, or the four-inch dew claws on each of her ankles. She offers us the kind of smile healthy cats offer to three-legged mice, and I can see that her tongue is black and forked.

"Hello, Mr. Dugan," she says, and her voice does not improve with proximity. "How nice to see you again."

"You are even more beautiful than before," replies Dugan, and Benny shoots me a look that says, *My God, what does she look like earlier in the day?*

"Who are your friends?" asks Anna.

"This is Harry the Book, my sometimes employer," says Dugan before I can whisper to him to make up a name, "and these are Benny Fifth Street, Gently Gently Dawkins, and Big-Hearted Milton."

"And what are you gentlemen here for?" she asks.

"It is Harry's fault," Dugan blurts out, so I figure I had better explain the situation.

"It would appear that Dugan, with the best will in the world, gives you a little keepsake that is not his to give," I say.

"I am just as happy to accept it from you, Harry," she says with a smile that makes me want to turn and race for the door and not stop running until I have reached Des Moines or Des

Plaines or some other distant municipality beginning with "Des".

"I will handle this, Harry," says Milton, stepping forward. "Miss Conda, charming and beautiful as you are, I am afraid I must insist that you return the three large to Harry, though you can keep a couple of Ben Franklins for your trouble."

"It was given to me in all earnestness, and I am not inclined to give it back," she says, and I notice that blue vapor is starting to pour out of her nose, which means that either she is losing her temper or perhaps her spleen has spontaneously combusted, and I will give heavy odds on the former.

"Then I am afraid I shall have to resort to stringent means of recovering it," says Milton.

"You do that," says Anna.

"Very well," says Milton. "Do not say that you weren't warned."

And with that, Milton begins chanting something in a forgotten language, and making gestures in the air, and otherwise conjuring up all of the black arts at his command, and finally he ends it with a cry of "Presto!" – and suddenly there are only four of us facing Anna Conda, and Big-Hearted Milton is nowhere to be seen.

"Where did he go?" asks Gently Gently.

"Beats me," I say.

"Get me the hell out of here!" says Milton's voice.

I look around, but there is no sign of him.

"Get you out of where?" I ask.

"This damned dimension that she hurls me into," says Milton's voice. "And hurry! It is cold and there is something very big sniffing at me and drooling on my face."

"I do not know how to magic you back," I say. "After all, you are the mage."

"Reach out and grab my hand, of course," says Milton.

"Reach *where*?" I say.

"Out!" yells Milton.

I reach my hand out, and sure enough a pudgy invisible hand takes hold of it. I give it a pull, and suddenly there is a *pop!* and then Milton is standing next to me, looking both relieved and annoyed.

He stares at Anna Conda with a combination of fear and awe. "Who does your protection?" he asks. "Whoever it is, he's *good!*"

"I need no protector," answers Anna.

"I can believe it," says Benny fervently.

"Enough of this chit-chat," I say. "I still want my money."

Dugan walks over and stands next to Anna. "Enough!" he says. "I will not stand idly by and let you pester the love of my life."

"Actually, she is more the love of your death," Gently Gently points out.

"Whatever she is," I say, "I am not inclined to supply her with a dowry one hour after collecting it from Longshot Lamont." I turn to her. "I hope you and Dugan will be very happy, and can find a hotel that caters to both of whatever you are, and I will even pop for a flimsy nightgown if you are going to tie the knot, but I still want my three large."

"And if I do not agree to part with it, will you put a hit out on Dead End Dugan?" she asks with a cold reptilian smile, and

I have to admit that the idea of putting out a hit on a dead man can best be called counter-productive.

"Milton," I say, "have you got any other tricks up your sleeve?"

"He has nothing up his sleeve except his arm," says Anna. "And if he tries anything, he will make me lose my temper. You will not be happy if I should lose my temper. The last time I lose it they blame what happens on Hurricane Katrina, and the time before that they invent Hurricane Andrew."

"Did you do Chernobyl too?" asks Benny curiously.

"No," she says. "That was my kid sister."

"I am sure I will love her too," says Dugan.

No sooner do the words leave his mouth than Anna gets all red in the face and lets out a shriek. All the windows break, my fillings fall out of my teeth, a bus half a block away veers and plows into a fire hydrant, and every dog with a mile begins howling.

"I am sorry," says Anna a moment later. "I have a jealous and passionate nature."

"To say nothing of cataclysmic and catastrophic and a lot of other words that begin with 'cat'," I agree.

"I see your friend is sprawled out on the floor," she says, indicating Gently Gently. "I hope I did not do him irreparable damage."

"If he can survive eighty-seven million calories," I say as Benny and I heave him to his feet, "he can survive a jealous scream."

"Where am I?" mumbles Gently Gently. "Are we at war? What day is it? Wait! I have it! Flyaway won and the world came to an end!"

"You'll be all right," I say. "Just stand there and try not to think."

"That should be very easy for him," says Benny. "Not thinking is one of the best things Gently Gently does."

Anna Conda turns to Dugan. "I am sorry I have upset your friends so much. I cherish our relationship, and to prove it I will return Harry the Book's money."

"While those are words I have been longing to hear," answers Dugan, "the part about cherishing our relationship, not the part about Harry's money, I am mildly surprised as our total time spent in each other's company has been only ten minutes, give or take."

"That is about seven minutes longer than most of my relationships last," says Anna. "I will be back with the money in a moment."

She goes into one of the back rooms, and Benny walks over to Dugan.

"I would be very careful with this girl," he says confidentially. "For example, when she suggests you go out for a bite, I will give plenty of eight-to-five that she is not talking about patronizing a restaurant."

Anna comes out and hands me a bag containing the three thousand dollars. "It is all there," she says. "You can count it if you wish."

"That is not necessary," I tell her. "Dugan would never cheat me, and if you would I prefer not to know about it, because then I will not have to do anything about it."

She gives me another of those smiles that are more frightening that a gorgon's grimace. "You are wise beyond your years, Harry the Book."

"And you are formidable beyond yours, Anna Conda," I say, bowing low, but not so low that I can't jump back if she changes her mind and reaches for the money, or maybe my neck.

As we are leaving, Benny whispers to me: "I know Love is blind, but until this minute I do not realize he is on life support."

And that is the story of Dead End Dugan's very special girl. I suppose their relationship was doomed from the start. I know that opposites attract, but there is nothing in the rule book about anyone quite as opposite as Dugan and Anna. They decide to go away for a weekend in the mountains. Dugan never mentions exactly what happens, except that he makes a mistake by remarking that the tour bus driver is very pretty, but I am told that when the next edition of Rand McNally comes out Pike's Peak will now be Pike's Valley.

"I have learned a valuable lesson, Harry," Dugan tells me when it is all over. "From now on, I will stick to my own kind."

And so he does. The next afternoon I am sitting in the third booth at Joey Chicago's, reading the *Form*, and the smell of rotting flesh is twice as strong as ever. I look up and there is Dugan and his new girlfriend, sidling up to the bar.

"What can I get you and this beautiful young lady?" asks Joey Chicago, managing to string together three misstatements in just three words.

"What will it be, my dear?" says Dugan.

"It's been so many decades since I've drunk anything at all, I can't remember," says his companion. "Why don't we let the bartender decide?"

"I've got just the thing," says Joey Chicago, pulling out a pair of tall glasses and little paper umbrellas.

"And what is that?" asks Dugan.

"A pair of Zombies," says Joey Chicago.

This story originally appeared in *Blood Lite*, Gallery Books, 2008.

Mike Resnick is, according to *Locus*, the all-time leading award winner, living or dead, for short science fiction. He is the winner of five Hugos (from a record thirty-seven nominations), a Nebula, and other major awards in the USA, France, Japan, Croatia, Catalonia, Poland and Spain.

He is the author of seventy-five novels, almost 300 stories, and three screenplays, and has edited forty-two anthologies. He currently edits *Galaxy's Edge* magazine and Stellar Guild books. His web page is www.mikeresnick.com.

THE BLUE CORPSE CORPS
JIM C. HINES

HALF THE GOBLINS under Jig's command died over the course
of the battle.

Given that goblin casualties were usually double that
amount, and more importantly, that Jig himself was in the half
that survived, he wasn't going to complain.

The rest of the survivors showed no such restraint. They had
gathered in the shade of some stunted pine trees on the way
back to the lair. Jig sat a short distance from the others,
dumping rocks and dirt from his boot as he listened to their
grumbling.

"It's not natural," said Valkaf, a younger warrior who had
lost her left ear during the fighting. "What do we care about
renegade human wizards and outlaws? Let the humans kill each
other. Just as long as they stay out of our tunnels."

"The only reason the king hasn't sent his army to kill every
goblin in the lair is because of the treaty," Jig pointed out.

Valkaf laughed, a nasty sound that brought back memories of Jig's younger days. He had been a small, scrawny muckworker, and had spent most of his childhood learning how to survive the torments of the bigger goblins . . . which included pretty much everyone. But those lessons had served him well as a small, scrawny adult.

"So instead, we do the human king's dirty work," Valkaf said. "Hunting his criminals."

"Only the ones who hide on our mountain," Jig mumbled.

Heat wafted from Jig's right shoulder as Smudge, his pet fire-spider, reacted to the growing hostility in Valkaf's words. Not that Jig needed the warning. The other goblins had already begun to split into two groups. Most gathered by Valkaf, the only exceptions being Braf, who appeared oblivious, and Skalk, who had taken several nasty wounds during the fighting.

Jig couldn't blame them. He was the one who had signed the treaty with King Wendel, naively hoping it would end the fighting between goblins and humans. Instead, it had simply shifted the war to a different front, one for which goblins were ill-prepared: politics.

Pages and pages of obligations. Taxes to be paid, and duties to be performed . . . including the defense of goblin territory against all outlaws. To neglect that duty was to violate the treaty. So the fighting had continued, only the goblins now paid taxes for the privilege. They were tired of it, and none moreso than Jig himself.

Braf scratched the inside of his nostril with his little finger. "At least we got to burn a human camp. And I got to punch a horse."

One of Valkaf's supporters laughed. "That was no horse, you

idiot. That was a donkey."

"I thought it was a cow," said another.

Braf's expression was a carefully crafted mask of vacant confusion. "Well, it was a *big* cow."

It was enough to break the tension. The goblins began to relax, boasting about their triumphs over the wizard and his magically cursed warriors who had refused to die. Jig caught Braf's eye long enough to give him a tiny nod of thanks.

"Hey, Skalk stopped whining!" Valkaf kicked the wounded goblin in the side. "Good timing. I'm hungry."

"We'll be back at the lair before nightfall," Jig said. "We could bring him back and let Golaka roast him properly, with that spider egg jelly she makes—"

"I'm hungry now," Valkaf shouted. "Unless *you* want to haul his carcass up the mountainside? Let's build a fire and toss him in."

"Save me some palm meat!"

"I want a leg. No, wait. How bruised are the arms?"

Jig's mouth watered. He *was* hungry after the battle, and—

Heat seared Jig's cheek. Smudge was growing hotter with every passing moment. The palm-sized spider paced a tight circle on Jig's leather shoulder pad. When one hairy leg brushed Jig's ear, it was hot enough to raise blisters.

Jig tugged the shoulder pad further from his face, nearly dislodging his spectacles in his haste. He perked his good ear and searched the woods, but he neither saw nor heard anything dangerous. So what was Smudge reacting to?

"Looks like one of the humans already started in on him." Valkaf pointed to a nasty bite on Skalk's shoulder. The blue skin had turned black, and blood oozed from the wound. "Let

Jig have that part."

"This might not be a good idea," said Jig. He stepped closer to the body. A tiny wave of red fire rippled over Smudge's back in response. "I've only seen Smudge this scared a few other times."

Braf hesitated. "But Skalk's so well-tenderized from the fighting."

Jig backed away. He didn't bother to argue further. They wouldn't listen. They might follow his plans in battle, because they knew he was good at surviving, but this was *food*.

Braf scowled and rubbed his stomach. "I'd better not. I had some bad dwarf yesterday, and my stomach hasn't recovered. If I eat Skalk, my trousers will regret it before the day's over."

Jig's stomach gurgled as the others began roasting Skalk's body. He scowled at Smudge. "You'd better be right about this . . ."

DESPITE SMUDGE'S FEARS, they reached the lair without incident. Jig relaxed somewhat as he left the moonlit sky for the security of the obsidian tunnels. His warriors exchanged boasts with the guards as they passed into the wide, sour-smelling cavern which was home to more than two hundred goblins.

Green muckfires burned around the edge of the cavern. The scent of fresh meat made his mouth water as he passed Golaka's kitchen, but that smell was soon overpowered by muck smoke, goblin sweat, and fouler things.

Jig kept his head down as he made his way toward a smaller cave at the back of the lair where goblins fought for sleeping space. He claimed an old blanket in a bumpy corner nearest the crack connecting this cave to the lair.

Sleep refused to come. Images from the day's battle blurred through his mind. Groaning human warriors who refused to stay dead. The memories blurred into fights from months and years before. No matter how many battles Jig survived, there was always another enemy. Dragons and pixies, humans and orcs, and of course his fellow goblins. He had survived for years on trickery, cleverness, and luck, but it wouldn't last forever.

The chief's voice echoed through the lair, jolting Jig from his memories. "Where is that runt Jig?"

The other goblins in the sleeping cave moved away as Jig groaned and stood. Whatever the problem, they wanted nothing to do with it. Smudge grew warmer as Jig trudged into the main lair.

"What is that?" Trok demanded, jabbing his sword toward the entrance where Braf, Valkaf, and one of the guards were fighting a battered goblin.

Jig adjusted his spectacles. "That's . . . that's Skalk. But he died."

"Does he look dead?" Trok was a fierce figure of a goblin, strong and well-armed. He had taken to filing his fangs lately. The tips were white and needle-sharp. "What happened to him?"

"We . . . kind of ate him. The other goblins did, I mean."

Skalk looked like a rag doll that had been devoured by tunnel-cats, then hacked back up. One leg was missing; the other ended at the knee. His left hand was gone as well. He was filthy, and the fingers of his right hand were bloody. He must have dragged himself back to the lair.

Blackened skin cracked and oozed as he fought the other

goblins. The few uncooked areas of skin were a sickly blue-gray. Jig could see a whitish film covering his eyes . . . just like the human zombies they had fought before.

"If you're hungry and want to eat one of your wounded, that's one thing," Trok yelled. "But *kill him first!*"

"We did!" Jig protested. "I mean, he was!"

Skalk groaned as Braf rammed a long spear through his ribs. It didn't slow him down. He reached out, trying to pull himself along the spear toward Braf even as Valkaf hacked off his other hand with her axe.

"The humans we fought were the same way." Jig swallowed. "When that human bit Skalk, it must have infected him somehow. You'll have to burn him or cut him into pieces to stop him."

Trok pursed his lips. "Warriors who don't die."

"They die," Jig said. "It just doesn't slow them down. They keep—Oh, no." He recognized the calculating look on Trok's face.

By now, Valkaf had grabbed the other end of the spear. She and Braf lifted Skalk off the ground. He let out a confused moan as his body slowly upended. His head swung to and fro over the floor. The stumps of his arms reached uselessly for the spear.

"Imagine an army of goblins who can't be killed," Trok said.

"Because they're already dead!" But it was too late. Others had overheard.

One of the closest goblins sprinted toward Skalk. "I want to be unkillable!" He tried to shove his arm into Skalk's mouth, but Braf kicked him away. More closed in, pushing and yelling in their eagerness to become zombies.

"You have to stop them," Jig said. "They'll attack anything, even their own kind. They won't obey orders. They don't care who's in charge. All they do is kill and eat."

"So they'll be no different than most goblin warriors," Trok said. He waded into the middle of the crowd, tossing the other goblins aside. He started to speak, and then his gaze fixed on Valkaf.

Skalk had gouged her arm in the fighting, but the wound wasn't bleeding like a normal injury. Instead, the cut oozed dark, mudlike blood . . . just like Skalk. Valkaf glanced down as though surprised.

"You're like him, aren't you?" Trok tapped Skalk's head with the toe of his boot.

"But she wasn't bitten," Jig protested. His stomach tightened. Valkaf *had* eaten plenty of Skalk the night before. No wonder Smudge had warned him against it.

"Behold the first of my zombie warriors," Trok shouted. "We'll call them Trok's Trudging Troops! The Blue Corpse Corps! An unstoppable army of blue death!"

"That's true." Valkaf's words were slightly slurred. She dropped her end of the spear, slammed her axe through Skalk's neck, then turned toward Trok. "You can't stop me, can you?"

"Oh, dung," Jig whispered.

Valkaf raised her bloody axe. "I challenge Trok for leadership of the goblin lair!"

GOBLINS HAD NO rules regarding challenges for leadership. Indeed, often the challenge wasn't even announced until after the challenger finished stabbing the former chief in the back.

Valkaf charged. Trok swore, grabbed the nearest goblin, and

flung him into Valkaf's path. She struck the poor goblin aside, but doing so tied up her axe long enough for Trok to draw his own weapon, a two-handed sword with brass spikes on the hilt and crossguard.

Jig pushed his way to the back of the crowd, where he could watch the fight through a protective layer of goblin spectators. Trok had already hit Valkaf twice, cutting her left arm and stabbing her through the gut. Neither wound affected her as far as Jig could see.

Jig frowned as he watched Valkaf fight. Against the humans, she had been vicious and gleeful, fighting with her own unique and terrifying style. Now that joy was gone, and her attacks were as straightforward as those of a child. Straightforward but powerful, and she showed no sign of weariness.

Trok backed away, earning jeers from the watching goblins, but Jig saw what Trok was doing. Every step he retreated brought him closer to one of the shallow muck pits, burning with foul-smelling green flame. If swords wouldn't stop Valkaf, fire would.

Heat pulled Jig's attention to Smudge, and then to the four goblins beyond who had broken away from the crowd. They gathered around the body of the hapless goblin Trok had flung into the path of Valkaf's axe.

Braf saw them as well. "Stop that," he shouted. "Wait until Golaka has the chance to cook him. And save some for the rest of us!" He started to reach for one of the goblins.

All four snarled, and Braf jumped away. Blood and worse dripped from the goblins' fangs, and they shared the same vacant, hungry expressions Jig remembered all too well from the human zombies.

Jig didn't move. He tried not to breathe until the goblins slowly turned their attention back to the corpse.

"Who starts with the head?" Braf whispered, sidling closer to Jig. "Ears are a chewy treat, sure, but there's so much better meat on the body. Brains are too slimy for my taste."

"The dead humans were the same," Jig said. "Unkillable, but they kept stopping to eat the corpses, especially the brains."

It had been a good thing, too. Ultimately, Jig had laid out five of his fallen goblins and waited for the dead humans to feed. Once they were all gathered together, it had been simple enough to encircle them in flames.

But these goblins were more alert than the zombies Jig had fought. Maybe they hadn't completely succumbed to whatever magic sickness they had eaten with Skalk's body, but all too soon they would be the rotted, mindless killers Jig had faced before.

The zombies snarled again, but this time their hostility was aimed inward. One jabbed a knife into another's chest, distracting him long enough for the first goblin to sneak in and snatch a bite to eat. They were like tunnel cats fighting over a meal.

"What do we do?" Braf asked.

"They're not the only ones we have to worry about." Jig searched the crowd. Where were the other survivors of his last battle? They would all be dying from the inside out as the magic took them.

The commotion was attracting attention away from Trok and Valkaf. One of the younger goblins pointed to the zombie with the knife in his chest. "Hey, there are more!" Before Jig could react, the young goblin ran toward the zombies. "Bite me, too!"

Jig caught Braf's eye. Braf inclined his head ever so slightly. As the goblin sprinted past, Braf extended the butt of his spear. The goblin hit the floor with a crack, but it was too late. Others were closing in, hoping either to be bitten or to eat the zombies, whatever it took to become undead.

Cheers broke out on the far side of the lair. Jig glimpsed Valkaf stumbling forward, bathed in green fire and missing an arm, but still fighting. If one zombie was giving Trok this much trouble, more would pretty well wipe out the lair.

"I've been bitten!" A gleeful goblin waved his arm in the air, showing off two bloody fang marks. "I'm unkillable! I'm—"

Jig stabbed him in the back. The other goblins froze. The one Jig had stabbed looked down, gurgled, and fell. Two of the zombies immediately broke away and began to feed on his body.

"Maybe he wasn't bitten hard enough?" one goblin suggested.

Braf punched him in the head.

Jig raised his voice. "These zombies can't make you unkillable. They're not . . . um . . . they're not ripe yet."

Braf sniffed. "They smell pretty ripe to me."

"Help me get the zombies to the kitchen," Jig said. "We can keep them in Golaka's slaughter pit until they're ready." The pit was as secure as any dungeon, both by nature of the pit itself and because anyone who escaped still had to get past Golaka.

"How do we get them into the pit without getting bitten?" Braf asked.

Jig glanced at the two corpses. He grabbed a sword from another goblin, jumped in, and swung, severing the closer corpse's head. "Jab the head with your spear and toss it into the pit. They'll follow."

"Gross." But Braf obeyed. He returned a short time later, wiping goo from his spear. "Golaka isn't happy about this. I told her it was your idea."

Jig grimaced. One more confrontation he wasn't looking forward to, but at least the immediate threat had passed. Over on the far side of the lair, the fighting was finally coming to a close. Valkaf had lost her weapon and three of her limbs. What followed wasn't so much a battle as simple butchery.

He reached up to pet Smudge, who was beginning to cool now that the zombies were gone.

"I've changed my mind," Trok yelled, wiping sweat from his face. "Kill every last one of those walking corpses."

Good. Let Trok finish cleaning up this mess. Jig would return to the sleeping cave and—

"And anyone who could have been exposed!" Trok added.

Anyone who could have been . . . Jig's chest tightened. He looked at Braf.

As one, they turned and fled.

"THIS IS THE STUPIDEST plan in the history of plans."

"Shut up," whispered Jig.

"It's not even a plan." Braf picked at the grime on the floor. "Of all the places to hide, you picked Golaka's slaughter pit?"

"Nobody's found us yet, have they?" Jig rubbed his knee, which had been badly bruised from jumping into the pit. Fortunately, one of the zombies had broken his fall. They were still squabbling over the brain of their last victim, but that wouldn't last long.

"And how do we get out?" Braf stabbed a finger toward the faint green light overhead. "The walls are too greasy to climb."

"I'm working on it!" Jig leaned back, banging his head against the rock. Braf was right, of course. It was a stupid plan. It hadn't even been a plan. More like blind panic. Eventually either Golaka would find them and toss them into her pot, or else Trok would figure out where they'd gone. At least Golaka would be quick, and she generally kept her knives sharp, so it shouldn't hurt as much . . .

In the end, it was Trok who peered down into the pit. "Not so clever after all, are you?"

"We didn't eat Skalk," Jig protested. "Neither of us has been bitten. We're not going to turn into zombies!"

"I'm not taking that risk. You saw what happened with Valkaf." He rubbed his shoulder, which looked like it had taken a nasty cut from her axe. "The last thing I need is an undead Jig walking around causing trouble with his zombie spider."

Jig's heart pounded so hard he could barely breathe. Braf's spear had broken in the fall, so he couldn't reach Trok. Jig had his knife. He could try to throw it at Trok, but that still left them trapped in the pit. Not to mention he had never had much luck with thrown weapons. On the other hand, it wasn't like things could get much worse.

Trok disappeared before he could try. A short time later, another body tumbled into the pit, landing with a sickly crunch. Several others followed, corpses and zombies both. Smudge flared to light, illuminating the groaning survivors from Jig's last battle.

"Now what?" Braf muttered.

"I don't know." Jig sagged against the wall. He had fought

more battles than he could count, but nothing ever changed. Kill the humans, and the goblin zombies tried to eat you. Get rid of them, and Trok sentenced you to death. It never ended.

"Get that filth out of my slaughter pit!" Golaka's shout echoed through the cavern.

"We will." Trok peeked back into the pit. "We were going to burn them all, but it was stinking up the lair. Easier to leave 'em down there to rot away."

Jig threw his dagger. It missed Trok by a wide margin, then clattered back down into the pit, nearly striking Jig's foot.

"Stupidest plan in history," Braf repeated.

JIG NUDGED SMUDGE'S fuzzy thorax, trying to scoot him up the wall to safety. Smudge kept climbing halfway up the pit, then scurrying back down to stare at Jig, as though wondering what was wrong that Jig wasn't following.

"Will you stop worrying about the stupid spider?" Braf snapped. The zombies were licking their fingers and fangs as they finished off the last of the corpses. One drooled as he studied Braf, who shook his broken spear in response. "Eat Jig first. Everyone knows his brain is too big."

"But Braf's meatier," Jig countered.

"Eat," said the closest zombie, slurring the word. She started toward Braf, who clubbed her back with the butt of the spear.

"Even if you eat us, you'll still rot down here," Jig pointed out. Flies had already settled on the zombies. Normally Smudge would have been in paradise, pouncing from the wall to cook the hapless insects, but he wasn't going anywhere near those goblins. "There won't be anything left but maggots and bones."

"That's your plan?" Braf asked. "You're trying to reason with the dead goblins?"

Jig sniffed the air. Over the putrefaction of the zombies, the scent of cooking meat filled the pit. The spices made Jig's eyes water. Golaka must have overspiced the meat, trying to overpower the rot from the pit.

The others smelled it as well. Undead or not, they were still goblin enough to prefer Golaka's cooking. They pressed against the wall, arms stretched upward.

"Probably leftover bear," Braf guessed. "Or maybe leftovers from the hunters who died killing the bear."

Jig's stomach gurgled. On top of everything else, he hadn't had a decent meal in at least a day. He had fought more battles than he could remember, and *this* was how he would die? Hungry and miserable, devoured by the rotting remnants of his own warriors? Meanwhile, with Jig gone, the treaty with the humans would follow. Trok would drag the goblins into all-out war within weeks, if not days.

"I know that look," said Braf.

Jig wiped sweat from his nose, then replaced his spectacles. "Hey, Golaka?" He called again, trying to pitch his voice so it wouldn't carry beyond the kitchen. After a third attempt, he heard footsteps approaching, and Golaka peered into the pit.

Golaka was the largest, strongest goblin in the lair. She could have killed Trok one-handed, but she had no interest in being chief. Her straggly hair had thinned in recent years, and her face was like cracked blue leather. She wore a heavy apron so stained it probably carried a meal's worth of food all by itself.

"You know the rules, Jig," she called. "If the food can't keep quiet, I dump the grease pot on its head."

"Wait!" Jig tried to force his voice down to a less frightened pitch. "You know you can't eat these goblins. They'll be rotting for weeks. It will stink up the whole kitchen. The smell will probably even get into your food."

Golaka said nothing. But she wasn't dumping hot grease on his head, which was a hopeful sign.

"Get me out of here, and I promise I'll—Ouch!" Jig rubbed his arm. "Get Braf and me out of here, and I'll take care of the zombies."

"How do you intend to do that?"

"I'll need you to cook something for me. One of your specialties . . ."

JIG CREPT OUT of the kitchen, both hands clutching a covered clay bowl. The buzz of voices died down as the nearest goblins noticed him.

Braf followed, clutching five leather leashes with both hands. Each leash was secured to the neck of a zombie, and all five strained to reach Jig.

He heard Trok's roar from the far side of the lair. Goblins split a path as Trok stomped toward Jig, flanked by armed guards. "I don't believe it! How in the name of all that's edible does a scrawny, miserable runt like you survive these things?"

A flicker of anger stirred in Jig's gut, or maybe that was just hunger. He straightened.

"You thought you'd try to turn the zombies on me, eh?" Trok eyed Braf and the leashed zombies. "You know they'll rip you apart before they even reach me."

"You think it's an accident I'm still alive?" Jig asked softly. "This scrawny runt has survived more battles in this past year than you have in your entire life."

Trok's eye narrowed. "Sure. Battles against *humans.*"

"And orcs. And hobgoblins. Even a dragon." Technically, someone else had killed the dragon, but Trok didn't know that.

"That will make it more impressive when I run you through."

"I'm not scared of you." To Jig's amazement, it was the truth. He had fought too many opponents, survived too many times, and Trok simply didn't frighten him anymore.

Trok pulled out his sword.

All right, maybe Jig was a little scared. Mostly though, he was just tired. "I challenge you for leadership of the lair!"

Trok laughed. "You don't even have a weapon."

Jig yanked the cover from the bowl. Steam rose from the red-gray sludge within. He flung the contents at Trok, doing his best to avoid splashing anyone else. Especially himself.

Trok wiped his face. His skin was a vivid blue, but the burns weren't serious. He raised his sword. "If you think hot gruel is enough to—"

"It's not gruel," Jig interrupted. "It's pudding. Minced bear brain pudding, spiced with fire-spider eggs."

Braf released the leashes.

Smudge seared Jig's ear as the zombies rushed past on either side, but they ignored Jig completely.

"I survive because I'm smarter than you," Jig muttered. He doubted anyone heard over the screams.

THE NEXT BATTLE came a month later. This time it was a band of human mercenaries, led by a young human in garish colors. Jig popped a fried lizard tail into his mouth and crunched happily as he watched them approach.

"How long until the attack?" asked Braf, settling in beside him.

Jig offered him a lizard tail. "Don't ask me. You're the chief."

"Don't remind me." There was just enough hostility in Braf's voice to make Jig scoot sideways. Jig's reign as chief had been the shortest in goblin history. He had named Braf the new chief before Trok's blood was even cool.

In a way, Jig owed Trok thanks. If not for Trok, it would be Jig himself down on the mountainside preparing for this battle. Instead, Jig got to watch from a small outcropping high above the lair, protected by rocks and gnarled trees.

The mercenaries reached the mouth of the lair. Jig heard shouts from within.

"There they are." Braf pointed to a handful of goblins running down a trail. Each carried a small, goo-filled bladder which they flung at the humans.

"We should find a better way to throw those," Jig said as the makeshift missiles exploded, splattering cold pudding on the mercenaries. Slings would be too messy. "Maybe handheld catapults?"

One goblin took an arrow to the stomach, and the rest scattered, earning taunts from the humans.

Braf snickered. "They think the goblins are running from *them*."

Jig could already see the first goblin zombie shambling up the path. "They look pretty well-preserved."

"Keeping them up in a colder cave was a good idea."

"So were the spiders." Jig had gathered all the spiders he could find, releasing them into the cave where the zombies were leashed and guarded. No fire-spiders; the cave was too cold for them anyway. But there were plenty of others to help protect the zombies from flies and other insects.

Jig reached up to pet Smudge. Trok might not have thought things through, but Jig had. Enthusiasm at joining the living dead had died out once the rest of the lair saw a few zombies in more advanced states of rot. Few were willing to risk their important bits falling off.

One zombie stopped to eat the fallen goblin while the rest closed in on the mercenaries, who had stopped laughing.

"You're sure they kept enough pudding in reserve to get them all back to the cave?" Braf asked.

Jig shrugged. If not, each of the zombie keepers carried a pointed skull-cracking hammer to use on whoever was responsible for forgetting. "They'll find a way to lure the zombies back."

"It won't last forever, you know."

"I know." Goblin plans rarely did. Sooner or later a zombie would escape, or one of the keepers would get careless, or the humans would find a way to destroy the zombies. When that happened, Jig would deal with it.

But until then, he intended to sit back, eat a few more lizard tails, and enjoy the well-earned rest.

This story originally appeared in *When the Hero Comes Home*, Dragon Moon Press, 2011.

Jim C. Hines's first novel was *Goblin Quest*, the humorous tale of a nearsighted goblin runt and his pet fire-spider. Actor and author Wil Wheaton described the book as "too f***ing cool for words," which is pretty much the Best Blurb Ever. After finishing the goblin trilogy, he went on to write the Princess series of fairy tale retellings and the Magic ex Libris books, a modern-day fantasy series about a magic-wielding librarian, a dryad, a secret society founded by Johannes Gutenberg, a flaming spider, and an enchanted convertible. He's also the author of the Fable Legends tie-in *Blood of Heroes*. His short fiction has appeared in more than 50 magazines and anthologies.

Jim is an active blogger about topics ranging from sexism and harassment to zombie-themed Christmas carols, and won the Hugo Award for Best Fan Writer in 2012. He has an undergraduate degree in psychology and a Master's in English, and lives with his wife and two children in mid-Michigan. You can find him online at www.jimchines.com.

LIBRARIANS IN THE BRANCH LIBRARY OF BABEL

SHAENON K. GARRITY

with apologies to Jorge Luis Borges

THE LIBRARY OF BABEL is one of those extrusions of pure logic into our universe that you get sometimes, a library of infinite size containing all possible books. Logically (and so actually), almost all these books are full of nonsense—meaningless collections of letters or even just random markings. Once in a very long while a book containing a few readable lines is found, and the people who find it rejoice. The search for meaning in the Library's honeycomb rooms is seldom rewarded, but really, most patrons just come in off the street to use the restroom, and the Library has plenty of restrooms.

I'm sorry. That was unfair to our patrons.

Carol and I worked at the Branch Library of Babel in Dublin, Ohio.

First:

THE BRANCH LIBRARY is infinite. All Libraries of Babel are infinite. The Branch Libraries are just smaller.

Which is larger: all possible numbers, or all possible even numbers? Logically, they're the same size. A fraction of an infinite set is still infinite, isn't it? By the same logic, it's possible for an infinite library in which every other book is, say, Stephen King's *Cujo* to still contain all possible books, same as the main library. It's just that you stand a 50% chance of getting *Cujo*.

I'm only using *Cujo* as an example. As you know, we did not work at an infinite library where every other book is Stephen King's *Cujo*. That library is in El Paso.

I know it's confusing. We used to have a laminated sign behind the front desk explaining the Library system, with all the math, but a few years ago someone stole it and by then we'd lost the laminating machine.

Second:

CAROL AND I WERE librarians at an infinite library where roughly 72% of books are *Moby-Dick*. Our library contains, within in its stacks, every edition of *Moby-Dick* that ever has been or will be or could be published. So does the main Library, of course, but at our branch the probability of coming across one of them is much higher.

The main Library, as I'm sure many of you know, is a sphere of infinite diameter packed with small, dimly lit hexagonal book-lined cells. Our branch in Dublin is a converted firehouse. Was. No, is. Inside is an endless labyrinth of whitewashed cinderblock rooms with all-weather carpeting and fluorescent lights. It has a faint smell of cat pee. We do not keep cats, out of consideration to our patrons with allergies or phobias; unfortunately, we suspect that a fractional but infinite number of the people squatting in the Branch Library stacks do.

In the Branch Library we have located two 1851 first editions of *Moby-Dick* from Harper and Brothers in the black cloth and orange endpapers, one with light foxing to title and text, the other significantly water-damaged and missing the front cover and part of the spine. We have also found a book that appears to be an 1851 first edition but contains no words, only hundreds of thousands of small hash marks with no meaning we can figure. We have found one volume of the three-volume slipcover with woodcuts by Rockwell Kent published in 1930, #496 in limited edition of 1,000 copies. Presumably the other two volumes are somewhere in the collection, and the 999 other copies of the set, and an infinite number of additional sets as well. We have found *Moby-Dick* in French, Swiss, Korean and a Vigenère encryption with several intentional misspellings to frustrate codebreakers (Carol cracked it). We have found a dog-eared Tor Classics paperback printed in 1996, signed by Herman Melville "with love to Kelly." We have found many, many copies of the CliffsNotes.

The readable *Moby-Dick*s, what we call the general-circulation copies, we used to shelve in the front rooms near the entrance for the convenience of our patrons. We were working very hard to make our library more convenient.

We had both subtly and spectacularly misprinted *Moby-Dick*s, *Moby-Dick*s riddled with misspellings and bad punctuation, *Moby-Dick*s where words disappear or run backward. I personally found eight copies with alternate endings. Three were gibberish and one was just the last chapter of *The Great Gatsby*, but the others weren't bad. We had two *Moby-Dick*s with sex scenes (Queequeg/Ishmael, Queequeg/Ahab). We had several about a black whale, and many where the whale was called Mocha Dick. If the deviations weren't too extreme—say, a few letter Es missing from one of the chapters like "Measure of the Whale's Skeleton" that everyone but Carol skips anyway—we used to shelve the book in front. Some of the others, the interesting ones, we kept in the back office. We felt we should do *something* with them. Not many of the *Moby-Dick*s we found were either useful or interesting. Most were seas of typographical babble from which rose, like coffins, floating phrases about sperm whales, shipbuilding and revenge.

Over time, working at the Branch Library, I came to think of all books as just misprinted editions of *Moby-Dick*. Carol told me she felt the same way.

I dwell in Possibility—A fairer House than Prose . . . Dickinson, Emily Dickinson, sorry. I do read things other than *Moby-Dick*, or used to.

Third:

THE DUBLIN CITY COUNCIL voted to cut off funding to the Branch Library of Babel.

I didn't get the news right away. I was in the deep stacks, the infinite network of unexplored, unorganized and uncatalogued rooms. At this point in my career at the Branch Library, an expedition into the uncatalogued collection required a journey of one to six weeks, round trip. Most times, I set out with a small team of assistant librarians and hired a local squatter as a guide. On this expedition I also took Ted, our star volunteer. Ted is an English instructor at the community college. I've heard a lot of people here say that no one uses the Branch Library except Melville scholars, but Ted's focus is the Transcendentalists, so there you are.

The room we were cataloguing had squatters, a fairly large encampment. They watched us warily as we set up camp, moving only to throw the occasional fresh book onto their cooking fire. We used to put signs up telling them not to do that, but it never helped. It's why I worked so hard to catalogue the Library—if I could save just a few more readable books from the squatters' fires or the walls of their papier-mâché huts or those flocks of rainbow-hued booklice that swarm every seven years, I would be doing my duty. The books deserved as much.

This particular encampment was non-hostile, I'm glad to say. Many are. We gave them a small electric cookstove as a peace offering, and they allowed us to bivouac in the opposite corner of the room.

It was not a fruitful expedition. We found two moderately irregular *Moby-Dick*s and a Nora Roberts novel. Nothing else in the room was worth adding to general circulation. We prepared catalog tags in silence, trying to stay cheerful. Statistically speaking, we could have done worse.

With our work done, we packed and began the long trek back through the already-catalogued rooms. Liz, one of our assistant librarians, handled the map and compass. She's still working on her master's in library science, but she has a BS in post-Euclidean topology.

On the third day of the return journey, the expedition was ambushed by hostile squatters. They wore shredded paper woven into their hair—I averted my eyes from the print, praying it hadn't been one of the legible books—and their faces were painted in blue and black ink and blood-red words: *Discarded, Second Notice.* I Tasered three before they fell back. Their crude spears . . .

Yes, yes, sorry. I'm getting off track.

Carol looked up from her coffee as we staggered into the front office, streaked with blood and dust. *But O this dust that I shall drive away / Is flowers and kings* . . . She took in the bandage on Liz's upper arm—a squatter's arrow had nicked her in the raid—and hurried over. "The books. Did they get the books?"

I opened my pack. "No, but it's just these three paperbacks."

"You could have given them the Nora Roberts."

"Carol!" I'd never heard her speak that way.

That was when she told me.

"The City Council's shutting us down?" It wasn't real. It couldn't be real. "But we've gotten so much cataloged this year! We've added so much to circulation!"

"They said they don't see the point," said Carol. "They said it's a, a waste of taxpayer money. They said nobody in Dublin wants to pay for people to look for old whaling novels."

"You talked to them? They were here?"

She shook her head. "I only found out about it when a reporter for the *Villager* called me to get a quote. I was like, they voted *what*? So I called them. Talked to one of the councilmen, I don't remember, Dan somebody." She trailed off, staring into nothing. I'd never seen Carol looking so small.

"We'll fight it," I said. "It's an infinite library, for the love of Pete! They're rare! We'll get it on the National Register of Historic Places! Or the world one, the World Heritage Sites!"

Carol smiled. "You get to work on that, Bev," she said.

I could tell she'd already given up hope.

Fourth:

IT IS SURPRISINGLY hard to get something onto the National Register of Historic Places.

Or any kind of registry, it turns out. I made all the calls. I filled out all the paperwork, when there was paperwork. More often, I got to the end of a long phone tree and an hour of hold music (the National Register plays the Beatles—isn't that odd?) only to be told to take it up with the government. Which I did. I wrote to both senators and our congressman. And now I'm here, so there's that.

Carol spent our last weeks wandering the stacks. I drifted around the back office, sorting and resorting the special collection. *Moby-Dick* as a play. *Moby-Dick* in space. *Moby-Dick* scrimshawed onto sheets of horn. They were very pretty, some of them. I always thought so. I wish I had some to show you now, but you know.

"We need an angel investor, is what we need," said Ted.

Ted and I were lingering late at one of the computer kiosks, combing the Internet for nonprofits that might have a little arts funding left. Earlier in the evening, Ted had given a PowerPoint presentation on Walt Whitman as a special event for our patrons, "to raise awareness," he said. It's so very Ted that he thought Whitman would get rear ends into seats.

Oh, well, it was a lovely presentation. Very witty. And a few of our regular seniors did show up. Mostly, though, it was nice to see more of Ted.

"We get a private investor with an interest in the library," said Ted. "There aren't many Libraries of Babel, are there? And this is the only one with all the *Moby-Dick*s."

"They all have all the *Moby-Dick*s," I corrected him. "Our library just has *more* of all the *Moby-Dick*s."

"It's unique, is what I mean. That's got to be worth something to somebody."

"Sell the library?" This was worse than Carol wanting to give up the Nora Roberts. "But it belongs to the people."

"Bev, the people have made it pretty clear what they want to do with it." He was right, as you all know. By then we'd gotten word of your plans to bulldoze the firehouse and put in an additional parking lot for the Marc's Discount Store across the street.

. . . Please, everyone. I'm not trying to start a fight. All water under the bridge now, isn't it? My point is, the firehouse was going to be torn down. And when the firehouse was gone, the library inside would go . . . wherever it came from, I guess. Scientists say the singularity collapses. I watched a video on it when I started work at the Branch Library, but that was a long time ago.

"I can't imagine what price you could put on an infinite collection," I said. "Anyway, who would want it? It doesn't . . . that is, on a strictly practical level, it doesn't *do* anything."

"It creates order," said a voice behind us. "It reverses entropy. It gives meaning."

Ted and I jumped like a couple of rabbits. We'd forgotten about Carol, and she should've gone home hours ago anyway. But I knew she hadn't left, and I'm sure Ted knew it too. Deep down I knew she hadn't left the library all week.

Hm? Where did she go? Anywhere. The stacks are infinite. There are campgrounds of colorful leather and cardboard, lean-to shelters of dismantled shelving, domed paper tents with gilt-edged windows, marketplaces where a library card can buy wonders. *A glorious court, where hourly I converse / With the old sages and philosophers. . . .* It's not my business, and it's certainly not yours. But it's dangerous, really dangerous, to go in alone. That's why we have Liz with the topology degree. Had Liz. You could wander there forever and never find your way out. That's how the library got its small but infinite population of squatters, and the cats I never saw but could always, faintly, smell.

There was so much more in the stacks than any one person could ever see.

Ted ran to Carol's side, and then I saw the ink in her hair, the smears of blood on her face. "Christ, Carol," said Ted, the first time I'd ever heard him take the Lord's name in vain. "Where were you?"

"You got into a skirmish," I said. "Are you crazy, fighting the squatters all by yourself?"

"I haven't been fighting anyone," said Carol. "I might be crazy. It's hard to tell. Did I hear you seriously talking about selling the library?"

"I have my doubts that anyone would buy it," I said, "but as a last-ditch effort—"

"Let some illiterate with too much money seal it off for his private collection?" Carol suddenly looked more alive than she'd been in days. "Let it get neglected and overgrown?"

"I don't see any other way, realistically—"

"That's not what libraries are for."

Ted put an arm around her. I'd always known he stuck around for her, really. It had been silly of me to invite him along on the expedition in the stacks, but I'm allowed a little silliness, aren't I?

"You know," Carol was saying, "my favorite chapters of *Moby-Dick* are the ones people say are boring."

Funny thing—I'd never heard her talk about the book itself before. "'Of Whales in Paint'?" I said. "'The Whiteness of the Whale'? 'The Right Whale's Head—A Contrasted View'?"

"That's right. All the stuff about whale biology and history and stuff. That's where the real story is." Carol's eyes were unfocused, like she was staring at something a long way away. Or maybe she was just exhausted.

I should have been sympathetic. I should have worried about the blood. But at that moment, Carol got under my skin. You know how that is, someone just getting under your skin? "And what do you think the real story is?"

Carol slid a *Moby-Dick* from the nearest shelf. Penguin paperback with French flaps, very recent edition. "*Moby-Dick*? It's about trying to categorize the uncategorizable. It's about trying to control something too big to be controlled."

"You said the library creates order."

"That's right."

"But it doesn't, Carol." It was late and I was so, so tired. "It's full of nonsense. Room after room of nonsense."

"Carol's right," said Ted. Of course he would. "Statistically, it contains significantly less nonsense than the main library." He thought for a second. "Significantly less nonsense than the rest of the universe, then."

"But still an infinite amount of nonsense," I said. "Can we go home? Let's all go home, Carol."

"I would prefer not to," said Carol. She laughed faintly. "We've never found 'Bartleby the Scrivener,' have we?"

With that, she wandered back into the stacks, swinging the paperback like a little purse.

We let her go, and I drove Ted home. "You want to know a secret?" I said as I pulled out. "I always skip those chapters Carol was talking about. I like the adventure story. The tragedy of Ahab chasing something he can never catch. And of course the funny parts."

"You want to know a secret?" said Ted. "I've never read *Moby-Dick* at all. I've been terrified of telling Carol."

That made us laugh, and I was glad to have him around again.

"But I thought Ahab did catch the whale at the end," said Ted.

"That's true," I said. "He did."

Fifth:

I DON'T WANT to be pushy, but I'd appreciate it if you could stop telling me to hurry it up. I'm trying to explain. . . .

Well, no, I don't know what happened. Not really. I have my guess, is all. Now may I have some quiet, please?

Thank you.

That night was the last time I saw much of Ted. He started following Carol into the stacks, at first because he was concerned about her, then . . . well, I'm sure he had his reasons. I ignored them and focused on saving the library.

The *Columbus Dispatch* did a little news item about the library closing, and we got a handful of supportive emails. At the eleventh hour, I drove out to the city for a weekend to meet with some people who had made noises about doing a fundraiser for us. It came to nothing. I won't bore you with the details, because it really was awful. Just a dead end, like everything else.

I drove back to Dublin the night before the Branch Library's last day of operations. We had activities planned. A trivia contest. A book sale. Liz had promised to hang crepe streamers while I was gone.

The last time I saw Carol? I don't remember. I know the last time I talked to Ted, though. It was on my drive back from Columbus. It wasn't like him to call. When I saw his name on the phone I was sure there was something wrong. But there wasn't. At least, he said there wasn't.

Now I think he was giving me an invitation.

"How'd the meeting go?" he asked.

"Badly. It's over, Ted. Tomorrow after we close I'm going to put in an application at Barnes & Noble. Kill me."

"Bev?"

"Urgh?"

"Why did you fight so hard for the library?"

The past tense shook me. "What do you mean? It's the *library*."

"I mean why did you, specifically, fight for it? You said it was just rooms full of nonsense."

"Did I say that?"

"What made you put in all that effort? What made you keep going back into the stacks, week after week?"

I was going to say something glib, about how it almost paid the bills and I had to use my master's degree for something, after all, but the tone of his voice made me pause. "I don't know . . . I think I like that the job never ends. There's always another room to catalog. Every *Moby-Dick* is different, and we'll never file them all."

"Why not?"

"Huh? It's an infinite library, Ted. You can't organize an infinite library."

There was silence on the other end of the line, and then Ted said, "I always admired how hard you worked."

"Why, Ted."

"You drive safely."

Somehow I felt like I'd failed a test.

Sixth:

WHY DO YOU care so much, anyway? You got what you wanted. We can't bring them back, we can't bring any of it back . . .

I'm sorry. I'm sorry. I'm not much of a public speaker. Ted could have done it. He did such a nice presentation on

Whitman. Look at me, I don't even have any visual aids, except my book.

I did drive safely. When I turned off the interstate, I thought briefly about stopping at the library, just to check up on everything. But it was so late. I went home and got some sleep instead. Maybe it wouldn't have made a difference. Maybe they were already gone by then.

I woke up early so I could set up for the last day. Like I said, we had activities planned. Liz had collected gift certificates from local businesses so we could do a raffle. Hair Today donated something, I remember that, and thanks very much, Trish. Yes, Jeff, and your garden center, that was very generous. Every little bit, you know.

What?

No, I can't tell you where they went. All I have is a guess, and I'm trying to explain where that guess comes from. It's about what Carol said that night. *That's not what libraries are for.*

What are libraries for?

Well, it depends on who's asking, doesn't it? To some people, they're for literature. To other people, they're for reference, for answers. Or for free computer access. For DVD rentals. I know a certain number of people who think they're for babysitting their kids while they shop at the Marc's across the street, and no, Kimberly, I'm not looking at you.

But Carol was a librarian. And for librarians, libraries are for cataloging. Bringing order to chaos, maybe. I don't know. I just know what Carol said.

I think Carol cataloged the Branch Library of Babel. The whole thing. And that made it . . . go away. Not back to where it came from. On to where it was going. I think she reversed entropy and collapsed the singularity that allows extrusions of pure logic into our universe. *Through Space and Time fused in a chant, and the flowing, eternal Identity* . . .

Yes, I know it's an infinite library. I know I told Ted you couldn't organize it all. But the Branch Library contained a fractional but infinite number of squatters. If Carol and Ted spent those last weeks making peace with the tribes and uniting them, had them pass the word along, showed them how to use the Library of Congress filing system . . .

A fractional but infinite number of librarians is the same size as a complete and infinite number of books. Isn't it? I wish I still had that sign we used to keep behind the front desk.

I remember punching the security code on the front door. I remember turning the key in the lock.

The inside of the firehouse was a whitewashed cinderblock room with all-weather carpeting. No other rooms. Nothing. Except for the book on the floor.

It's not even one of the nice editions. I mean, look at it. 1985 trade paperback from Watermill Press, with, frankly, kind of an ugly cover illustration of the *Pequod* under attack. You see it in a lot of used bookstores.

But the text is perfect *Moby-Dick*, no hiccups or irregularities, from beginning to end.

The first edition of *Moby-Dick* was irregular, you know. That 1851 edition. It came out in England first, and the English publisher put out this terrible, typo-riddled book. They even left out the Epilogue. The critics all gave it bad reviews, and Melville's masterpiece—I do think it's a masterpiece, even if I skip the boring parts—was forgotten for almost a hundred years. I used to like to imagine the Branch Library was trying to fix that old mistake by putting out an infinite number of irregular editions, with one perfect one, the way it should have been, mixed in somewhere.

Well, they're all shelved correctly now, all the good *Moby-Dicks* and bad *Moby-Dicks* in the universe. And all the books that aren't *Moby-Dick*, although to me all books are *Moby-Dick*, it's just that some of them are really badly misprinted. They're all in order now, and our librarian and star volunteer keep them that way, in a cinderblock pocket universe that's infinitely less chaotic, infinitely more meaningful than this one. I really do believe that. And I only am escaped alone to tell thee.

That's from the Bible, originally, you know. That line. Is it all right to mention the Bible at a city council meeting?

Well, that's good to know. Thank you very much. It's from Job. And I guess you can go ahead and tear down the building now.

This story originally appeared in *Strange Horizons*, 2011.

Shaenon K. Garrity is an award-winning cartoonist best known for the webcomics *Narbonic* and *Skin Horse*. Her prose fiction has appeared in *Strange Horizons*, *Lightspeed*, *Escape Pod*, and *Daily Science Fiction*. She lives in Berkeley with two birds, a baby, and a man.

THE QUEEN'S REASON
RICHARD PARKS

THE COURTIERS AND SERVANTS did their best to conceal the truth, but that was a losing battle. The final straw, so to speak, was when their beautiful young queen managed to elude her Ladies in Waiting and greet the South Islands Confederation ambassador while wearing only a skirt made of broom straw and a gardenia pot for a hat. After that incident there was little point in denying the obvious: Mei Janda II, newly crowned Queen of Lucosa, was barking mad.

The Chief Assistant, a youngish man who was the second son of an earl, conferred with the Head of the Privy Council, an oldish man who held the rank of duke, as they walked through the palace gardens.

"Lovely roses," said the Chief Assistant, by way of conversation.

"I hate roses," said the Head of the Privy Council in the same spirit. "Pity about Her Majesty, though. Do you think the nuns knew?"

Mei Janda had spent the last five years in a convent, according to the wishes of Their Late Majesties. The Privy Council had ruled in her name until her eighteenth birthday, whereupon the coronation had taken place. All had gone as planned. Except for the "barking mad" part.

"The Sisters of Inevitable Sin? Almost certainly, though I'm not sure I blame them for keeping it quiet. Still, if it wasn't for that business with His Excellency the Ambassador ... well, water under the bridge."

"Usually the royal family is better about hiding such things," the Head of the Privy Council said.

The Chief Assistant nodded. "Quite so. Have you ever considered that when a Royal goes lunatic, it's usually a sort of, well, *specific* madness? For instance, do you know why the former king and queen put their daughter in a convent at age thirteen?"

The Head of the Privy Council scowled. "It was said that they wanted her to be raised away from palace intrigue."

"Rubbish. The real reason was because the princess asked what those two dogs in the courtyard were doing, and her parents became hysterical; she was packed off to the convent that very night. Or consider her great-grandfather, Omor III. He believed that the stones of the palace were eavesdropping on him. Some lathwork and plaster, a few well-placed tapestries, and he was perfectly fine. Ruled well for over fifty years. Yet the fog around Queen Mei's brain doesn't seem to obey any strictures whatsoever."

"Have you consulted the Royal Magician?"

The Chief Assistant made a rude gesture. "That charlatan? I asked him what we should do about the queen's illness. You know what the old fool said? He said that there was nothing wrong with her! I'm afraid he's gone senile."

"Quite," said the Head of the Privy Council.

His terseness could perhaps be explained by the sudden presence of the Queen, who chose that moment to come skipping through the gardens with a garland of wilted morning-glories around her head. She was stark naked otherwise. Being experienced courtiers, the two men just bowed and pretended not to notice.

"Good morning, Your Majesty," they said practically in unison.

"How do you like my dress, ducks?"

"Quite becoming, Majesty," said the Chief Assistant. Which was true enough. Unlike many in her bloodline, Queen Mei's heredity agreed with her. Except, again, for the "barking mad" part.

"You think so? Then I shall wear it at my wedding," she said.

The Chief Assistant exchanged glances with the Head of the Privy Council. "Wedding, your Majesty?" again, nearly in unison. Still, being individuals of a sort, they never quite managed a true unity of speech, but that didn't seem to matter.

"You didn't know? We sent out the invitations ages ago. Of course you two are invited, never doubt it!"

"Thank you, Majesty," said the Head of the Privy Council, on his own this time. "Might one inquire when the joyous event is to occur?"

"A week next. On Whitsunday."

"We shall clear our schedules, of course," said the Chief Assistant. "As the message containing the details has apparently gone astray, might one also inquire who is to be the lucky groom?"

The queen frowned then. "That's the only strange thing about it," she said. "I don't know who he is. Isn't that odd? Still, he is coming and there is much to do. My bouquet, for a start. I need more flowers!" The queen began plucking stems at random from both sides of the path, ignoring both thorns and briars even while her hands began to bleed.

The two men withdrew to a discreet distance.

"She's coherent enough," the Head of the Privy Council said, "considering that she's speaking pure nonsense."

"She thinks she's getting married," said the Chief Assistant thoughtfully. "This might be the solution to our dilemma."

"How so?"

"The management of the kingdom is in good hands as it is. Yet we have a Queen now. At some point she's going to be making decisions and asking people to do impossible things that will, nevertheless, be treason to disobey."

"That's only sense," said the Head of the Privy Council.

"Further, the Council cannot take that authority away from the Crown, even if she is barking mad. That would be treason as well."

"I never suggested such a thing!" the Head of the Privy Council said. Granted, he had thought about it, but he had never suggested it.

"So you see our dilemma?"

"Of course I do!" said the Head of the Privy Council. "What I don't see is how the Queen's delusions of a wedding have anything to do with solving it."

"Simple, Your Grace: We have a real wedding."

The older man blinked. "We what?"

"Think about it. Her Majesty is currently the only living member of the royal family. For the stability of the kingdom, she simply must produce an heir."

"Well, yes. Preferably several," the Head of the Privy Council conceded. "In due course."

"We don't have that luxury. Word of Her Majesty's condition will soon spread. What sort of suitors will she attract then?"

"The same sort as before," the older man said dryly. "Penniless second and third sons, greedy princes, ambitious monarchs intent on absorbing our ancient kingdom into their own territories. We'll be lucky to end up as a sixteenth sinister on someone else's coat of arms." He stopped because the Chief Assistant was nodding vigorously.

"Precisely so," the younger man said. "In her present condition, the Queen is incapable of sorting the wheat from the chaff. Unless we look at this situation as more than simply a problem—it is also an opportunity. I'm almost certain that Her Majesty sent no invitations. So we send our own. Have the Privy Council draw up a list of eligible men of good character, and these and only these will be in the palace on Whitsunday.

As they will be the only men permitted to be present, the Queen is sure to pick one of them."

"In her current state, she's just as likely to marry the Archbishop's podium," the Head of the Privy Council said.

The Chief Assistant dismissed that. "Even the Queen, sane or otherwise, cannot overrule the church on a point of theology, and the marriage between a human woman and a lectern is currently not sanctified. I admit my plan has no guarantees, Your Grace, and certainly will not solve all our problems. If this works, however, it will ensure that at least *one* person on the throne is sane, plus create the reasonable chance of an heir. That would be a vast improvement, no?"

"Yes," the Head of the Privy Council said. "Very well. I shall present your plan to the Council."

His Grace quickly did so, and as the Council had no ideas of their own, they agreed. Nor was it a great surprise that all the eligible bachelors in the Privy Council put their own names on the guest list, as well as that of the Chief Assistant. After that, likely candidates were more sparse, but the Privy Council did manage to put together a respectable list, to the number of two hundred and three men of reasonable standing and at least passable character, most of whom, like the Queen herself, awaited the coming Whitsunday with great anticipation.

"TELL ME AGAIN why this gown won't do?" The Queen was admiring herself in the full length mirror in her chambers. The Royal Magician sat patiently on a stool in the corner. He neither ogled nor pointedly *didn't* ogle, even though the Queen was still stark naked.

"Because it's not a gown, Majesty. It's your own bare flesh."

"Well," she said, "I admit it is a bit form-fitting."

"Being your own skin, that stands to reason."

The Queen sighed. "I'm not so good with reason these days, Magician. I mean, everything makes perfect sense when I do it, but later I begin to wonder. For instance, I knew this gown was just too comfortable. Even the prettiest, best-fitting dress pinches somewhere. Still, the Head of the Privy Council and the Chief Assistant both liked it."

"I'd question their eyesight otherwise," the Magician said. "They are both good men at heart, Majesty. Even if they don't listen very well. So. Why don't you wear the white gown with the yellow brocade? It belonged to your mother. It might need to be taken in a bit for you, but I think it would look splendid."

The Queen frowned but held up the dress in question so that she could examine it against her skin using the mirror. "It's very nice," she said finally. "Not quite so well-fitted as the one I'm wearing, but I do like the colors. Do you really think I should wear this or just have the one I'm wearing now dyed to match?"

"Definitely your mother's dress," he said. "You have many seamstresses, but the best dyers are in Aljin, and that's more than a week's travel. You'd never get the dress back in time."

"I suppose," said Queen Mei. "I'm fortunate to have your counsel, Magician. You're so wise. Is that because you're... archetypecast?"

"*Archetypical*, Majesty," the Magician corrected politely. "And yes, I think so."

"What does that mean, anyway?"

"It means that I have a role to play. We all do. It just so happens that mine is to at least appear to be wise and to do my best to make sure things turn out as they're supposed to."

"Who decides how things are 'supposed to turn out'?"

"No one. Or perhaps everyone."

She sighed. "I don't understand, but I guess that's because I'm barking mad."

The old man's smile was not unkind. "Actually, no, Your Majesty. No one really understands this, and I do not exclude myself. I merely realize that some things are not to be understood—they are to be acknowledged. Just as we sometimes recognize the roles we play even as we play them."

The Queen looked pleased. "That means I must have a role, too! Do you know what it is?"

"For a start, to get married on Whitsunday."

The Queen looked less pleased. "That does sound like fun, but it doesn't really seem very important."

The Magician smiled again. "Majesty, in this instance it is the most important role of all. The future of our country depends on it."

"Very well. Did you attend to the invitations?"

"Yes, I did send out the invitation, Majesty."

"Invitation? You meant invitations, didn't you? As in 'more than one'? I mean, I know I'm barking mad and all, but shouldn't there have been more?"

"I sent the one that mattered. Trust me, Majesty— There will be plenty of guests."

"Well, if you're sure." She pulled the dress aside to gaze at her own reflection again wistfully. "Pity about the dyers, though."

THE TRAVELER, a handsome, roguish fellow, entered Lucosa the day before Whitsunday. Perhaps it was merely a coincidence that both the Head of the Privy Council and the Chief Assistant happened to be visiting their respective tailors for fittings on that same day. Perhaps there are no coincidences. Whatever conclusion one draws, the fact remains that they were present, with their haughty attendants, and the Traveler cheerfully greeted them there.

"Good day to you, gentlemen," he said.

"I am a Duke," corrected the Head of the Privy Council.

"And I am a knight, the son of an earl," said the Chief Assistant. Their attendants, as was proper, did not speak, but to a man they fixed the Traveler with Looks of Disapproval.

"Well, then it was clearly wrong of me to refer to either of you as a gentleman, and I apologize," the Traveler said. "Rather, then, Your Grace and Good Sir Knight."

"That's better," said the Chief Assistant as he eyed the youth with some distaste. The Traveler's face and clothes were dirty, his dark hair unkempt, and his brown traveling cloak tattered and worn. "What business do you have with us, fellow?"

"I merely wished to ask what time the Queen's wedding was to take place tomorrow, as you two fine personages seemed the sort who might know. The invitation was a bit vague."

"Wedding?" The Chief Assistant frowned.

"Invitation?" The Head of the Privy Council frowned even more.

"Frankly," said the Traveler, "I'm as surprised as you are. I have not been in Lucosa, so far as I can recall, since the year of my birth. I have no friends or family here that I know of, and yet," he said, fumbling inside a pouch in his belt. "Ah, here it is."

The youth held up the paper so that both could see. "It says only the date, which is tomorrow. Not even the name of the groom. I do not know why I should have been invited but saw no reason to forego the experience. I've never been to a Royal Wedding before."

The two men just studied the document in silence for a few moments.

"That's not like ours," the Head of the Privy Council said finally.

"No. This one actually has the Queen's seal," the Chief Assistant replied. "Pray, young man," he asked. "How did you come by this?"

"Odd about that—a red hawk dropped it on me. In broad daylight. At first I thought the wretched bird had dropped something more odious, but that did not turn out to be the case."

"I don't like where this is going," muttered the Head of the Privy Council.

"You said you had no family here?" asked the Chief Assistant.

"Well, not that I *know* of, you understand," the Traveler said. "I don't remember much before my time on the road."

"Uncertain origins," said the Head of the Privy Council, nodding, though he was talking to the Chief Assistant, and his tone was pure "I told you so."

"I suppose you've traveled far and wide, seen all sorts of things?" the Chief Assistant asked the younger man.

The Traveler's face lit up like a beacon. "Oh, yes. From the South Islands to the frozen north, the burning west, and the sultry east. I have met such people, tasted such food, seen such wonders, experienced such marvels... Even if your esteemed selves were content to listen, we'd miss the wedding entirely merely recounting half of it."

"And now you're here, by Royal Invitation, a penniless, homeless nobody," said the Chief Assistant.

"I'd be insulted," the Traveler said, "had not every word you had just muttered been the absolute truth. As I said, it puzzled me as well."

"Oh, I'm not puzzled," the Chief Assistant said. "Clearly there is a Destiny upon you. Wouldn't you agree?" He turned to the Head of the Privy Council for confirmation.

"Extensive travels? Obscure origins? Animal messengers? Do you even need to ask?" confirmed the older man.

The Traveler frowned. "What sort of Destiny?"

"Something involving the Queen, I fancy," said the Chief Assistant. "But don't let that concern you just now. You are here by Royal Invitation, but the wedding is not until tomorrow. As faithful servants of the Queen, we certainly cannot let you sleep on the streets."

"Well, I was really considering a lovely game park I saw on the way in ...."

"I won't hear of it." The Chief Assistant signaled two of his burlier attendants. "Please escort this man to the palace. He is our guest."

"Too kind," said the Traveler.

Before they led the young man away, the burlier of the burly two leaned close to the Chief Attendant and whispered a question. "Dungeon?"

"Of course."

The Chief Assistant and the Head of the Privy Council watched the young man being led away.

"That was bloody close," said the Head of the Privy Council.

"Agreed. It's all well and good for penurious young men of destiny to win the hand of a beautiful young queen in a fairy-tale," the Chief Assistant said. "But how in good conscience could we let our kingdom simply be a reward for the position of the stars at this stranger's birth? I mean, really. For all we know he's the long-lost heir of some ancient enemy, or an ogre or worse in disguise. I like our plan better."

"That goes without argument," said the Head of the Privy Council. "I do love your new tunic, by the way. Quite fetching."

THE TRAVELER WALKED into the cell calmly enough. It wasn't that he didn't recognize a dungeon when he saw one. It was more that, first of all, he judged his chances against his escort if he chose to resist and didn't like what his eyes and common sense told him. Second, while it was true that the Traveler had seen a dungeon, he had never been in one. It was his nature to experience everything he could, and especially the new and different. He had sought both out for as long as he could remember. He did not understand why and never had, but the inclination bordered on irresistible, and now it led him to walk through the cell door and experience the clang of an unbreakable door shutting behind him.

He looked around his new quarters with the same eye for detail and curiosity that he approached everything. While he had little experience of dungeons, he rather got the impression that this was one of the nicer ones. The straw on the cold stone floor was at least relatively clean, if old, and smelled a bit musty but no worse than that. The Traveler judged that this particular dungeon didn't get a great deal of use, which he thought spoke well of the Queen and her kingdom.

The Traveler spent a relatively comfortable night on the straw in his cell. Truth to tell, he'd had worse nights' sleep under the open sky. In the morning, a surly guard brought him a passable breakfast of cold peaseporridge and water.

The Traveler had no idea why the two noblemen he had met felt the need to confine him. He hoped they would at least inform him of this in due course. Something else to understand and experience, even if such experience turned out to be his last.

"One would almost judge this a friendly, welcoming sort of place," he said. "Except for the bars on the door of my accommodations."

"Ah, there you are. I thought I might find you here," said a high, piping voice with no obvious body attached to it.

The Traveler looked about. "Who said that?"

"I did. Down here, young man."

The Traveler looked down into the beady black eyes of a stout, brown, frost-whiskered rat. It stood on its hind paws by a break in the stone, which it had apparently used to gain entrance.

"Well, then, it would hardly be a respectable dungeon at all without at least *one* rat," the Traveler said, "but I wouldn't expect that rat to talk. Strange, because I hardly think I've been confined here long enough to go mad with despair and loneliness. Such things, I thought, took time."

"You're not mad," the rat said patiently. "The Queen might be, but you're certainly not. I'm here to help you."

"I've heard rumors of such things," the Traveler admitted. "Ferocious tasks and animal helpers. Are you saying I'm a Prince in disguise?"

The rat sighed. "No, Traveler. You are no prince, nor am I a rat. I'm the Court Magician. I've merely taken this form so that we can have a little chat. I trust you received your invitation?"

"Unless I miss my guess, you know I did. Weren't you the hawk, too?"

The rat grinned, showing sharp, chisel-like teeth. "Clever, but I would expect no less. Yes, Traveler, I was the hawk as well. I brought you here ...." At that the rat paused and looked around the cell. "Well, not *here*. That was the Chief Assistant and the Head of the Privy Council. Don't think too harshly of them, by the way. They mean well. Mostly. Though I suppose the chance of becoming king has skewed their judgment just a tad."

"Am I supposed to understand what you're talking about? If so, I may need to ponder a while. At the moment it makes no sense."

"Right again," the rat said cheerfully. "Forgive me for rambling about matters that do not yet concern you. Your current task is to get out of the dungeon so you won't be late for the wedding."

"But why? Am I to marry the Queen?"

"I didn't say that either. I said you need to get out of here and make it to the wedding. I can't tell you why because then you'd say that *I'm* mad, and there wouldn't be any recourse to reason that would convince you otherwise. Frankly, Traveler, we just don't have that kind of time. Say rather that you really don't want to miss a Royal Wedding, do you?"

"No," said the Traveler. "I don't. And I really don't understand that part either."

"Would it help if I told you that after you attend the wedding, you will understand why you were supposed to be there?"

"Maybe," the Traveler said. "I really would like to. Understanding things makes me happy. Learning makes me happy. Seeing things I have never seen before makes me happy."

"Come to the wedding," the rat said, "and I guarantee that you'll hardly be able to contain your joy."

"Fine to say, but how? The door is locked."

"Have you tried it?"

The Traveler's eyes grew wide for a moment in open astonishment. He took two long steps and put his hand on the door.

"There is still much to learn," the Traveler said as the massive door swung open.

"If you're indeed fortunate, that fact will never change," the rat said. "The ballroom is two flights up. You still have your invitation, don't you?"

"Yes."

"Show it to the guards at the door and go on in. I will meet you there."

THE QUEEN WORE her mother's wedding dress into the grand ballroom. She had to admit that the Magician had been right; the looks of envy from the women and admiration from the men told her that much even if her reason wasn't available to do the same. A long green swath of carpeting marked the central aisle leading to the makeshift dais where two thrones sat.

One for my husband, I suppose. I hope he isn't late.

The Queen moved in stately procession down the aisle, her two Ladies in Waiting keeping sharp eyes on the train of her gown so that it didn't snag. It was hard for the Queen to remain so solemn, when what she really wanted to do was to stick out her tongue at the Duchess of Corns, or moon the Archbishop now standing in the center of the dais beside the thrones, his book ready. Yet something told her that this would be wrong, and nothing had ever told her that before. At least, not so that she could remember. Today was different. She tried to think about that for a moment, but her thoughts, as they always did, swam away from her like little frightened fish. Sometimes she believed she could almost see them darting away.

I'm meeting my intended today. Maybe that's why. So where is he?

The Queen ascended the dais, nodded to the Archbishop with perfect decorum and turned around to face her guests. The Magician had been right about that too. There were a goodly number; in fact, the ballroom was nigh to bursting. That was nice. Yet none of it would make sense even to a barking mad queen, unless...

"Ah. *There* you are. But why are there three of you? I don't think the Archbishop will allow that."

The three dark-haired, handsome young men in threadbare clothes had just entered through the main doors, looked about themselves with awe and curiosity, and were, apparently, very slow to recognize that the Queen was speaking to them. At this point, the Duchess of Corn and all the rest of the duchesses—and not a few of the Earls present—screamed.

"A rat!"

"Where?" asked the rat who had just scampered up to sit beside the leftmost empty throne. "Oh, me. Right." In a blink the rat was gone, and the Court Magician stood in its place. "Sorry I'm late, Majesty. Had a run in with the Royal Moggie. Had to singe his whiskers a bit."

"Why are there three grooms?" Queen Mei asked.

By this time the Chief Assistant and the Head of the Privy Council had pushed forward. "Really, Your Majesty, we must insist—"

"Silence, the both of you," the Queen said. "Honestly, ducks, you'll get your turn. Right now I'm talking to my Magician." She turned back to the Royal Magician. "Why?" she asked again.

"I'm afraid it's a test, your Majesty."

"Isn't that a little presumptious of you? I mean, I'm barking mad and all, but I *am* the Queen."

"Precisely, Majesty. Yet once this thing was begun, certain rules began to apply, which neither you nor I can gainsay. While the Traveler has had some minor travails, the fact is that, right now, this isn't about him. As I said before: *you* are the one who matters here. So this test has to be for you."

"Oh," the Queen said, "well, that's all right, then. What sort of test?"

"You must recognize your intended."

"Or?"

"Or you will be separated from him forever. As this would be quite disastrous, please choose well."

"Are you barking mad, too?" the Chief Assistant blurted at the Magician. "The Queen is in no condition—"

"The Queen," said the Queen, "will decide for herself what she may or may not do, and what her condition allows."

"Of course, Majesty," said the Head of the Privy Council. "Yet even the Queen, if she is wise, will listen to the advice of those who best understand the situation."

The Queen glanced at the Magician, who merely shrugged. "True, so far as it goes, Majesty," he said.

The Queen turned back to the Chief Assistant and the Head of the Privy Council. "Well then, gentlemen, which of the pair of you understands this situation better than I do, barking mad though I am?"

The Head of the Privy Council just scowled. The Chief Assistant opened his mouth as if to speak, then apparently thought better of it, since he slowly closed it again. The Queen nodded.

"That's what I thought." She turned again to the three identical Travelers, who all this time watched everything unfolding before them with eagerness if not, the Queen judged, full comprehension.

"I'm having a remarkable run of coherent thought at the moment," she said. "And I think you three gentlemen have something to do with that. Yet I wonder why that is."

It wasn't exactly a question, but the three Travelers didn't show any sign of having an answer. If anything, they seemed more and more confused as each noted the presence of the other two as if he had never seen them before.

"Strange," they said, almost in unison.

"Don't start that," the Queen said firmly. "I'm not sure how long this coherence will last." She turned to the Magician. "I must choose? As they are?"

"You may ask one question of each," the Magician said, "if that helps any."

"Your Majesty," began the Head of the Privy Council, "Surely you can't—"

"I'm barking mad, Your Grace," the Queen said. "Not simple. Now, I did ask you to be quiet. I really must insist."

The Head of the Privy Council fell silent and the Queen stepped down from the dais and approached the three young men as her two Ladies in Waiting followed behind. She turned to the first young man. "Who are you?" she asked.

"I'm the Traveler," said the first. "Such wonders I have seen, such wonders still to be seen! Too much for a lifetime, but I must try in the short time I have."

"Sounds marvelous," the Queen said, then she turned to the second young man. "Who are you, then?"

"*I* am the Traveler," he said. "I don't know who these upstarts are, but I am the one, the true Traveler. Everything that false face just said applies to *me*."

"If you say so," the Queen said and turned to the third. "Young man, who are you?"

The third Traveler met the Queen's gaze squarely. "I don't know."

The Queen frowned. "Oh?"

"I thought I did," the young man said. "I was the Traveler. Then I stepped into this room and beheld Your Majesty for the first time. At least, I think it is the first time. I cannot remember another, and yet I do not think I can go back to being a simple Traveler again. I think that time has passed."

"I've missed you," said the Queen. "Welcome home."

She embraced the third young man before the assembled guests and kissed him on the lips. In another instant he was gone, along with the other two false images. Vanished, as if they had never been. Alone now except for her two attendants, the Queen glided regally back to the dais and took her place in front of the throne. For a moment or two she simply stood there, a deep frown creasing her brow. Just as the guests began to get restless, the Queen spoke.

"Friends and Honored Guests, I know you came today prepared to witness a wedding. I'm afraid I must disappoint you in this. We will be having a celebration as planned, but no wedding ... at least, not today. The feast, however, will commence shortly and of course you are all invited, so please make your way to the banquet hall now. It seems I will be in need of partners for the dance, so perhaps this will be our chance to get to know one another better."

The guests were, for the most part, pleased with Her Majesty's speech, even if they didn't have the slightest idea of what had just occurred. They began to file out of the ballroom on their way to the banquet. The Chief Assistant and the Head of the Privy Council, however, were not content to be confused. The Head of the Privy Council was still under a stricture of silence, so the Chief Assistant was the one who asked.

"Majesty, what just happened here?"

"You already knew that my reason had left me. Today it came back."

"Your reason?"

"I'm sure Your Majesty remembers the details well enough now," said the Royal Magician. "But to save your strength for the dancing tonight, perhaps I should explain?" The Queen nodded assent and the Royal Magician continued. "Five years ago, Her Majesty was given into the safekeeping of the Sisters of Inevitable Sin."

"Everyone knows that," said the Chief Assistant.

"What everyone doesn't know is that the Queen was stuck in a twilight existence there, neither free to leave nor in training as one dedicated to the Order. She was learning nothing that would be of any use to her as the Queen she was destined to be. I separated her from her reason," the Royal Magician said, then went on when he saw the horrified looks on the two men, "at her own request. I gave her reason a separate existence and sent it out into the world with a magical directive of *curiosity*, so that it would do and experience all the things that she could not."

"Leaving her Majesty barking mad!" said the Chief Assistant.

"Sir," said Queen Mei, "it's not as if I actually *needed* my reason before now. It wasn't doing me much good in the convent."

The Magician smiled. "Just so. When the time came, her reason was invited to return, bringing everything it had learned with it. Their meeting was expressed as a wedding simply because, well, I had to put the matter in terms consistent with Her Majesty's then-current level of comprehension. That was the tricky bit—she still had to be able to recognize and acknowledge that part of herself when it returned, else they could never be whole again. It was a risk, but fortunately Her Majesty acquitted herself wisely."

"Well, of course we were not questioning ...." began the Chief Assistant as the Head of the Privy Council vigorously nodded agreement, but the Queen cut them both off flat with a wave of her small hand.

"We understand that you had the good of the kingdom at heart," the Queen said, "even if neither of you would have minded being king. To make up for your disappointment, Your Grace shall have the first dance tonight. After that, Sir Chief Assistant. We believe that is the correct order of precedence."

"Too kind, Majesty," said the Chief Assistant, already planning his charm and small talk.

"Afterwards, you can keep each other company in the dungeon." She smiled then at the look of horror on each man's face. "Oh, calm yourselves, Sirs. Your confinement will not last through tomorrow morning. After a hearty breakfast of water and peaseporridge, you will both be expected to return to your duties. We would merely suggest that you remember this coming night," she said. "If either of you is ever tempted to insult Our reason again."

There was a healthy mixture of both relief and fear in the two men's eyes as they gratefully withdrew with the other guests. The Queen sent her two attendants ahead to prepare a more appropriate gown for the dance. When they were quite alone, the Magician turned to her again.

"Gratitude is sometimes best with a leaven of fear. That was well done, Majesty," he said.

"Was it? I had hoped so, but wasn't entirely sure. Perhaps reason and I can reach accommodation, then. Yet I must say ... it feels very strange to be sane."

"Majesty," the old man said, bowing. He then nodded at the retreating men. "To give them their due, neither would have made a bad king," he said.

"I'm not sure that either the kingdom or I personally should settle for a consort who is merely 'not bad,'" the Queen said. She remembered the handsome features and dark eyes of her newly returned reason. She remembered what he remembered, and her face adopted a wistful expression. "Though I'm not certain I'm the best judge of that yet. Perhaps I should make my own better acquaintance before I go wearing this gown again. Or is that barking mad of me?"

The old man smiled, and bowed again to his queen. "Not in the least, Majesty."

Queen Mei smiled too. "Just checking."

This story originally appeared in *Lady Churchill's Rosebud Wristlet*, 2010.

Richard Parks's work has appeared in *Asimov's SF, Realms of Fantasy, Beneath Ceaseless Skies, Lady Churchill's Rosebud Wristlet*, and several "Year's Best" anthologies and has been nominated for both the World Fantasy Award and the Mythopoetic Award for Adult Literature. The fourth book in the Yamada Monogatari series, *The Emperor in Shadow*, is due out from Prime Books in September 2016. He blogs at "Den of Ego and Iniquity Annex #3", also known as www.richard-parks.com.

THE BEST LITTLE CLEANING ROBOT IN ALL OF FAERIE
SUSAN JANE BIGELOW

WHEN EVERYBODY ON the bridge of the interstellar mercenary cruiser *Zinnia* fell into a magic sleep, I was busy using my scrubber attachments to attack the usual stains under the captain's chair. There was a sudden series of thuds, and I noticed that everyone had either slumped over in their chairs or fallen to the floor.

At that moment the doors opened and about fifty tiny, filthy, hairy, gross little *things* streamed out, shrieking in some language I didn't know. They started bashing in the consoles, whacking unconscious crew members upside the head with oversize clubs, and getting grit everywhere.

"Hey," I said, boosting upwards on a cushion of very clean air. I waved my tentacle attachments in agitation. "Knock that off!"

But they didn't. I hesitantly thumped one of them on the backside with a tentacle; it turned and hissed at me, hitting my shiny surface with a cloud of noxious breath and spittle.

"Goblins! Begone!" shouted someone from the doorway. A tall figure, cloaked in shadow and mist, stood there. Lightning crackled from his fingertips. A stiff wind blew in from the doorway. The goblins shrieked and ran out the emergency stairwell, down towards engineering and the pool.

The mist and shadow ebbed to reveal Lt. Hob, the captain's aide, standing awkwardly in the doorway.

"Oh, dear," he said glumly. He was tall, pale, gaunt, and had stringy blond hair.

He also, I noticed, had pointed ears.

"Did you do this?" I asked. "Is this some kind of mutiny?" Ships in the Senecan Mercenary Fleet sometimes mutinied. It happened. I didn't like the idea of Hob in charge, but I'd deal. "Why did you change your ears?"

He turned and wiggled his fingers at me. Sparks flew, and for a split second my vocal processors cut out. Shocked, I frantically tried to reroute power and switch on repair programs. But then, a moment later, my voice returned.

"Don't do that!" I said, thrown. I raced through five hundred thousand possible ways he could have done it. None of them made sense. I partitioned off a piece of my memory to keep working on it.

Hob tapped a long, thin finger on the side of the chair. "Well. That explains that," he said. "You're resistant. You're the only Type-7 robot on board, yes?"

"Yeah," I said, feeling a little defensive about it. "Why?"

"That means it's just you and me," he said portentously. "Just the two of us, against the full power of the Nightmare Duke. We're doomed."

"Huh?" I asked.

"WHAT KIND OF alien are you, again?" I asked as we made our way down the hallway towards his quarters. He walked, I hovered next to him. I'm sort of round and flat with lots of attachments, so I have to hover.

"I'm not," he said. "Like I told you, I am a *hob*."

"I thought your name was Hob," I said.

"It is," he said. "'Hob' is also the name of my species." Goblins raced gleefully by, toting loot from sleeping crew. He glowered at them. "I am a member of the Court of the Ten Stars, or... I was. Before the Nightmare Duke banished my people, scattering all of us to the four winds."

"That's real fascinating," I said.

"I didn't think a tentacled hot plate like you would be interested in my travails," he retorted. "The short version is that I came here and joined this fleet. It was a natural fit for me."

"A mercenary fleet?" I asked. That didn't seem likely. Hob had always kind of stuck out with this bunch.

"Yes. We hobs are good at keeping watch over those who need it most. We're skilled at serving and cleaning."

"But I do all the cleaning," I said.

"Yes," he said darkly. "I've noticed."

"So that's why you have those ear points, right?"

"Indeed," he said. "I removed my glamour. It's magic."

"Magic," I repeated, still disbelieving.

"If you don't believe me, go inside my cabin and tell me what you see."

I zipped through the door to his cabin. I'd been in here dozens of times before, and it had smelled like an old man and some kind of spice I couldn't quite air freshen out, but there hadn't been anything weird.

That had changed.

A howling vortex swirled beside his tottery shelf of cheap knick-knacks. Some choice scents and sounds wafted from inside; the smell of summer rain, the sound of firewood crackling, and the distinct aroma of rotting garbage.

"It stinks in there," I concluded.

"Well, yes," Hob said. "My people have been exiled from Faerie for five hundred years. The garbage does pile up."

So much garbage to clean. I tapped my tentacles against the floor in anticipation. "Why is this attacking us now?"

Hob blushed. "There was a message board. I... posted a few things... videos about him. I wasn't very nice. He finally found them and now he's very angry."

"So you pissed him off and now he's trying to get back at you and us. Great. Can I just shove you through there and let him have you?"

He looked afraid. "Kidding," I said lightly, though I wasn't. "What's the plan?"

"We wake someone up," he said. "That's the first thing. Then we go in there and close the portal."

"Oh!" I said. "I know just the person."

* * *

HOB DID NOT like my idea.

"Not her!" he exclaimed when I toted the unconscious body of Sgt. Ndala into his room. "No. I won't. Take her away this instant!"

"She gets stuff done," I said. And it was true. She was startlingly good at being a mercenary. "If anyone can fuck up Faerie and what's-his-name, it's her."

Hob considered this. "Put her on the table."

I used several of my tentacles, which were wonderfully strong, to toss her onto his table. It creaked and groaned when she hit it, but held. He bent over her and waved his hands around, speaking some kind of language that wasn't in my data banks.

Nothing happened and I prepared to deliver a gloating speech about how his magic was all crap.

But then Sgt. Ndala coughed and sat bolt upright. She looked wildly around, spotted Hob, and grabbed him by the throat.

"Why the hell am I in your *quarters* on a *table?*" she demanded.

"It's not like that—!" he squawked. She squeezed harder.

"Let him go," I said after a long few seconds of enjoying myself. "He's okay."

She grinned. "Hey, Ms. Clean!"

I like Sgt. Ndala. She gave me a name beyond Fleet Cleaning Robot SFN-7894-Z, and she gave me a gender. I'm a fan of both of them. She is one of the few members of the crew I never have fantasies about spacing, and as a reward I make her often-filthy cabin extra shiny.

"Hey yourself," I said. "We've got a weird situation."

"I'll say," she said, dropping Hob. "This place smells like shit."

"That's from the vortex," I said, gesturing with a few of my tentacle-like arms.

Her eyes widened. "Pretty," she said. "Where'd you get it?"

"It is a gateway to Faerie," said Hob with his characteristic aristocratic arrogance. "You wouldn't understand what that is."

"You mean there are *real* fairies? Like from holovision fairies? In there?" Ndala gaped, then grabbed and fondled Hob's ears. "You got points! Are you a fairy, Hob?"

He yelped and shoved her away. "I am Fae, yes," said Hob, rubbing his ear points.

"He's *a* hob," I filled in. "Which is a fairy that cleans things less well than I do."

He shot me a dirty look.

"Also, the rest of the crew is in a magic sleep," I added.

"Magic!" Ndala looked positively rapturous at the possibility.

"I'm trying not to think about that," I said. "We have to close the portal to wake them up."

"Aw. We have to?"

"Yes," said Hob. "The goblins will destroy us if we don't."

She huffed. "Fine. How?"

"We must go into the portal itself," Hob intoned. "There is great danger in the crossing. Once there, we must travel across the Plains of Suffering until we reach the Gorge of Blood. We find a way to cross that, and then we must climb the Mountain of Dread, battle the Host of the Duke, and then ascend the Tower of Woe itself. There we must steal the Orb of Knowing from the Nightmare Duke and use it to close the portal."

"And if we don't?" asked Ndala skeptically.

Right on cue, another little hairy guy wielding a battleaxe dove out of the portal, screaming a banshee berserker battle cry.

"Holy shit!" yelped Ndala, snatching her sidearm from its holster and blasting away at the goblin. She managed to shoot holes in the bed and a knick-knack collection, but finally hit it before it could whack any of us with the axe. An instant later it was a smoking pile of fur.

"Whoa," Ndala said.

"My things..." said Hob, picking up a few pieces of smashed knick-knack. "I collected those figurines over centuries."

I quickly moved over and sucked up all the fragments. Hob looked like he might cry. I deposited a neat little waste cube near his feet to make him feel better.

"So those things will keep coming if we don't do something?" Ndala asked. "Gross. I guess we gotta go in there."

"It will be an adventure, but I will guard us. I have swords and armor in the closet," said Hob grandly. "I am skilled in fencing and the manly arts."

Ndala gave him a disdainful look. "Swords? This isn't the Middle Ages, Hobbsie." He twitched—he hated that nickname. "I've got a better idea."

THE MZ-27 SPRINGBOK SUPERTANK rumbled up the wide corridor, scraping metal away on both sides. Ndala sat at the controls, a manic grin on her face.

"How did you get that *up* here?" I asked. The lifts didn't seem wide enough. Neither, to be fair, did the corridor.

"These things go out into *space!*" she said, clearly thrilled. "I had to blow a hole in the gym to get back inside, but it was so worth it."

"You did check to make sure no one was inside, first, right?" I asked.

"Well, nobody floated by," said Ndala, unconcerned.

The tank groaned to a halt outside Hob's room.

"You can't possibly mean to take *that* into Faerie!" Hob gibbered.

"Why the hell not?" asked Ndala.

"Faerie is a magic land! That is a tool of science!" said Hob, aghast. "The two don't mix! And you can't even fit it through the door to my room!"

"Well, I bet science is gonna kick magic's ass," said Ndala. "And as for getting into your room, stand back."

She popped back into the tank and the big gun swiveled toward the bulkhead between the corridor and Hob's room.

"No!" cried Hob, but it was far too late. Ndala blew a hole in the wall, and the tank rumbled through.

HOB AND NDALA had the seats. I was awkwardly taped down in the back. In human ships, all the chairs are made for humans.

"Ready?" she asked. "Let's go!"

I wrapped all my tentacle arms around the nearest pylon as Ndala hit the throttle and the tank lumbered forward into the whirling vortex.

There was a dreadful lurch. Ndala actually gagged, but held her lunch down. Hob turned paler. But then there was a sharp shock, and the tank ground to a halt.

"There! I told you!" crowed Hob. "Your scientific—"

Ndala pressed a button and the great honking engine of the tank roared back to life. "Sorry. Just stalled it." She grinned at Hob. "Science!" Then she glanced out the window and whistled. "Whoa."

"Welcome to Faerie," said Hob sulkily.

The world around us was bright, shocking green. Ndala popped open the roof of the tank so we could look around. The smell of rotting garbage was everywhere, but that didn't distract from the sheer beauty of the place. Beyond a tottering tower of garbage was the most pristine lake I'd ever seen, a tall white mountain, and trees of every color imaginable and then some.

But what really threw me was the fact that there was no roof at all overhead. I compressed myself on the floor of the tank. It felt, for no good reason, like I might drift off into that barrier-free sky at any moment.

Who builds robots with anxieties?

"This looks like back home!" Ndala said, wide-eyed. "Like Cascadia!"

"Yes," said Hob, eyes bright.

"Let's go, let's go," I said.

Ndala clapped her hands together with enthusiasm. "All right, troops! Let's get this show on the road. So this is a magic planet, huh? Cool."

"It's not a planet," Hob tried to explain, to no avail. Ndala was bad at allowing anything contradicting her original notions to penetrate her skull.

I liked her for that, too.

FOR THE FIRST HOUR or so, we didn't see anybody besides a few goblins running full tilt toward the portal. Ndala took a shot at one but missed. It dove cackling into the undergrowth and out of sight.

"Get him when we go back," Ndala promised.

As we went I busied myself by cleaning up in the tank to avoid having to deal with the scenery and the alarming lack of a ceiling. Whoever had last operated the tank had left it a pigsty. I slurped up garbage, turning it into harmless puffs of water and tiny waste cubes, which I was happy to store in a neat pile over in the corner of the tank compartment.

Ndala started keeping up a running commentary, just to annoy Hob. "Hey, another secret-whispering tree! Shut up, tree! I bet your mom's a spruce or something." Or, "Hey, is that puddle made of ice cream? Eww! It's been out in the sun! Why is your home so gross, Hob?"

He eventually put his hands over his ears to block her out. She just talked louder or used the loudspeakers. And so we reached the first trial with Hob pissed off, Ndala in a great mood, and me convinced I was about to fly off into space.

"THERE IT IS," Hob intoned gravely. We looked out onto what seemed to be a massive field full of writhing objects, shards of glass, and mean-looking plants. "The Plains of Suffering."

"Let's go around," I suggested.

"That is the only way to the heart of this duchy of Faerie," said Hob. "We must cross it if we are to prove ourselves worthy." He glanced down at me meaningfully. "There are magical protections. I will chant us a spell of invisibility so that we may pass unseen between the spires. Bring what materials you dare, but don't bring too much."

Ndala folded her arms across her chest giving him a sardonic look.

"I did bring the swords," he said hopefully.

"Dude," she said, patting the metal dashboard. "Supertank. Remember?"

"There are magical creatures and carnivorous plants out there!" he protested.

"And if any come at us, we'll shoot them. This thing has triple-plated Radovan steel and synthetic mesh shielding, treads that could go up a damn mountain and back, and six heavy ion cannons. Plus the big gun, which punched a hole in a starship a couple hours ago." Ndala fixed him with a sardonic look. "And you brought some swords?"

It was seriously easy. The tank rolled right over the shards, and when the Doursnakes came at us Ndala blew them into little magic snake bits. By the time we rumbled out of the plains a half an hour later Ndala was cackling with unrestrained joy, while Hob looked like his dog had died.

"THE GORGE OF BLOOD is a rapid, rushing river of boiling, human blood," said Hob as we drew near. "It's fast, wide, and *hot*. There's only one way across, and that's to answer the questions of the Ferryman."

"So why's there a river of blood?" I asked. That seemed very untidy.

"And where'd all the blood come from?" asked Ndala. "Is there some sort of big thing that grinds up people, like an orange juicer, somewhere? Or maybe a blood bank?"

"It comes from a spring in the ground in the Highlands of Yawl," said Hob.

"So the people juicer is underground?" asked Ndala.

"No! It's—it's a magic spring! It just *is*!"

"You can't make something from nothing," I pointed out.

"Conservation of mass and energy, dude," said Ndala.

"You two don't get it," said Hob. "But you will. Here's the Gorge."

The river was in a steep canyon. It was full of dark red, steaming, sticky-looking fluid. Bubbles floated to the surface and popped. I was reminded of the floors when the ship made port and everyone got really drunk.

"Stinks," observed Ndala, wrinkling her nose.

"We have to find the Ferryman," said Hob. "I doubt the tank will be allowed to cross."

He looked pleased by that possibility.

"Nah," said Ndala. "We'll just go through it."

The roof clanged shut above us and the airtight seals engaged. "Hang on!" called Ndala. She hit the throttle and the tank leapt forward—right down the side of the gorge.

"No!" shrieked Hob as we plunged over.

"Relax!" shouted Ndala, that manic look back in her eyes. "Let your seat belt and the inertial dampeners do the work!"

We hit the blood and sank quickly to the bottom. It was impossible to see anything.

"Exterior temperature's 50° C and climbing," said Ndala. "That's a hot mess out there."

"You idiot!" cried Hob. "Now what do we do? We're stuck here!"

"Stuck? Not even close," said Ndala confidently. She engaged the tank's aquatic mode. Slowly, sluggishly, the tank began to move again. "Ha! Science kicks magic's ass again!"

There was a sudden jolt, and we stopped dead. Then there was a groan as the tank started drifting back down towards the bottom.

"What the hell?" Ndala exclaimed, jabbing buttons frantically. "Shit! Nothing!"

"Blood-sprites!" said Hob, pointing out the heavily reinforced window. A sinuous, fanged creature had attached itself to the front of the supertank. There was an angry orange glow all around it. "They're dropping us back to the bottom!"

"Gonna electrify the exterior," said Ndala. "Stand clear of the walls." Hob jumped back from the console as Ndala hit a control, and the water around us sizzled with electricity.

The blood-sprite on the screen wasn't thrown clear. Instead, it grinned toothily at us and doubled in size.

"Crap," said Ndala.

Hob glanced at the sensor readings. "We're covered in them. At least two dozen and more are coming."

They began banging on the hull, which started to groan ominously.

"Gonna fire the escape thrusters!" said Ndala, suddenly all business. "Everybody strapped in?" She hit another control. Nothing happened. "Oh, man."

The temperature in the tank's cabin was climbing rapidly. We'd settled at the bottom of the blood river and had begun, terrifyingly, to sink into the muck below. The sprites banged on the tank's hull; they were close enough that we could hear their eerie, distorted chanting.

There was a *crunch* and the lights went out. Somewhere I could hear liquid pouring in, and the cabin suddenly got much hotter.

"Hull breach!" Ndala shouted as the emergency light came on. "Damn it! Escape pod, come on, get out, get out!"

She dragged us into a narrow tube and hit the big red button. I curled all my tentacles around her and held on. The door closed, and then there was a lot of noise, jolts and terror as the pod rocketed out of the tank.

"GET IT OFF ME!" Hob was shouting.

"Ow," Ndala said. She kicked at the door twice until the explosive bolts caught and blasted it up and away from us. Light flooded in. We were alive and on land.

"Damn it."

"Get *off!*" Hob screeched.

I realized that at some point I'd wrapped all my tentacles around his face. I lifted off and out of the blood-covered capsule. "Sorry."

Ndala scrambled out after me, followed by a weary, disheveled Hob. I followed the two of them to the edge of the

Gorge. There were little bubbles and a patch of oil where the doomed supertank had gone down.

"So much for science," said Hob, not unkindly.

"Yeah, well," said Ndala grouchily. "That was a dumb idea."

"Uh," I said, scanning around. "Guys?"

"It would have worked if not for those blood-sprites," continued Hob. "And at least we got to the other side."

"True!" said Ndala brightly. Her face fell again. "Aw. That tank's gonna come out of my salary, I bet."

"Guys!" I said, adding a note of urgency to my voice.

"What's up, Ms. Clean?" asked Ndala, glancing back at me. Her eyes widened. "Oh."

A horde of goblins surrounded us. They stretched as far as the eye could see, cackling and rubbing their furry little hands together in anticipation.

"Hey, Hob?" asked Ndala as they turned and stood, hands raised.

"Yeah?"

"You still have those swords?"

THEY TRUSSED US UP like turkeys, hung Ndala and Hob from poles, and trooped us off towards the looming castle of the Nightmare Duke. Me they weren't sure what to do with, so they put me in a cookpot and magically sealed the lid. That was fine. I didn't want to get out.

I did clean the goo out of the bottom of the pot with the few tentacles I could wriggle free, though.

We clanked along for hours until at last the lid came off the cookpot and I was dumped unceremoniously onto the cold stone floor of a vast outdoor amphitheater. Hob and Ndala, still tied up, were surrounded by goblins with big, nasty-looking axes and pikes. In every space of the amphitheater sat a screeching, cheering goblin.

A hush fell over the crowd as a magnificent Fae wearing a swirling black cape descended from the sky. He was tall with skin nearly bleach-white, hair the color of gold, and finely pointed ears. His cruel features betrayed nothing remotely soft or welcoming.

"Well then," he said, coming to rest directly in front of Hob. "Welcome back."

Hob looked utterly wretched.

"You're the Nightmare Duke," I said.

"Yes, machine. It is I." He gestured to the goblins with the pikes. "Untie them."

The goblins wiggled their fingers and the ropes fell away. More magic. I snapped a tentacle at one who got too close; he bonked me with his pike.

As soon as she was free Ndala snarled, "You fucker! Wake up our crew!" and leapt for him, sidearm drawn. He yawned and flicked his wrist—Ndala went flying across the floor. Several goblins immediately surrounded her, keeping her pinned with the business end of the pikes.

"Mortals," sighed the Nightmare Duke. "So easy, so easy. Ah, Iassando Showerrain. You came home."

Hob glowered at him. "Dad."

"How are you, my boy?" asked the Nightmare Duke.

"Not well, since you banished my entire race from this part of Faerie," he said sulkily.

"Well, you know how it is when your mother and I fight," the Nightmare Duke said with a lackadaisical shrug. "I expect I'll allow you back within the millennium."

"Oh, so—" I started to say.

"Nightmare Dude is Hobbsie's dad, and he's a real prick who is probably gonna kill all of us just to make some dumbass point," said Ndala from the ground. "Right? Get with the program, Ms. Clean."

Both Hob and the Nightmare Duke looked impressed. "She's astute," said the Nightmare Duke.

"You don't have to kill *both* of them," said Hob. "Maybe just the robot?"

"That's hardly any fun," said the Nightmare Duke. He bared his sharp, silver teeth at us. "Especially when I can keep your crew asleep until they all die of starvation. Perhaps we can store our extra garbage there. I'd love to know what you're going to do about it. *Hobbsie.*"

"That's it!" cried Hob. He pulled a short dagger out of his belt. "I challenge you to—"

The Nightmare Duke hit him in the chest with a bolt of lightning.

Hob staggered, then spoke a few arcane words into the air. A crowbar appeared and started smacking the Nightmare Duke in the thigh.

But the Nightmare Duke was too fast. He changed into a hawk and soared overhead, diving at Hob's head. The goblin crowd cheered.

There was a sizzling blast of plasma from Ndala's direction. She'd rolled to her feet and fired her sidearm while the goblins were distracted. She missed the Nightmare Duke by millimeters, and the goblins tackled her.

"Kick his ass, Hobbsie!" she cried as she went down.

Hob turned into a tiger. He growled and leaped at the hawk, which turned around and *shattered* into a thousand pieces.

"Never catch me this way!" crowed the teeny bits of the Nightmare Duke. "Any of us you catch, there will be a thousand more!"

A zillion little Nightmare Dukes ran around on the stones of the amphitheater, just like bugs, while the horde of goblins cheered.

I hate bugs. And when I see bugs, I do what I do best:

I clean them up.

I raced around at lightning quick speed, sucking up every one of the Nightmare Dukes I could see. He was so surprised that he forgot to change himself back—or, maybe once he lost some of his parts, he couldn't.

I didn't care. In less time than it could take the goblins to react I'd finished my run, emitted some very pleasant water vapor, and stacked a neat pile of waste cubes there on the ground. Nothing else of the Nightmare Duke remained.

The crowd of goblins gasped.

"You... you killed him!" said Hob.

"Science!" shouted Ndala, triumphantly pumping a fist in the air. "Woo!"

The goblins roared, jumping up and down in fury. Suddenly the little guys with the pikes were all around us again, and they were not happy.

"Crap," Hob said, quivering.

* * *

"THAT WAS REALLY great, how you begged for our lives," I said to Hob as we picked our way through the piles of garbage leading to the portal. A phalanx of grumbling goblins escorted us.

"I liked it when you cried," added Ndala.

"Shut up, both of you," muttered Hob.

"It was nice of them not to kill us," I said.

"Wasn't it?" agreed Ndala brightly. "And all because Hob's the Nightmare Duke now!"

"It doesn't work that way," Hob sighed. "The title goes to my second cousin, but I get a certain amount of influence and a time-limited claim on pieces of the title while I'm in Faerie. It's... complicated."

"Still, we're not dead," I said. "Just exiled forever."

"Which is fine with me," said Ndala. "This place sucks! But Hob, you can return. Lucky."

"I suppose," said Hob. He looked a lot glummer than I'd expected.

We arrived at the portal and the goblins pointed me and Ndala at it with their pikes. I took one last longing look at the massive piles of garbage and zipped forward across the event horizon. Ndala and Hob were right behind me.

"Well," said Ndala once we were on the other side. "I'm bushed. I'm gonna go take a nap."

Hob looked back through the vortex. "This is going to require some explaining," he said. "I wonder. Maybe a ship like this isn't a good place for a Fae like me. Maybe I should learn to live in the world I'm from and acknowledge who I am. Or maybe I can be a bridge between worlds!" His eyes lit up. "Think of that! Real connections between Faerie and this world! Oh, just imagine how glorious it could be."

Ndala looked at me, and then back at him.

Then she shoved him back through the vortex. It obligingly shut an instant later.

"Nice work," I said. Shouts of alarm and irritation echoed from all over the ship, followed by high-pitched shrieking. The crew of the *Zinnia* was waking up and getting down to the business of slaughtering whatever goblins remained.

"Fairies on a spaceship are a bad fucking idea," said Ndala.

"Agreed," I said, and began to clean.

This story originally appeared in *Apex*, 2015.

Susan Jane Bigelow is a fiction writer, political columnist, and librarian. She mainly writes science fiction and fantasy novels. Her short fiction has appeared in *Strange Horizons*, *Apex Magazine*, and *Lightspeed Magazine*'s "Queers Destroy Science Fiction" issue, among others. Her Extrahuman Union series is being republished by Book Smugglers Publishing in 2016. She lives with her wife in northern Connecticut, and is probably currently at the bottom of a pile of cats.

SUEDE THIS TIME

JEAN RABE

PRINCE WASN'T CHARMING.

Not as far as I was concerned.

He stood in the middle of the castle drawbridge, his wheat-blond hair a mass of tangles, his jowls sagging, and his vacuous black eyes fixed unblinkingly on me. As I returned his stare, a thick strand of drool spilled over his lower lip and stretched down to pool between his front paws. A threatening growl rumbled up from his barrel-shaped chest, and he tipped his snout to display his sharp teeth.

No, Prince wasn't charming at all.

Though I was several yards away, on the far bank of the moat, I could smell him. The early morning breeze pummeled me with the redolence of whatever long-dead thing he'd found to roll in. I could well imagine he had fleas—a burgeoning colony of them—as when he wasn't watching me, he was usually scratching at himself with his hind legs or vigorously rubbing his rump against a post. He probably had mange, too.

It was my master who named the wretch "Prince," just three weeks past—the day he spied the grubby mongrel looking so apparently hungry and forlorn and whimpering so damn theatrically.

How my master could find this creature even remotely "adorable and oh-so-cute" was a mystery.

How he could take this insidious cur into our magnificent castle . . .

How he could let this filthy animal sleep at the foot of his bed . . .

How he could feed this . . . *thing* . . . choice bits from the table . . .

And how he could fashion a collar of the finest leather and the most exquisite sapphires for the beast's thick neck (the jewels being the only princely aspect of the fiend) . . .

. . . was well and truly beyond the scope of my considerable intelligence to grasp.

The worst of it—Prince wasn't even a dog.

Oh, he certainly looked like a dog, even to my keenly perceptive eyes, a wavy-coated retriever of some sort or an overgrown water spaniel with a fanciful plumy tail. He could bark with the best of them, shake "hands," roll over, even play "fetch" when the mood struck him. And he was quite practiced at passing wind under the dining room table when guests were present, and hiking his leg against the castle's walls when none of the guards were watching.

But to call him a dog would be an insult to lowly canines everywhere.

"Prince" was an ogre.

I accidentally discovered his dark secret late last night. And mere minutes later—before I could reveal him for the monster he is—he chased me out of the castle just as the drawbridge was rising, forcing me to spend the night beyond the moat on this chill, damp ground. When the bridge was lowered just an hour ago to greet the dawn, he immediately sidled out, no doubt to keep me from getting back in and warning my master about him. You see, I can speak the human tongue when I've a mind to. And the moment I tell my master the truth about his dear "Prince," he will order the ogre captured and slain.

I would attend to the killing myself. Unfortunately, "Prince" is a tad smarter than his departed brother was. I dealt with that particular ogre a few years ago.

I suppose I should explain.

I am Minew Milakye, a chartreux of some distinction. For those of you regrettably unknowledgeable about the finer points of cats, the chartreux is an ancient and esteemed breed that originated in France and was raised into numbers by a sect of Carthusian monks. All of my kind are known for our splendid and wooly slate-blue coats, bright orange eyes, even temperaments, and sharp wits. My wit is sharper than most.

It was my dear mother who named me Minew.

It was my master who drolly and fondly dubbed me Puss, as in 'Puss 'N Boots.' My good friend Charles Perrault reasonably accurately penned the story of how I came into my master's company—a far better telling, I might say, than he rendered of the sagas of that cinder girl and the child who looked quite silly in the vermilion ridinghood.

The curtailed version of my story: I 'belonged' to a miller who died. The miller's will made provisions for his eldest son to receive the mill, his middle son to acquire the donkey, and his youngest son to be given me.

The youngest son struck off, saddened by his lot and unappreciative of my company until I revealed that I could speak his simple language. I took pity on him, and so I promised that I would make him rich—if he would buy me a fine cloak, a velvet hat, a small bag, and a pair of shiny black leather boots for my back paws (on occasion I enjoy walking on two legs). He was reasonably quick to attend to my requests, and I was quick about my schemes.

Decked out quite nicely, I presented the nearest king with various sundries, claiming them all to be gifts from my master the handsome and noble Marquis de Carabas. (What a grandiose title I created for the lad!) When the King's curiosity was suitably piqued, and when he began toying with the notion of arranging a marriage between his beautiful daughter and the mysterious Marquis de Carabas, I invited the royal family to visit my master in his castle.

Now my master didn't have a castle, but I'd heard tell of an ogre who owned a magnificent one. All I had to do was take the castle away from the brute. So I paid a visit to the ogre, a quite magical if dim-witted creature, and I told him that I'd heard he had great arcane powers.

"Yep, I sure do," the ogre replied. "I can change into things . . . a lion . . . an elephant . . . ya know, things."

"That's wonderful!" I played along. "But you're so tall! I bet you can't turn into something tiny." I furrowed my brow. "Say . . . a blackbird. Or even more difficult . . . a mouse. That would be impossible even for one of your magical talent, wouldn't it?"

"Nope. Not impossible," he shot back. "I can do a mouse. Watch this."

On the spot the fool cast a spell and transformed himself into a little gray one, which I snapped up, chomped its head off, and swallowed.

Before the hapless beast had a chance to give me indigestion, the "Marquis" had a magnificent castle to show off to the King and the Princess. And, soon after, the "Marquis" had a beautiful royal wife, and was able to attract a staff of servants and two dozen well-armed and armored guards.

It looked like the lot of us would live happily ever after.

That is until three weeks past when my master brought "Prince" into the castle, and until late last night when I accidentally caught "Prince" prowling through the kitchen for a late-night snack. "Prince" was walking on two olive-tinged legs the size of tree-trunks and had shed all of his doggy-hair in favor of his natural warty ogre hide. No wonder the dog had smelled odd, not like other canines I'd been downwind of. Unfortunately, "Prince" spotted me, and because of that I'm standing here on this chill, damp ground rather than lounging on a pillow high in the castle waiting for breakfast to be served.

How was I to know the ogre whose head I bit off had a brother?

How was I to anticipate that said brother would use magic to show up at the castle looking like some overgrown, sad-eyed water spaniel? And that he would be standing guard on the drawbridge at this very moment, turning the pool of drool at his feet into a veritable lake?

How was I to know?

Quick-witted though I am, do not expect me to be omniscient. So of course I couldn't have known about "Prince." Still, I felt some responsibility to warn the Marquis about the detestable creature. I had put the Marquis de Carabas in the castle after all.

I glided closer to the drawbridge, trying to gauge whether I might be able to race past "Prince" and into the castle proper before he could catch me. The beast's eyes lost their empty look and glimmered darkly.

"Ya ain't comin' in, cat," he whispered just loud enough for me to hear. His voice sounded like bits of gravel jostling around inside a bucket. "I heard whatcha did to my brother. Word gets 'round ya know. So ya ain't never comin' back in. This's my castle now." He punctuated the sentiment with a loud dog-belch that added to the evil smells assaulting me.

"Your castle?"

"Yeah. I inherited it. From my brother who you killed."

"Inherited. Big word for an ogre."

He growled and scratched at a plank.

"Fine. Your castle," I hissed. "Then I suppose I have no alternative but to leave." I turned tail and sauntered into the bushes. To myself, I added: "But it is *not* your castle. There is no way you're claiming the place with the Marquis, his royal wife, and all those guards traipsing around. Ogres are powerful. But not powerful enough to deal with that many people."

Still . . . ogres live a very long time. Perhaps the lout was going to remain a dog for the next several decades, waiting until my master grew old and died and the castle was abandoned—provided the Princess did not produce an heir to pass the castle along to. Or perhaps the ogre intended to remain a dog forever. Maybe he found the ghastly form an improvement over his natural one. Maybe he liked sleeping at my master's feet. Maybe he liked the Princess cooing over him and scratching his ears, maybe he liked hiking his . . . .

Maybe he had something sinister planned.

I needed to get inside and talk to the Marquis. I knew the Marquis' brother was coming to visit today—the middle son who had inherited the donkey. Perhaps I could sneak in with him, hop into a pack or something. But he might not arrive until the afternoon, and I didn't want to wait that long.

Neither did I want to wait out the ogre-dog, hoping he'd grow bored of standing on the drawbridge and go elsewhere, giving me an easy way in.

No, I couldn't afford to wait. And so I decided to make an arduous sacrifice. I drifted deeper into the foliage and began circling the castle wall, paralleling the moat. I breathed deep and steadied myself for what I had to do. I located a suitable spreading fern, and beneath it I carefully placed my boots, cloak, hat, and bag for safekeeping. Then I continued on my route until I was behind the castle, where "Prince" couldn't see me.

I padded to the moat's edge. The breeze sent faint ripples across the water, making my reflection shimmer and dance and seem somehow mystical on this early morning. Water—the thought of it made my throat instantly dry. A shiver raced down my spine as I urged myself into it. Some say the part of the cat that hesitates is the paws. Especially over the prospect of getting wet. But I know it is essentially the whole of the cat. Every inch of me wanted to stay on this dry, chill ground. Every inch except one very small and persistent part that made me again pity the young man I'd turned into a Marquis. And it made me want to warn him.

"No recourse," I said as I somehow found the water lapping over my toes, then against my stomach, as I somehow found myself practically submerged and swimming oh-so-quietly toward the rear of the wall that circled the castle. I felt something brush against my side, and for an instant I wondered if there were foul beasts lairing in this foul water. But nothing grabbed me, no toothed snout appeared, and no carnivorous fish dared to strike at my churning legs. And so moments later I found myself on the opposite bank, wet, cold, wet, thoroughly miserable, and thoroughly drenched. I started to rub against the tall grass that grew against the castle wall, then quickly stopped myself when I recalled where "Prince" tended to relieve himself. I most certainly would rather be wet and miserable than. . . .

I glanced up at the crenellated wall. Though I'd lived inside the place for the past few years I'd never appreciated just how imposing that wall was. Thick and impossibly tall, ogre-sized naturally—likely constructed to keep out whatever huge creatures might threaten ogres (never mind keeping out small clever cats).

"No recourse," I repeated, as I stretched against the wall and began climbing, claws digging into the hardened mud mortar between the blocks of stone. My muscles were screaming in protest before I'd reached the halfway point, and my chest felt like a fire being stoked. The small part of me that had urged me into the moat was delighting in this. For too long I'd been sedentary, enjoying the pampering of the Marquis and the Princess and the servants. My walks were brief ones, my lounging considerable, and my food heavy on the tasty aspect and light on nutrition. Often someone carried me up and down the stairs.

I should be carried up and down the stairs, I told myself. *I should be pampered.* "Why ever am I doing this? Why? Why? Why?" I hesitated, clinging fast and working hard to catch my breath. *I'm doing this so I can be carried up and down the stairs*, I decided. *I'm doing this to oust "Prince."*

I don't know how long I hung there, waiting for the fire within my chest to die down just a bit. It seemed like an eternity, my paws aching fiercely, but I knew it was only minutes. By the time I resumed my climb, and by the time I'd made it to the top, my fur was still dripping.

The small part of me that had impelled me up the wall rejoiced in the exertion. The rest of me simply rejoiced in the view. It was all so amazing from the top of the wall, the lush greens of the woods and meadows spreading away in all directions, the water of the moat looking like a silver ribbon festooned with beads of sunlight. The breeze carried the scent of wildflowers, the small fragrant ones that hung on at the close of summer, and I could hear the faint twitter-song of swallows. Turning inward, I could see the castle and the service buildings around it—the stable, blacksmith's stall, and the barracks. Workers busied themselves scurrying about while the guards stood like statues—two on either side of the archway that led to the moat, two on either side of the castle door, two more on parapets. The castle itself stood in the midst of it all, made of white granite shot through with glistening veins of black, a turret rising above this wall with a pointed conical roof looking like a spear jutting into the cloudless sky. There was a window high in the turret, and I'd never thought to perch in it before and absorb the view.

I would now, after "Prince" was dealt with and I'd retrieved my clothes and boots. I'd make that windowsill my favorite spot, and from it I would survey this glorious countryside—after I climbed the stairs to reach it, of course, making sure that small part of me was satisfied that I'd gotten some exercise. An ogre did not deserve such a magnificent place, and could not appreciate the beauty of the land. An ogre would not enjoy the view. So the ogre had to go . . . now.

The castle was trimmed around the windows and balconies in pale blue, the Marquis' favorite color. But the trim had been burnt orange and was chipping dreadfully when I'd acquired the place from "Prince's" brother. The ogre hadn't done much to keep the place up. His brother would do no better job. I felt bile rising in my throat as I continued to think of the ogre-dog that was likely still on the drawbridge.

I started down the other side of the wall, using the cover of the castle to hide my presence. It was a little easier climbing down, and easier still to rush across the ground and dart inside the kitchen door that was timely being opened by a cook.

"Puss!" she said, as I shot past. She'd made a motion to pet me, but I hadn't the time for such pleasantries. "Where's your hat and . . . ."

I was well beyond her and her trivial prattle, through the dining room and into the gallery before I came to a stop behind a suit of decorative plate armor. Here I listened for the beat of the place. Every castle has a heart. Sometimes it's a strong one—like those great ancient edifices belonging to important kings. Sometimes it's a small and feeble one, like a few places I'd slipped into during my kitten days, pretentious castles built for men who have titles but lack the miens and brains for leadership. This castle, I'd learned shortly after its previous owner's demise, had a dark heart. Its beat was hard to hear, but if you were a chartreux and if you listened for it, you could manage.

Its steady thrum spoke of its long decades on this land, of its deep foundation filled with dungeons and treasure chambers, of the blood-stained floors in its secret rooms. It beat with the brush strokes of paintings stolen from merchant caravans, with the stitches of great tapestries fashioned by human slaves, with the last gasps of the lives lost to the ogre who once held sway here. And it pulsed with the presence of the damnable ogre-dog.

Why couldn't he have stayed on the drawbridge?

I could hear the beast in the room beyond, nails clicking rhythmically over the stone floor, breath coming short and even. He must have come in from the drawbridge shortly after I'd given up that route, and was now patrolling the main room and the winding stairway that lead up to the chambers where the Marquis was most likely to be found.

His ogre-heart beat in time with the castle's, not as strong, but darker, I sensed. The Marquis would deal with the monster today, I vowed. Then perhaps the beat of the castle's dark heart would be silenced and a new heart would replace it—one that beat in time with mine.

I slipped back into the kitchen and made my way up the narrow stairs that lead to the cook's room. Faintly, from below, I heard the clacking of the ogre-dog's nails. Could he sense me as I sensed him? Could he smell my pleasant musky odor as I was forced to stomach the stench of him?

I moved faster, darting beneath the cook's bed while I listened more carefully. The clacking was coming up the stairs.

Faster still and I was out of the meager room and into the hall beyond, rushing toward a wider staircase that would lead to the sitting room the young Marquis and his Princess favored. My sides were aching from the exertion of the swim across the moat, from climbing the wall, from now climbing these stairs. The small part of me that was oh-so-proud at my efforts would be prouder still when the ogre met his demise.

Faster.

"Puss!" the Princess exclaimed as I slipped into the massive sitting room filled with stolen paintings and slave-made tapestries, scented tapers and the soft glow spilling in from high narrow windows. "Puss, you're wet! And you've lost your cloak and boots!"

The clacking was louder, the beast closing.

I glanced about for the Marquis-I'd-made. I'd never spoken to the Princess, only to my young master. Speaking to her now—and about a horrid ogre—would yield nothing but a shocked look on her pretty face. She'd hear my words but she wouldn't listen to what I had to say.

The clacking and . . .

Humming! The young Marquis was humming in the room beyond, the music room he called it, a polished marble place filled with poorly-strung harps and ill-tuned lyres. I was a blue-gray streak past the Princess and into the next room, a chartreux blur heading straight toward my master sitting on a plush velvet chair, a skidding mass of fur as I scrambled to come to a stop.

"Puss!" he exclaimed. "You've been out all night! You're wet!" His tone became playfully scolding. "You've lost your cloak and boots. I'll have to buy you new and . . ."

"No." It was the only word I could manage at the moment, and it wasn't in reference to his offer of new attire. "No." The word was directed at what was swirling around his feet. There were puppies, eight of them—writhing balls of golden hair and shiny black noses, wagging plumy tails and merry yappings. "No. No. No."

"So you don't want to wear clothes anymore?" He reached down and picked up one of the pups, cradled it in his lap and twirled his long fingers around its ears.

They weren't puppies. I could sense it as I could sense the castle's heartbeat. Ogres, all of them.

"They're not puppies," I started. The words were coming fast now. "I never told you the whole story of how I got this castle for you. There was an ogre. . . ."

"Yes, yes," he said. "I remember. You somehow managed to slay the vile monster after a fierce battle."

I inwardly groaned. I never told the Marquis de Carabas the truth, that I'd tricked the brute into transforming himself into a mouse. The slay-the-vile-creature-after-a-fierce-battle-story seemed much more glamorous at the time. The Marquis didn't know that ogres could magically assume different shapes. Didn't know about the mouse. Didn't know about the true nature of the dog he'd brought into the castle. I'd only told the true story to Charles Perrault and a few stray cats, all good friends.

"Ogres are magical creatures," I began, deciding there wasn't time to explain everything. I was listening for the clacking of Prince's nails, but I couldn't hear it anymore. My heart was pounding too loudly.

"Not so magical as you," he kindly returned.

Much more magical, actually, I thought. Aloud, I said: "They can turn into things."

He cocked his head in polite curiosity and reached down to pick up a second pup.

"Things like dogs and puppies," I continued. "Those aren't real puppies. They're ogres. All eight of them. And Prince is an ogre, too. Last night . . . ."

The Marquis laughed then, loud and long, throwing back his head and cackling upward so his voice bounced off the ceiling. When the mirthful cacophony finally subsided, he fixed his eyes on mine. "You're clever, Puss, trying to make me think these delightful creatures are ogres. You probably want me to toss them out of the castle."

"That wouldn't be good enough," I said. "They'd come back. How'd they get here to begin with?"

"The pups? They came in yesterday late in a farmer's cart. He was as surprised as the cooks that they were hiding behind the bushels of potatoes. Aren't they . . . charming?"

"They're ogres," I repeated. "You'll need to drown them. Or behead them. Skewer them with a long spear and . . . ."

He laughed again, but curtly this time. "I know cats don't care for dogs, Puss, but you're being a little ridiculous." One of the pups stretched up and licked his chin. Another, between his legs and where he couldn't see, raised its lip in a silent snarl directed at me.

I snorted. "Ridiculous? I'm being realistic. They're ogres, the pups *and* Prince—warty green-skinned smelly monsters that will find a way to . . ."

He drew his eyebrows together and studied me.

"That will find a way to . . ." I so hated to talk in front of the ogres, but what alternative did I have? ". . . to get rid of the guards and deal with the servants, chase you out of this wonderful castle. Kill you maybe. Probably. Ogres kill people." The heart of the castle beat with the last gasps of dozens of humans the previous ogre-owner had slain. Perhaps the heart was too dark to change.

"They're puppies, Puss, charming, adorable puppies." He offered me a slight smile. "And they're staying. The princess and I discussed it, and we've agreed to keep them all."

"You can't, you . . . ."

"And you'll have to accept them."

I shook my head, droplets of moat water flying away from me. "I can't. I won't. They're ogres and . . ."

"Then you'll have to leave."

What? I stared at him incredulously. *What did he say?*

"If you can't accept the pups and Prince, you'll just have to find a home elsewhere."

I heard the clacking again, glanced over my shoulder and saw "Prince" standing in the doorway behind me. He was looking at the Marquis, tail wagging a greeting.

"There's my good boy," the Marquis gushed. "Prince" trotted over and settled in next to his chair.

I needed time. I had to think. There must be a way to get the Marquis alone. Perhaps I could again catch "Prince" prowling in the pantry late at night, get my master to see the monster for its true self. But there were nine ogres now, a formidable force. Nine ogres would be more than enough to handle the servants. But nine ogres might not be enough to tackle the Marquis' armed and armored guards. There was still time to deal with this threat, especially if the ogres were attacked while in pup form. Kill them as I had swallowed the mouse. Still time and . . . .

"Dear!" The Princesses' lilting voice carried in from the sitting room. "One of the maids says she's found more puppies—a half dozen. Isn't that wonderful!"

"No." I had to think. I whirled and bolted from the room, a blur of blue-gray that was in an instant beyond the Princess and out onto the landing, was racing up steep stone steps that added to the ache in my sides.

"Puss?" the Princess called.

"Leave him be." This from the Marquis. Though I was putting distance between myself and the lot of them, my hearing was acute enough to pick up the conversation. "Puss doesn't like the pups. But he'll get used to them. He'll have to."

"He'll have to if he wants to stay here," the Princess finished. "The pups are . . . charming."

Charming. The word rattled 'round inside my head. *Charming.* Perhaps that was it! Perhaps the oh-so-magical ogres had cast a charm spell on the Marquis and the Princess. Perhaps that was why my master wouldn't listen to reason, *he couldn't listen to reason,* couldn't see the pups for what they really were.

How could I get my master alone? Or at least catch him when none of the ogres were around. Six more of them! Fifteen in all. I skidded to a stop on a higher landing. Fifteen ogres could defeat my master's armed and armored guards. Fifteen ogres would be enough to take back this castle. To wipe out the servants. To kill the Marquis and the Princess.

I sensed the castle's dark heart beating more strongly, even as my own heart hammered wildly in my chest. It was no longer a matter of dealing with the ogres. It was a matter of getting my master and his wife and as many others as possible out of the castle before the ogres made their move. I turned to retrace my steps, deciding to make another attempt at reaching the Marquis-I'd-made, when I saw a ball of golden fur bounding up the stairs toward me. The pup's expression was pure malevolence, and I wasted no time in heading back up the stairs.

How was I to know that the ogre whose head I bit off had a brother?

And that the brother had fourteen ogre-friends?

Before I reached the next landing, even the small part of me that had been delighting in all this exercise was complaining. My lungs burned, my chest heaved, my head pounded and my legs throbbed. I wanted desperately to stop, to lie down somewhere and rest. But I forced myself on, and at a faster pace still, as the ogre-pup that chased me was far from winded.

The stairs were narrowing now, as we were in the narrowing turret, and they were becoming steeper. While at first I considered that an advantage, as my agile cat legs could better handle them than awkward pup feet, a look behind sent my head to pounding more. The pup had cast a spell and transformed itself into a dog, one similar to "Prince," though even uglier. Within moments, I suspected it would be on me. It would chomp my head off and devour me. It would reclaim this castle before my body had a chance to give the monster indigestion.

"Faster!" I shouted, and somehow my legs complied. "Move!"

Then I was at the highest landing, through a narrow door, and up on that very high windowsill that provided a glorious view of the countryside. I had no time to absorb the splendor, however, as the ogre-dog burst into the small, round room, snarling and snapping and dribbling saliva on the floor.

Though the sill was oddly high, he could perhaps reach it—barely—if he stretched up on his hind legs. I would go out the window, climb down the stone. In fact, I started to do just that—until I spied three sleek-coated pointers far beneath me. I couldn't smell them, but I was certain they were ogres, too. I spun and looked about the room. There was an iron chandelier hanging from the ceiling, and if I sprang just right I could catch it, pull myself up and get beyond the ogre-dog's . . . .

I bunched my leg muscles and prepared to leap, then I stopped myself when his ugly eyes caught and held mine.

"Ya talk too much, cat," the dog said. Twin strands of drool spilled from his mouth. "Ya shouldn't've went blathering like ya did to the Marquis. Shouldn't've exposed our secret, not that he believed ya. Shouldn't've suggested he drown us. Wasn't polite, cat. An' here I surmised that you were a critter with some brains."

Blathering. Surmised. Big words for an ogre, I thought. Perhaps they weren't all so utterly stupid as the one whose head I . . . .

"Them stray cats we caught a month or so back, they seemed pretty smart—and real tasty. 'Fore we ate 'em they talked to us 'bout how you killed the ogre what used to live here. Ya shouldn't've told them cats 'bout it."

No, I shouldn't have, I agreed. I risked another glance at the chandelier. It was higher than I'd ever jumped before, but perhaps I could . . . .

"If ya had kept your mouth shut, we wouldn't've known. Grizwald wouldn't've learned ya ate his brother, my second cousin once removed and Ratigan's and Zebedee's best friend. Griz wouldn't've got us all together and had us come here. Should've kept your mouth shut, cat. 'Cause now I'm gonna see if you're tasty, too."

"I guarantee you I'm all gristle," I replied. If I missed the chandelier, I'd fall right in front of him. There had to be another way out . . . .

The dog sat back on his haunches, watching me. "Should've kept your mouth shut," he repeated. "At least the Marquis didn't swallow a word ya said. At least . . . ."

"What are you going to do to him?" Despite my master's unwillingness to believe me, I held a fondness for him.

The dog made an exaggerated gesture that approximated a shrug. "Griz . . . Prince . . . likes the Marquis well enough. So we probably won't kill him. Probably keep the human tied up in the dungeon. Bring him out and set him to waving at merchant wagons to lure 'em in."

"And everyone else?"

Another shrug. "Once upon a time we ogres was peaceable sorts."

Not any longer, I knew.

"So I 'spose we'll kill 'em. Maybe we'll keep the Princess and one or two others around to cook for us. Maybe we won't. Ratigan can cook when he puts his mind to it."

The dog's tongue lolled out and his eyes took on a hungry gleam. As I contemplated my options—either the chandelier or climbing out of the window, both bad options—I saw him change. The fur melted off him like butter, seeping into the cracks of the stone floor and disappearing. The skin beneath was a pale green, dotted with warts and festering boils. There were muscles, and they were growing as I gaped. The entire dog was growing, and its limbs were changing, becoming manlike and thick and long. Arms extended and front paws turned into massive hands with fingers ending in ugly, cracked nails. The chest became defined and impressive, and the head became hideous. The ogre's face was shaped like an egg, hairless save for a dozen uneven strands that jutted from the top. His eyes were crooked, the right being slightly higher and larger than the left, and the nose was wide and puglike, looking as if it might have been broken a few times. The lips were large and bulbous, licked by a wide black tongue.

"I like gristle," he said in a sonorous voice that echoed off the walls.

He gave a chuckle then and reached for me, and in that instant I abandoned the chandelier notion and leapt from the windowsill and into the room. In a heartbeat I was through his legs, speeding across the floor and out the door, scrambling over the landing and down the stairs. I was a blue-gray blur heading toward the music room, intent on trying one final time to get the Marquis to listen.

"Puss!" the Princess exclaimed as I ran past her. She was still ensconced in the sitting room, a half-dozen golden-furred ogre-puppies around her dainty slippered feet. "Dear kitty, have you . . . ."

I barreled into the next room, my clawed feet skittering over the polished floor and taking me to my master.

"Father's cat!" A sneeze. "You still have father's cat."

My master had company, the new voice belonging to the middle brother. The man was sitting several feet away from the Marquis, leaning against an enormous harp and sniffling into a handkerchief.

"Yes, Puss is still with me, and . . ."

"Listen," I blurted, eyes darting from one pup to the next to "Prince," who had taken a discreet position behind the Marquis. "You have to listen to me!"

"Father's cat talks?" Another sneeze. And another.

"Yes, brother, and sometimes he . . . ."

"Listen! They're ogres. All of the pups are ogres. And if you and the Princess and your brother and the servants and the armed and armored guards don't leave, you all could be dead by nightfall."

The Marquis didn't laugh this time, and for a moment I thought I'd reached him. That notion vanished, however, when his eyes narrowed to thin slits.

"You listen to me, Puss."

The brother sneezed quite loudly this time.

"And you listen good. I like these pups. I like Prince. I like them better than you."

What? His words were daggers, and I heard them well, just as I heard the castle's dark heart beat faster and stronger, just as I smelled the stench of the ogre-pups. I was reeling from all of it.

"I never liked you, Puss. I only tolerated you because my father liked you. Then I tolerated you because you got me this castle and the Princess."

The brother sneezed again and again.

"I don't like *any* cats, Puss. Never did. In fact, I hate cats. They're too aloof. They're too independent. Can't stand the hairballs and the finicky behavior. Dogs, Puss. I like dogs. No. I *love* dogs. All of these pups and Prince are staying, and . . . ."

"Ahhhhhhhhh-choooooooooooooo!" The brother was caught up in a sneezing fit.

". . . and you're leaving, Puss," the Marquis continued, raising his voice. "You're leaving right this very instant."

"I'm leaving, too, I'm afraid." The brother stood, handkerchief over his nose. "I can't sit here another moment. I am so allergic to dog fur." His eyes watered as if he'd been to his best friend's funeral. "I can take the cat with me if you'd like. I rather fancy the notion of having a talking cat."

"The pups," I tried one final time, catching the angry gaze of the Marquis. "They're ogres. They're going to . . . ." Then I felt myself being lifted and held beneath the middle brother's arm. He stuffed the handkerchief in his pocket, sneezed again, and petted me with his free hand.

"You're damp," he said to me, as he carried me out of the music room and paused in the sitting room to bow to the Princess. "However did you get so damp?" he continued, as he started down the stairs. "And you're out of breath. I bet those pups were chasing you."

"Yes, chasing," I said.

"No pups will chase you in my house," he returned. "It's a good house, sturdy and small, nothing like this castle. But you'll like it."

"No dogs," I said.

"No. No dogs. I'm so terribly allergic to them. I've a donkey, though. He doesn't talk, but you'll like him."

"I'm sure I will," I replied, as he carried me out of the castle's front door, strode to the stables, and deposited me on the donkey's saddle.

"Your paws!" he exclaimed, taking note of the rest of my condition. "You've got a few broken claws, and your pads are bleeding."

All the running, I thought, the climbing up and down the wall, the scrabbling up the stairs. I wasn't used to it, and my paws were paying the price.

"Perhaps I should buy you some boots," he continued, as he led the donkey across the drawbridge.

Behind us I could hear the playful yip of the fourteen puppies and the loud bark of "Prince." Fifteen ogres. Eighteen if the three pointers outside the window were ogres, too. A veritable force of monsters! The Marquis' guards couldn't possibly . . . .

Then my breath caught, as on the grounds beyond the moat I saw seven more dogs, a motley looking crew—terriers, shepherds, and a one-eared shaggy sheepdog. They smelled just like "Prince." Thankfully they waited until we were over the drawbridge and headed away from the Marquis' lands before they scampered across and hurried to join the other ogres. The Marquis would be going to the dogs, all right. I fervently hoped at least some of the people within the castle walls could find their way free before . . . .

"Did you hear me, Puss?"

"Minew, my name's Minew Milakye."

"Would you like some boots, sweet Minew?"

My eyes took on a faraway look as I thought of the fine cloak and hat, bag and boots I'd lost beneath the spreading fern.

"Yes," I answered with fervor. "I indeed would fancy a new pair of boots. Suede this time."

This story originally appeared in *Magic Tails,* DAW, 2005.

USA Today bestselling author **Jean Rabe** has written more than thirty fantasy and adventure novels and more than eighty short stories. When she's not writing, which isn't often, she edits ... more than two dozen anthologies and more than one hundred magazine issues so far. She's a former news reporter and news bureau chief who penned a true crime book with noted attorney F. Lee Bailey. Her genre writing includes military, science fiction, fantasy, urban fantasy, mystery, horror, and modern-day adventure. She shares her home with a Labrador retriever, a graying pug, and a lively young Boston terrier. Visit her at www.jeanrabe.com.

IF YOU ENJOYED these stories and would like to read more, *Unidentified Funny Objects* publishes an annual volume of stories just like these. Many of the authors featured in this book are regular contributors. There is also fiction by Robert Silverberg, George R. R. Martin, Esther Friesner, Piers Anthony, Jody Lynn Nye, Kevin J. Anderson, Gini Koch, Neil Gaiman, and many other excellent and very funny writers.

Also look for *Funny Science Fiction* (2015), *Funny Horror* (2016), and *Funny Science Fiction 2* (2017).

ABOUT THE EDITOR

Alex Shvartsman is a writer, anthologist, translator, and game designer from Brooklyn, NY. He's the winner of the 2014 WSFA Small Press Award for Short Fiction and a finalist for the 2015 Canopus Award for Excellence in Interstellar Writing.

His short stories have appeared in *Nature, Intergalactic Medicine Show, Daily Science Fiction, Galaxy's Edge*, and a variety of other magazines and anthologies. His collection, *Explaining Cthulhu to Grandma and Other Stories*, and his steampunk humor novella *H. G. Wells, Secret Agent* were published in 2015.

In addition to the UFO series, he has edited the *Humanity 2.0, Funny Science Fiction, Coffee: 14 Caffeinated Tales of the Fantastic* and *Dark Expanse: Surviving the Collapse* anthologies. His website is www.alexshvartsman.com.

Made in the USA
Charleston, SC
07 May 2016